Nancy –

Congratulations on
winning my Goodreads
Giveaway!

Bullets and
BONFIRES

TAKE A RISK OR LOSE THE CHANCE.

AUTUMN JONES LAKE

I hope you love
Liam & Bree's Story ♡

♡

Autumn Jones Lake

REQUEST FROM THE AUTHOR

You may not realize this, but reviews are vital for Indie Authors like myself. Without the support of a publisher, Indies rely on reviews to help get the word out about our books and to prove to retailers that we should be given visibility.

If you love a book, please consider taking a few minutes to *write* a quick review. It doesn't have to be fancy or long. Just a few short lines, can mean the world to your favorite author.

Knowing that readers appreciate what we do also inspires us and helps us continue writing when we want to give up!

ABOUT BULLETS & BONFIRES

The one man she's always wanted is now the sexy sheriff of their hometown.

Battered but not broken, grad student Brianna Avery returns to the childhood home she abandoned four years ago. With her abusive ex behind bars, Bree needs the summer to relax and recover before returning to school. But her overprotective brother decides she needs someone to babysit her in his absence, and he picks the one person guaranteed to drive her nuts.

She's the one woman he can't have.

Telling Bree no has never been easy. Four years ago, Liam Hollister did it to preserve his friendship with his best friend—Brianna's brother. Now, no matter how she tempts him, he's determined to do the right thing. As deputy sheriff of their rural area, Liam is torn between protecting Brianna and wanting her for himself.

Take a risk or lose the chance.

Spending so much time alone together challenges them both. Old feelings and hurts resurface immediately. With each hot, sweaty day it's harder to deny their attraction.

It's going to be a long, hot summer.

COPYRIGHT

Bullets and Bonfires
Copyright © 2017 by Autumn Jones Lake
Print Edition
Print ISBN: 978-1-943950-19-5

All rights reserved.

Edited by: Vanessa Bridges
Edited by: Lisa Connelly
Cover Design by: Letitia Hasser, RBA Designs
Cover Photo: Wander Aguiar Photography
Cover Model: Andrew Biernat
Formatting: BB eBooks

Visit my website at www.autumnjoneslake.com.

ACKNOWLEDGMENTS

This crazy-awesome Indie book community has brought so many wonderful people into my life. More than a few of them are directly responsible for helping me bring Bullets & Bonfires to you and here is where I'd like to say thank you.

I'm always a nervous when Iza Matei has one of my books in her hands. However, I need to thank her for reading an early, rough draft of Bullets & Bonfires and enthusiastically encouraging me to keep going.

I'm indebted to Elizabeth Kelly for painstakingly going through Bullets & Bonfires and providing me with her honest insight.

Andrea Florkowski who also read an early incarnation of Liam and Bree's story and wanted more.

Tanya Skaggs and Sue Banner for having faith in me to write anything.

Before I even stepped foot into the world of Indie publishing, I met some wonderful women through my local RWA chapter who helped shape and guide me along my writing journey.

KA Mitchell spent many, many hours helping me work on this book back when it was called *Alone Together*.

Thank you to Cara, who shredded the first version of *Bullets & Bonfires*, forcing me to dig deeper. She deserves extra thanks for saving my bacon and giving *Bullets & Bonfires* a solid read-through at the very end.

My awesome crit partners, Cara, Kari, and Virginia for unanimously agreeing that the first pages I brought to critique group needed work.

Letitia Hasser for being so patient with me while I figured out what the heck I wanted for my "first" non-Lost Kings MC cover.

Wander and Andrey for patiently listening to me describe what I wanted for the cover photo and then helping Andrew nail it.

My Lost Kings MC Ladies for loving my work enough to give a non-Lost Kings MC book a chance.

All of my awesome readers, thank you for following me on this journey. I'm looking forward to giving you many more stories for years to come.

And always and forever, Mr. Lake. I couldn't do any of this without him.

DEDICATION

If you're no longer afraid of monsters,
because you survived loving one, this is for you.

CHAPTER ONE
LIAM

THE ONE DAY I need to be on time.

And I'm late.

My best friend doesn't ask for favors often.

This morning, he called from whatever far-off spot his company sent him to this month, and asked me to stop by his house to let his sister in. Apparently she'd be crashing there for a few days.

I hadn't asked for details.

Didn't need any. For Vince and Bree, I'd pretty much do anything.

Bree.

Haven't seen her since two Christmases ago. Shares an apartment with her boyfriend, so even though it kills me, I keep my distance.

Not that I'd ever disrespect my best friend by messing around with his sister.

Never again.

No matter how much I might want her.

A flash of blue in the form of a hatchback blows through a stop sign, nearly sideswiping my patrol car and putting an abrupt end to day-dreaming about Bree.

"You've got to be kidding," I grumble. Pulling the careless driver over will only make me later. The paperwork alone will take another half hour.

But leaving this menace on the road doesn't sit well with me either.

The car drifts to the left, making my decision for me. Probably some asshole texting.

I flip on the lights, but the car doesn't pull over right away. Uncooperative drivers piss me off. I'm running down my mental list of tickets to write when the car finally jerks onto the shoulder and comes to a stop.

Usually, I'd let them sweat for a few minutes while I call the traffic stop in to dispatch and dawdle over my paperwork. But I'm still hoping I can make it to Vince's house before Bree arrives.

I step out into the boiling June afternoon. The weight of my uniform increases the temperature by at least another ten degrees. My eyes scan the vehicle as I slowly approach, taking note of everything. Engine still running. Female driver. Alone. Backseat stuffed with boxes and clothing.

As I'm about to tap my knuckles against the glass, the engine shuts off and the window slides down.

I brace my arm on the roof and lean over. "Good afternoon, miss—"

"Liam?"

It takes me a few seconds to realize the careless driver I pulled over is Bree. And when it clicks in my brain, my heart stutters all over itself. She's thinner than I remember, and I have the urge to drive her straight to my mother's for a dose of home cooking. Always a beautiful girl, Bree's now a striking woman. The long brown hair I've admired since we were kids on the playground is tied into a ponytail flowing down her back. Messy, windblown tendrils beg my fingers to tuck them into place. The long-sleeved, tight, pink T-shirt she's wearing leaves a lot of cleavage on display. Something I shouldn't notice, admire or pay attention to at all.

"You ran a stop sign back there." I keep my voice light.

"I'm sorry. I'm so frazzled—" She pushes her sunglasses up on her forehead.

The bruising around her left eye hits me like a fist in the gut. My gaze drops to her split lip and her tongue darts out, nervously slicking over the injured spot. I don't remember Bree as a particularly clumsy girl. No, the damage to her face looks like—"Jesus, Bree. What happened?"

She slips the shades back into place, but I can't unsee the damage as easily. "Vince didn't tell you, huh?" she says in a tone devoid of any emotion, staring straight ahead.

"Brianna," I say, using my cop voice. "What. Happened?"

"Can we talk about it at the house?" Her voice wobbles as if she's close to tears. The last thing I'd ever want to do is make her cry. I used to be the one she'd come to when she needed cheering up.

I'm torn in two. I want to comfort her. But I also want to shake her and demand answers right now. The rational side of me decides the roadside isn't the place to have this conversation.

"I was on my way there when you almost plowed into me," I tease, hoping to lighten things up. Instead, she seems even more distressed.

"My head...I have a bad migraine. I'm a little out of it." One of her hands flutters against her temple and my gaze strays to the bruises ringing her wrists. Defensive marks? Restraint marks? I can't tell. She notices me staring and yanks her sleeves down, covering the marks.

Someone hurt her and my body shudders with beastly rage. My hand strays to the gun at my hip. Rolling my shoulders, I tilt my head side-to-side and flex my hands. No. No gun required for what I plan to do to the person responsible.

"I'll be careful," she says softly.

It's unprofessional, but Bree's a friend not a vic, so my fingers brush against her shoulder. Just a quick touch meant to reassure her. Nothing more. "I'll be right behind you."

She nods. "Okay."

I hold my hand out to stop her from turning the key in the ignition. "Just watch where you're going, okay?"

"Will do, Deputy Hollister," she answers. There's none of the joy or sass I remember in her voice. If anything, she sounds defeated.

Vince has a lot of explaining to do.

As soon as I'm inside my car, I dial his number. My gaze never leaves the back of Bree's car while I wait for her brother to answer the phone.

"Hey, you at the house yet?" he answers as Brianna steers her car onto the blacktop.

Trained to multi-task, I pull onto the road and keep a moderate distance behind Bree's car while answering his question. "Almost. I ran into Bree on my way there. What the hell happened?"

"What do you mean?"

"I mean," I say, not bothering to mask my irritation, "she's sporting a black eye like a motherfucking boxer went at her." My voice explodes in the confines of the patrol car, drowning out every other sound.

"Shit," Vince shouts on the other end. In the background there's a crash. "The hospital said she'd been in an accident. All she told me was she got into a fight with that dickwad boyfriend of hers while she was trying to move out and needed a place to stay. She made it sound like she tripped down the stairs or something. Not that he touched her."

"That didn't happen from a fall down the stairs." Don't need to be a doctor to know her injuries have nothing to do with stumbling on some stairs, smacking into a door, or anything else she might try to claim.

A string of curses erupts from my best friend as I pull into the driveway next to Bree. "I can't leave, Liam. I can't get another manager here to supervise this project for at least a week. I need you to handle this for me and keep her safe."

I'm already compiling a list of favors to call in before Vince says, "And if that stuck-up, pretty-boy boyfriend of hers did it—"

"I'll take care of it."

"Thank you." He laughs a wry, almost pained sound. "Can you stay at the house with her? I don't want her alone."

He doesn't have to voice his reasons. Although I don't know if the two of us alone together is the best idea, I reassure my friend anyway. "I can do that."

"You need to play big brother until I get home. Keep her out of trouble. Any guys come sniffing around, nip that in the bud. The last thing she needs is to get involved with another loser."

While I'm insulted he thinks so little of Bree, I choke out a sound of agreement, because honestly, I'd do that anyway. Not because I think of her as a little sister.

None of my feelings for Bree are brotherly.

"Liam!" Vince barks into the phone. "You there?"

"Yeah, I'm listening."

"Can you do this?"

"I already said yes."

"Good." He breathes a sigh of relief. "You're the only person I trust to look out for her right now."

I'm not sure if it's a compliment or a warning.

Brianna

SHAKING WITH NERVES and embarrassment, *and* hyper-aware of Liam riding my tail, I do my best to maintain my car at the speed limit. Even though my arms and wrists ache, I manage to keep the steering wheel straight.

Of course Liam had to pull me over the second I arrive back in town. The only person whose opinion matters to me more than my brother's. Why wouldn't he be the first one to see me in this shape? Heap on more humiliation at the worst time of my life?

I couldn't get stopped by crotchety old Sheriff Stevens. Nope. Not me.

Even though it's less than five miles to the house, Liam falls behind. Probably calling my brother so the two of them can decide how to handle me.

My car sputters as I pull into the driveway. As if it doesn't want to be here any more than I do. After my mother's funeral, I swore I'd never spend another night in this town. Yet, here I am.

Figures my big brother is away and all I'm returning to is an empty house.

My brows draw down, and I immediately wince as pain spears my cheek. Flipping down my visor, I stare into the small vanity mirror. My dark sunglasses hide most of the damage, but not all. Mottled bruising extends above and around my eyebrow.

At least most of the swelling has gone down, and I can open my eye today.

Hooray for progress!

Shame slithers over my skin as I remember the expression on Liam's face. How do I explain that my boyfriend's response to "let's break up" was to use my face as a speed bag?

Liam never seemed to care for Chad, and my brother definitely didn't like my boyfriend. I can almost hear the chorus of "I told you so" I have coming my way.

The visor thumps against the ceiling as I flick it out of my way. Now I'm left staring at my childhood house through my filthy windshield.

Isn't that appropriate.

A longing for something or someone familiar fills my chest. I can't believe Vince won't be home for at least a week. To be fair, I may have fibbed on some of the details of my recent hospital stay. I doubt the full truth would have made Vince come home any faster, though.

Staying in our childhood home alone will be a challenge. So many painful ghosts live between those walls, it's hard to believe there's any room for me.

Luckily—or unluckily, depending on my mood—I'll bet anything Vince tasks his best friend with playing babysitter for me. If our earlier encounter is any indication, Liam will pester me with questions I don't want to answer during the day, and I'll be left to battle old memories all night long. Alone.

In the four years since I left, the neighborhood hasn't changed all that much. Well, our childhood home looks different. Cared for. That has to be my brother's doing. It sure as hell hadn't looked this nice when we were kids.

Gravel crunches next to me. My scared heart slams against my ribs, sweat trickles down my back.

Not Chad. Not Chad. Not Chad.

My left hand curls around the steering wheel so tight, my knuckles hurt. In my other hand, I grasp my keys. *Chad's in jail.*

Finally, it registers that it's Liam's patrol car pulling in.

I'm safe.

Deep breath. In and out.

I glance over and a shaky smile curves my lips. Liam holds up a few fingers, indicating he's on the phone and will be right out.

Take your time.

No doubt he's on the phone with Vince. A mixture of joy, relief, and a few complicated emotions I can't name, war inside me.

Liam's here. For me.

Correction, Liam's here to do a favor for my brother.

A few seconds later his door swings open and he stalks toward my car. My stomach flips with anticipation. I haven't been near Liam in so long.

For the millionth time, I wish I'd said *no* when the hospital told me to call my brother. Mortification twisted my insides the whole time I tried to explain to him what happened. He ordered me home like I was a naughty teenager instead of an adult. Now Liam's here to make my humiliation complete.

How many times did my brother and I take refuge at Liam's house when my mother went on a bender or one of her boyfriends smacked her around? Turns out, I'm no better than she was.

I wheeze out a painful breath. Allowing Liam to see me in this condition almost hurts more than my actual injuries. I've idolized him, crushed on him, *loved* him since I was a kid. Resisting his masculine beauty, wicked sense of humor and habit of protecting me was impossible.

I may have fallen for Liam a long time ago.

But he was never going to catch me.

I know that, and yet I can't stop the fluttering in my stomach.

I'd never be more than little Bree to him. Vince's baby sister. Not Brianna who finished near the top of her high school class and was accepted into a competitive psychology program. Not the Brianna who's been accepted to a prestigious university to finish my master's degree.

Now? He'll see me as pathetic and broken Brianna. Crawling home after her boyfriend beat the crap out of her. As a deputy sheriff in our small hometown, I'm sure he sees women like me all the time. Pathetic, weak, and stupid women who mistake smooth lines, out-of-control jealousy, and lavish gifts for love.

I let out a final sigh and paste on a fake smile as I step out of my car to greet him. My stupid heart stumbles all over itself as I take in every masculine inch. In the sunlight, copper highlights glint throughout his familiar coffee brown hair. It's long enough for me to run my fingers through—not that he'd ever allow that. His full lips may look soft and inviting, but I know all too well how firm and obstinate they can be. All the boyish charm I remember has been replaced with a hard-faced, and hard-bodied—but I choose to ignore that for the moment—*man*. Liam's easy swagger radiates confidence and safety. Two things I desperately need at the moment.

As he meets my eyes, his lips curve into a tender half-smile, reminding me why I'm here. The small spark of excitement at seeing him fizzles. Pity, plain as day, is written all over his handsome face. He holds out his arms to me. "Come here, baby girl. I haven't seen you in forever."

My traitorous body quivers at the sound of his smooth, deep voice. For a brief second, I'm thrown back to the night of my high school graduation when he used those same arms to shove me away when my brother caught us kissing.

Apparently, my body forgot the sting of rejection, because I rush into his waiting arms. Throwing myself against him, I allow myself a few seconds of safe, simple comfort. His familiar woodsy scent conjures up a lot of fond memories.

The moment his sturdy arms band around me, a ragged sob tears out of my throat. He runs one big hand over my hair, and makes soft soothing noises.

"I got you, Bree. You're safe now."

I never want him to let me go.

CHAPTER TWO
LIAM

RAGE BOILS INSIDE me at the sight of the once-vibrant girl in my arms. Big, bug-eyed sunglasses or not, I caught another glimpse of the bruises on her face before she buried her head against my chest.

"Tell me what happened, Bree. Who did this to you?"

Her muffled whimper makes me regret questioning her so soon. But I have to know who did this so I can plan how to kill them.

My hands curl into fists and I struggle to straighten them out and keep running them over Bree's back. If I could carry her pain, I'd do it. No question.

She flinches, and I hesitate. Where else is she hurt? An unfamiliar, out-of-control sensation threatens to blow the top of my head off as I consider the possibilities.

Nothing in my professional training prepared me for this. Maybe that makes me a shitty cop. I don't know. I've dealt with DV victims before. Locked up plenty of husbands who were too quick with their fists.

It made me angry every single time.

But nothing like this.

"Honey," I say gently, trying to keep my voice calm and professional. "Is Chad the one who hurt you?"

It'll take everything in me not to hunt Chad down and beat the living fuck out of him if he did this to my little Bree. I need to know every single detail so I can fix this for her.

One more sniffle from Bree threatens to shatter me, and I wrap my arms around her tighter.

Against my body, she seems fragile and tiny. What kind of "man" hurts a woman?

Slowly, she unwraps her arms from around my waist before I'm ready to let her go.

Shoving the sunglasses up and settling them on top of her head, she brushes a few stray tears off her cheeks. One look at the full extent of the bruising sends me back into murderous-rage territory.

She must sense my fury, because she quickly tugs the sunglasses back down. "It looks worse than it feels. I'm okay, really."

I was in enough fights as a teenager to know she's lying. Her bright blue eyes may have temporarily lost the sparkle I remember, but her courage reassures me.

"Thank you for being here, Liam."

"I'm always here for you." Sure wish I'd been there to prevent this.

Our eyes lock and I nod, hoping to encourage her to tell me what happened. "Tell me the truth. Did Chad do this?" I ask again.

She nods slowly and I suck in a deep breath, willing myself to stay calm. "Where is he now?"

"Empire County Jail," she whispers.

"Good."

My eyes take more of her in. I haven't seen her in at least two years. Bree isn't a little girl anymore. She's grown into a stunning woman.

A woman who just got knocked around by her boyfriend, dickhead.

"Please don't—"

"Don't what, Bree?"

"Get involved. He's in jail and the judge denied bail. I'll be fine. I'm okay," she says, but I'm not sure if she's trying to convince herself or convince me.

Okay my ass.

Unwanted memories of her high school graduation flood my brain. Sweet little Bree had curled herself around my body, stared up into my face, and informed me she wasn't a kid any more before asking me to be her *first.* Like an idiot, I'd given in and kissed her. Wanted to do a hell of a lot more.

Vince catching his best friend making out with his sister behind their house had *not* gone over well.

In the academy, I'd been tasered, tear-gassed, and pepper-sprayed, but pushing Bree away to save my friendship with her brother remains the hardest thing I've ever done.

Because I really, really wanted to be her first.

How would things have turned out if I'd followed my instincts? Told my best friend to fuck off, mind his own business. Explained that I was crazy about his sister and he better suck it up?

But she was barely out of high school. About to leave for college when I had no plans to leave our small town. She was off limits in so many ways.

Now, she's home to recover from something horrible. Not to be manhandled. No matter how much I want to keep my arms around her, I have to let her go. It's the right thing to do.

She's not only Vince's little sister, she's my friend. And I want—no, I *need*—to do everything possible to help her through this.

Coming on to her is *not* helpful. It's not what a good friend would do.

"I don't have a key anymore, so I guess that's why Vince called you?"

I'm struggling here. Unsure of which role to slip into. Detached cop consoling a victim? Friend? More-than-friend?

Definitely not the last one.

"He called early this morning. I would've found someone to cover my shift, if…"

If I'd know the reason for her return, I would have called in to work and hauled ass to Empire County Jail to beat the life out of Chad.

"I'll be fine. I can entertain myself."

"I'm sure you can." To stop myself from pulling her into my arms again or something stupid, I lean over to check out her car. "Packed pretty full."

"I kind of left my apartment in a hurry. All my worldly possessions are in there." She lets out a short laugh. "It's not much."

So much for not saying anything stupid. Before I can apologize or reassure her in some way, she spins and opens the trunk. I jam my hand in my pocket, pull out Vince's key, and go prop open the front door.

When I return, I find her bent over searching for something in the trunk.

"Go on inside. I'll take care of everything."

My voice startles her, and she bonks her head on the trunk lid.

"Ouch!"

"Sorry." I reach out and run my hand over her head to soothe the bump.

She leans into my touch and whispers, "I'm just jumpy."

A searing rush of protectiveness surges through my body, twisting and clawing at me. I'm furious. At the man who did this to her. At myself for not keeping better tabs on her. Hell, I'm even pissed at Vince for not being here when his sister needs him.

"I can carry my own stuff," she protests.

Arguing with Bree is the last thing I want to do today, so I grab the heaviest boxes and allow her to take care of the rest.

"What do you think of the house?" I ask after setting the last box down in the entryway.

"It's—wow."

"Vince gutted it and redid everything."

"He sent me a few pictures. But it's totally different to see it in person." She sweeps her gaze over the boxes. "Oh, I forgot something."

In case whatever it is weighs as much as the last box I brought in, I follow her outside.

Mistake.

She opens the driver's side back door, bending over and halfway crawling across the seat to grab something.

"Fuck me," I mutter while staring at the sky. How had I missed those tiny, fucking micro-shorts that leave zero to my overheated imagination? I drop my gaze in time to find her backing out of the car.

And catch the smattering of bruises on her thighs. Small. Like fingers.

From rough sex? Manhandling? Something worse?

What the fuck? Without thinking about how inappropriate it is, I reach out, skimming my fingers over her leg.

She inhales a sharp breath. "What are you doing?" she asks.

"Your legs are bruised. Did he...? What happened?"

Her cheeks flame pink. "It's nothing." She slaps my hand away. "I'm fine."

Shit. What the hell was I thinking putting my hands on her? I'd never touch a vic like that.

She's not a vic. She's your friend and she's hurt. Stop being a creep and get a grip.

She stalks into the house while I check in with the station. I need a minute to gain control of myself, but no matter how hard I try, I can't erase the image of her bruised skin from my mind.

Brianna

I CAN'T STOP gawking at the house. Shiny hardwood floors instead of the beer-stained, cigarette-burned, avocado-colored carpet we'd grown up with. Soft blue walls with crisp, white trim instead of peeling wallpaper.

"Vince works on it every chance he gets," Liam explains. His voice jolts me out of my childhood memories, chasing the bad vibes out the door.

"I guess so. It's beautiful." I laugh when we enter the living room. A giant flat-screen television takes up most of one wall. That's my brother. I can vividly imagine him sprawled out on the brown leather couch, shouting at the screen during Sunday Night Football.

The pain of missing my big brother hits me hard. Why didn't I visit more often?

Pointless question. I know the answer. *Chad. Chad. Chad.* He never liked me spending time with anyone except *him*. First, he alienated me from my friends. Then my brother, and especially Liam, once he knew I'd had a crush on him.

Oh, Chad pretended he was concerned about me having enough time to study. Overwhelmed with my boyfriend's single-minded focus, it took me a while to catch on to his act. For someone who was supposed to be so smart, I'd been awfully stupid.

Liam's voice cuts off my trip down Bad-Decision Lane. "Vince said you should take his room. He hasn't set up a guest room yet."

"Oh, okay." A glance shows that Liam's watching me intently. Unable to stand the scrutiny, I head down the hallway. Away from him.

Each step I take stirs up a new memory that threatens to unhinge me.

A lump forms in my throat as I pass the bathroom. Teenage Vince had installed locks on that door to keep out one of my mother's sleazy boyfriends who'd offered to "help" me at bath time.

I pause before stepping into what had once been my mother's room. Well, mine *and* my mother's old rooms. Gone was the one thin wall separating her room from mine. The wall that had provided quite an education before I even understood what all the men coming and going from her room meant. Gone was my tinier room where I'd spent a lot of nights under my bed with my fingers plugging my ears. My brother knocked down the wall and turned both spaces into one big master suite.

"Wow." The gleaming hardwood floors continue into the bedroom, warmed by braided throw rugs. "I'm impressed with Vince's good taste." I point to the navy and orange comforter tossed over the bed. "Except for that."

Liam's quick bark of laughter chases away the gloom that had settled over me.

"He spends a lot of time reading those DIY magazines and watching home improvement shows," he explains.

A picture on the dresser draws me closer. Vince, Liam, and me on the night of my high school graduation. Hours before I made the dumbest mistake of my life. Without thinking, I brush my fingers over my lips.

I catch my reflection in the mirror over the dresser. Well, second dumbest mistake.

"I have the same picture," Liam says, gently taking the photo out of my hands. "I was so proud of you."

Yeah, right. I'd embarrassed the hell out of myself that night by propositioning Liam after my graduation party. That kiss meant more to me than any gift I received that day. Until my brother ruined it. And Liam chose his friendship with my brother over me.

Vince accused me of being drunk. Wish I could say that was the reason I attempted to seduce Liam in my clumsy, girlish way, but I hadn't even tasted alcohol at the time.

A good girl through and through.

At least I was.

Now, I'm a battered girl.

"If only you'd known what I'd turn into," I blurt out.

"Hey," Liam says, gently gripping my shoulder. "You've turned into a smart, beautiful woman."

Does he really see me that way? My gaze lands on the sleeve of his uniform shirt—that his arm stretches almost to the limits—then shifts to the Empire County Sheriff Department patch he sports on the left shoulder. Liam always wanted to be a sheriff. And now he is.

I always wanted to be a successful professional, far away from the upstate New York town I grew up in.

Yet, I'm right back where I started.

"I don't know about smart or beautiful, but I am a woman," I joke back. It's a lie though. Standing next to big, strong, has-it-together Liam makes me feel like an awkward little girl all over again.

He sets the photo back on the dresser without responding. A quick glance at his face yields nothing. He could be mentally agreeing with me or planning how to get the hell out of here.

Hard to tell.

The thought of being left alone in this house full of memories of all my screw-ups turns my stomach upside down. There's no way I'd ask Liam to stay over. He'd think I was throwing myself at him.

I can't handle being turned down by Liam again. Even if it's for something as simple as friendly company.

"You probably want to get home," I say, holding my hand out for the house key.

He drops a shiny silver key into my hand. I let out a sad laugh at the tiny, pink crown key chain it's attached to. Liam loved calling me princess when I was little. Around thirteen, I decided I hated it and asked him to stop. Now, it only brings back pleasant memories.

"I'm sure you have lots of things to do. Thanks for stopping by to—"

He cuts me off before I can offer him an excuse to leave.

"Yeah, you know me. Gotta get home to feed the chickens and slop the pigs."

I stare at him for a second before it kicks in that he's teasing me.

"Well, I'm sure there's some lucky girl waiting on you."

He shifts away. "There's no girlfriend, Brianna. I *do* have to go back to work, though."

"Oh." I squirm and flick a bead of sweat off my forehead.

"Damn. I should've turned on the A/C. It's supposed to be in the eighties this week."

I can't help staring at him in disbelief and following him to the control panel in the hallway. This house had only ever had window fans that barely brought in a breeze. I watch as Liam flicks a switch and the low hum of machinery kicks on. A slight, cool breeze drifts over my shoulders.

"He installed central air last spring," Liam explains.

Something I'd have known if I ever visited my brother. Liam doesn't say that, but the thought hangs between us. I shiver, but not from the cool air.

"Come on, you must be tired. Why don't you rest." His tone conveys it's an order not a suggestion.

"I can't. I need to keep busy."

His mouth twists and he glances down the hall. "I have a few more hours left of my shift, but why don't I take you out to dinner when I'm done?"

He holds out his hand, inviting me to walk him outside. I so badly want to take it. Have him wrap his fingers around mine, but the thought of going out in public when my face looks like I've endured a round with an MMA fighter freezes me in place.

"I don't think I'm ready to show myself around the old stomping grounds," I mumble, pointing in the general direction of my messed-up face.

Anger ripples over his features, but his words are gentle.

"I'll bring groceries and stock the fridge then."

"That's sweet. Thank you."

He shrugs as if it's no big deal, but to me it is. I can't envision myself doing something as simple as navigating the grocery store right now.

"Get yourself settled. If there's something in particular you want, text me."

"Your garlic mashed potatoes?"

"You got it." This time he takes my hand and tugs me toward the front door.

"I'm so sorry for keeping you…for interrupting your work day."

He pats the radio at his side. "All's quiet in our little town—"

A burst of static interrupts him and I laugh. "You had to say it, didn't you?"

"Never fails," he mutters as he listens to the request. "I have to go," he says, hurrying toward the front door.

Nervous, even though I know he won't be gone long, I follow him.

He seems to sense my unease. "I'll be back in no time." He points at the door. "Lock this. I have another key."

Hell, I'd shove the couch in front of the door if I thought I could move the damn thing. "I will."

He steps onto the porch, but I stay behind the door. Almost as an afterthought, he turns, pulls me forward and places a gentle kiss on my forehead.

The back of his hand lightly strokes my cheek and I savor the gentle but brief contact. "I've missed you, Bree," he murmurs before hurrying down the stairs and sliding into his car.

Confused from the emotions bubbling up inside me, I stand there and watch him drive away before closing the door.

CHAPTER THREE

Brianna

UNPACKING KEEPS MY mind off of being alone, but how will I survive night after night here by myself until my brother returns?

I'm too restless to check out the television. Too nervous to scavenge for food in Vince's cupboards.

All my boxes cluttering up the entranceway make me feel like an intruder in the house I grew up in. Except for a few bags of clothes and personal items, I shove everything into the hall closet. Something heavy clatters on the floor, and I lean in to pick up my brother's old shotgun.

Knowing my brother, the shotgun's probably loaded, so I carefully place it in the corner and back away. Vince always wanted to teach me to shoot and I'd always said *no thanks*. I wanted to be an educated city girl who didn't need to keep a shotgun in the closet to feel safe.

Joke's on me, isn't it? Because right about now, if Chad came at me again, I don't think I'd hesitate to blow a hole in him.

Shaking off the morbid thoughts, I head to Vince's room to unpack. My anger isn't as easy to shake off.

The feeling that I'm trespassing increases as I prowl around Vince's tidy bedroom. I don't belong here. I don't belong anywhere.

Eventually, I push my unease aside and search for an empty drawer to stash my clothes.

As I suspected, Vince keeps almost nothing in his dresser. Each item I stuff into a drawer gives me a silly feeling of accomplishment. I shake out shorts, tank tops, and other new clothes I bought on my way here. For far too long, I've been living in baggy, shapeless garments to appease Chad's jealousy. It'll be nice to look like something other than a homeless nun for a change.

"Fuck you, Chad," I whisper as I close the drawer.

I reach for the very bottom drawer and stop myself. I shouldn't get too comfortable. Vince will have a shit-fit when he comes home and finds my girly stuff all over his manly house.

"Really making yourself at home there, huh?" Liam's amused voice startles me and I let out a sharp scream, throwing socks and underwear in the air.

He drops the bags in his hands and reaches for me.

"Shit, I'm so sorry, honey. I thought you heard me come in the house."

Embarrassed for acting like a nutjob, I squat down and scoop up my scattered unmentionables, stuffing them into the bottom drawer. "I didn't," I mumble.

"I'm such a clumsy ox, I thought for sure you heard me thumping my way down the hall."

Clumsy. That's not a word I would use to ever describe Liam. "You're not clumsy. You're the most graceful big guy I know."

"That *sounded* like a compliment, but I'm not sure if I like being described as *graceful*," he says, teasing me with my sincere observation.

Laughter spills out of me. Liam's probably the only person in the world who could make me laugh today.

"I tried calling you," he says as I follow him down the hallway to the kitchen. "You had me worried."

"Oh." I pat my pockets, searching for my cell phone. "My phone must be in my purse."

Liam's face shifts from protective friend to hardened cop. It's a look I'm not used to seeing on him and I'm not sure how I feel about it.

I sense I'm about to be on the receiving end of a lecture.

"I need you to keep your phone close. In case of an emergency."

No reading between the lines needed. "Chad's not coming here, Liam. I'll be fine. He wouldn't dare."

His expression darkens. "I'm sure you thought he wouldn't dare hit you either."

19

The painful truth—that this wasn't the first time Chad hit me—isn't something I can share with Liam. Don't think I can ever share it with anyone, but especially not Liam.

"The judge denied bail," I say weakly.

"I know." By his tone, I suspect he used the few hours away to do some investigating. I'm not sure if I'm relieved to have someone in my corner or embarrassed about whatever intimate details he might have learned.

"Come on." He forces a smile and points to the grocery bags lined up on the counter. "I've got a big sack of potatoes with your name on them," he encourages.

A mundane task like peeling five pounds of potatoes sounds perfect right about now.

LIAM

WHY THE FUCK didn't I yell out a greeting or do *something* so I didn't scare the shit out of Bree when I returned to the house?

Then I lectured her, when I'm sure that's the last thing she wants.

I'm torn. Fucked-up because I don't know how to handle this. If this were a case I'd been handed—easy. Follow protocol.

Bree? I don't know how to handle myself around her. I'm burning with the urge to do something meaningful—kicking the shit out of Chad would be a nice start.

Logically, what's best for Bree?

Be her friend. Keep her safe.

So that's my plan. For now.

"Are you throwing a party?" she teases as she checks out the over-flowing bags of groceries.

"Nah." I force some enthusiasm into my voice. "Need to make sure you eat more than twigs, berries, and bunny food." The words still came out way more somber than I intended. Turning, I give her a lopsided grin so she knows I'm teasing. "Vince said you still won't eat red meat?"

She nods. "You talked to him again?"

I hesitate before answering. "We spoke." After I tracked down information about the domestic disturbance that landed Bree in the hospital and Chad in jail. The most painful details I kept from my best friend. They've been churning in my mind all afternoon, though. Now that I know more of the story behind her bruises, I'm even more enraged, and struggling to keep myself calm. The last thing I want to do is embarrass Bree.

From my training and experience, I'm aware there's a good chance she might return to Chad and I'll be damned if I give her a reason to push me away.

So, I'll keep what I learned to myself.

She rolls her eyes and reaches into one of the bags on the counter. "I don't need a vivid imagination to guess how *that* conversation went," she grumbles.

"Hey." I place my hand on her arm, stopping her from opening the refrigerator. "What are you talking about?"

"'Uh, how bad is she? She's pretty messed up, bro,'" she mimics her version of my conversation with her brother in a ridiculously lousy impression of both of us.

"Your man-voice needs work."

She snorts and pulls out of my grasp.

"You're not messed up. That's not what I said to him."

"Why didn't he call *me* and ask *me* how I was doing?"

"Maybe he *did* and you didn't answer."

I said it jokingly, but it *is* odd Vince hasn't called to check on her. I know they spoke at some point—she called her brother from the hospital, and he called me.

"Nope," she says, strolling back into the kitchen. She waves her phone at me. "Nothing from my brother."

"I'm sure he'll call later." The look on her face makes me want to take her into my arms again.

"I can't believe the kitchen," she says after a few minutes of silence.

"It's nice, right?"

21

"It's certainly homey." She runs her fingers over the countertop. "Not like when we were kids and used to heat up our own microwave dinners and ate on the floor in front of the television."

Even though I've known both Vince and Bree since we were all kids, those little details aren't things Vince and I would ever talk about. Bree stating it so plainly leaves me unsure of what to say to make it better.

She spins in a slow circle, taking in every detail. "It looks like something out of *Martha Stewart Living.*"

"Don't tell him that. I think he was going for *Country Farm Boy.*"

She chuckles and runs her hand over the built-in window seat. "I always wanted one of these in my room."

"Well, when you're settled, let him know. He built it himself."

She lets out a soft snort. "Settled. Yeah."

"Bree, you're—"

She cuts me off before I can offer any reassuring words. "I had no idea Vince was so handy."

"Come on, stop trying to shirk potato duty."

She huffs out a laugh and joins me by the sink. We work together for a while. When she's done peeling and slicing potatoes, she curls up on the window seat and watches me work.

Her phone jingles, and I glance over. She frowns and squints at the screen. Her lips flatten into an angry line and she bangs out a reply.

"Everything okay?"

"What?" Her head snaps up, confusion all over her face.

Something's off. Chad shouldn't be able to contact her from jail, but after a few years with the department I've learned to expect just about anything. "Who was that?"

She won't answer or meet my eyes right away.

"Bree," I prompt.

"Why are you being so nosy—"

"I'm your friend," I snap, cutting her off.

She glares at me for a second before relenting and answering me. "Chad's brother. Harassing me to drop the charges."

"Like fuck," I say, striding over with my hand out. "Give me that."

She tucks the phone in her pocket. "No."

"Bree. I'm not fucking around. If he's harassing you, we'll get a restraining order."

"I can handle it."

Yeah, right.

"Why are you being so difficult?"

She lifts her chin toward the stove. "You're doing enough for me. I don't need to drag you into my mess."

"*Drag* me…are you serious, Bree?"

A soft sigh leaves her lips. "His parents know a lot of people. I don't want…I don't want them to try to screw with your job or something."

I let out a sharp bark of laughter, and she narrows her eyes. The investigator assigned to Bree's case already warned me all about the deep pockets and connections Chad's family has. Entitled pricks who beat up their girlfriends didn't tend to earn a lot of respect with law enforcement.

Squatting down next to her, I take her hands in mine. "Listen to me, I know people too. I'm good at my job. There's not a damn thing his family can do to me. And even if there was, it wouldn't matter. You're more important to me than any job."

"This is all my fault," she mumbles.

"No, it's not." I shift to sit next to her and pull her into my arms. When she quiets, I hold out my hand. She slides the phone into it and sighs.

"Good. Now where does the brother live? Empire?"

She nods.

"Okay. I'll have someone I know down there talk to him. And I'm going to get a transcript of these texts in case we need to get a restraining order against him too."

I work my fingers over her phone. "For now, I'm going to block his number."

"Thank you, Liam," she says softly.

"You don't have to thank me, baby girl."

Once that's taken care of we don't talk about anything to do with her ex. I've got plenty of questions, but I'm already a live wire of emotions. Bree's going to have to repeat her story enough in the coming weeks. Right now, she needs to relax and feel safe, not be interrogated.

She sets the table and waits for me to finish making dinner.

"Do you remember the day we met?" she asks after heaping mashed potatoes on her plate and sitting at the table.

"How could I forget? You were the prettiest girl on the playground."

Her fork stops moving through the potatoes and she meets my eyes. "That's not true. I was picking myself up off the ground after Matty Cantwell knocked me down."

"Yeah, and I was coming over to see if you were okay and then on my way to kick Matty's ass. Little bastard needed a lesson on treating girls with respect."

The corners of her mouth quirk up. "I told you not to bother because Vince would beat up Matty on the way home."

I chuckle, remembering how fierce but vulnerable seven-year-old Bree was. How she matter-of-factly brushed the dirt off her skinned knees, then burst into tears when she realized her dress was ripped.

"Gee, here you are sixteen years later doing the same thing." She sets her glass of milk on the table with a thump and sits back in her chair.

"What's that?"

"Rescuing me."

I grind my teeth, swallowing down my irritation. I'm far from *rescuing* her from anything. No, I'm picking up pieces after the fact because I didn't know what was happening to her.

"You rescued yourself, Bree," I say instead. My elbow bumps against hers. "Eat your chicken. You need the protein."

She picks at the chicken. "I don't have much of an appetite." After a few more bites she sets her fork down. "Chad's always telling me I'm too fat."

My fists clench, but I manage not to explode. "He's an asshole."

"That was your first day at our school," she says, sidestepping any more Chad talk. "Right?"

"Yup. We'd just moved here and I thought I'd be bored to death."

"You and Vince were tight from day one."

"Well, I wanted to stay close to his pretty sister, so…"

She glances up, disbelief in her eyes. Although I said it teasingly, there's some truth to that. Vince and I were in the same grade and shared similar interests, but Bree's the one I was drawn to. Even then she seemed older than most of the kids I knew.

"At least you two always let me hang around. Remember Lucy and Emma? They were always jealous of me because their brothers ignored them."

Bree wasn't like other kid sisters and Vince wasn't like any of the boys in our class. He was fiercely protective of his sister and always included her in whatever he was up to.

"You were fun to be around."

"And *you* were a good influence on my brother."

"He was a hot-headed little shit," I agree, making her laugh. As a kid, I'd helped Vince avoid plenty of fights. Got dragged into a bunch of brawls because of him too. Vince had a hell of a temper.

Dinner with Bree brings both bittersweet and pleasant memories. I've missed her. We haven't spent time with each other in years. Not like this. Except for the occasional Christmas visit and her mother's funeral, once Bree escaped our small town, she rarely came home. She sent me a few impersonal emails, texts, and the yearly birthday phone call, but not much more than that.

Despite the murderous rage welling up inside me every time I'm confronted with the bruises on her face, I'm happier than I've been in a long time.

I work hard to keep my expression blank. Deny the emotions warring inside me. A skill we're trained to do in the academy and hone on the job. In no way do I want her to feel self-conscious around me, so I lock all of my emotions down.

Now that I know some of the reason she kept her distance was her controlling boyfriend and not one hundred percent my fault, it somehow makes me feel worse. I'd have to be an idiot not to know how much I hurt her feelings when I pushed her away after Vince caught us kissing the night of her high school graduation. Bree's always been a brave and proud girl. Vince embarrassed the hell out of her and I, like an idiot, only made it worse. She left for college early in the summer. By the time I found my balls and went to see her, she was involved with Chad and blew me off.

Vince hated Chad, and I hadn't been impressed with him either. But deep down where I refused to acknowledge it, I knew I didn't like him because I was jealous. That, more than anything, pisses me off. Maybe if I'd been thinking with my brain instead of my dick and my ego, I would have seen what was happening and done something to protect Bree.

Maybe if I hadn't made her feel like shit about herself, she would've come to me for help when Chad started hurting her.

The thought makes me sick.

And while I'm busy mentally flogging myself, why didn't I tell Vince to *back off* that night? Was doing the honorable thing—respecting my best friend's wishes—really worth throwing away my chance to be with Bree?

Seems pretty stupid in hindsight.

I'd been caught off guard that night. Mesmerized by the moonlight shining on Bree's skin. Slightly embarrassed because she had more courage than I did to admit how she felt. Excited by the words she whispered in my ear. Lost in her drugging kisses and soft warm body.

Completely disoriented when Vince grabbed me by the back of my neck and yanked me away from Bree. She'd jumped in between us and they'd shared some ugly words. To keep the peace, I'd shrugged off our encounter as a lapse in judgment. Played down the kiss that meant everything.

Would I have ruined my friendship with Vince if I'd told him how I really felt? Would I have slipped a ring on Bree's finger by now?

Glancing up, I find Bree staring at me. A pretty flush colors her cheeks, marred by the bruises trailing from her left eye.

"What are you thinking about?" she asks.

"You." It's almost on the tip of my tongue to spill it all to her. How much I regret my cowardice that night.

But that's not what she needs right now. Her being home isn't some second chance for me. It's not about *me* at all.

It's about her. This time I'll do what's right for her.

She holds my gaze for a brief second before pushing out of her seat and grabbing the plates.

"You don't have to do that. I'll take care of it after you go to bed."

She pauses, then turns. "Are you planning to stay over?"

Well, this is awkward.

Maybe she wants her space and some time alone. But I'm not comfortable leaving her by herself. Staying together in this house probably isn't my brightest idea, but I swore to Vince I'd take care of his sister and I'm not about to dodge that duty. Nothing could drag me away from her, even if this arrangement tests every single bit of my boundaries and willpower.

"Yeah, I promised Vince I'd look after you until he gets home."

A flash of anger crosses her face. Brief, but I still catch it. Little Bree always had an independent streak too wide for her own good.

"Thanks." Her jaw's so tight, she doesn't sound very thankful.

"Is that okay with you?"

"It's fine." She returns to the dishes. "It'll be nice not to be alone," she says so softly I almost don't hear her over the rushing water.

I stand, unsure of what to do. Finally, I come up behind her and gently place my hands on her shoulders. "You're not alone."

She dips her head. "Thank you."

"Go on. Find a movie or something for us to watch. I'll finish the dishes."

This time she doesn't argue with me, she ghosts out of the kitchen and a few minutes later the television blares to life.

When we were kids, I relished teasing the hell out of her, riling her up, and watching her stomp off. Now? I want to comfort her and do anything to make her smile.

So far I'm not doing a very good job.

CHAPTER FOUR

Brianna

LIAM'S LITTLE ATTEMPTS to make me feel better during dinner had their intended effect. I can almost forget about the horror-show my life's become. Until I see Liam's jaw clench every time he looks at me.

I'm disgusted with myself for being so needy. For almost crying in relief when he said he was staying over.

Liam scans my outfit when he joins me in the living room. "You changed."

Self-conscious in one of Vince's over-sized shirts, I tuck my knees up underneath it and curl into the corner of the couch, placing my head on the overstuffed arm. "I'm tired."

"You want to go to bed?"

"Not yet."

I should. I haven't slept more than a few hours in days. Up late packing before Chad came home from a bachelor party weekend away with his buddies. Worrying about his reaction when I told him we were done had kept me up the rest of the night. After regaining consciousness, my two nights in the hospital hadn't been restful. Every time I dropped off, someone came in the room to question me or poke me with a needle.

For the first time in days, I just relax and drift. The television creates nice background noise that drowns out the constant ringing in my head. I'm aware of the couch dipping. Of my feet resting up against Liam's warm leg. The hesitant way he places his hand over my foot and gently rubs his thumb over the tops of my toes.

"Mmm…that tickles."

"Sorry." He stops the restless movement and slides his hand to my ankle.

Feeling safe and secure, I finally allow the warm, black cover of sleep to envelope me.

LIAM

CURLED UP LIKE a kitten, Bree finally drifts off to sleep. Her phone buzzes and I reach over to grab it off the end table before it wakes her.

Big Bro.

"Hey," I answer in a hushed voice. A glance at Bree shows she hasn't moved. Her breathing's still deep and even. Gently moving her feet from my lap to the couch, I stand and move to the kitchen.

"Why're you answering her phone?"

"She's sleeping." I almost add *jackass*, because I don't appreciate his tone. He asked me to watch his sister, I'm doing it, and now he's slinging attitude at me.

"You're staying there?"

"Yes, you asked me to. Remember?" I answer with a healthy dose of slow sarcasm.

"Tell me that motherfucker's still in jail."

"They're supposed to give me a head's up if he's released. His brother's been harassing her though. Sending texts and shit."

"Jesus Christ."

"I've got it handled."

"Thank you." He hesitates before asking, "How is she?"

"Somber," I blurt out the first word that pops in my head. "Still got that feisty streak, though. She'll be fine."

"Just…keep her away from him. She wants to visit him or drop the charges or something stupid, tell her no."

"Christ, Vince, she's not a fuckin' kid. She's smarter than that. Besides, I can't exactly order her around like she's a five-year-old."

"Sure you can. Someone obviously needs to."

That attitude's more likely to push Bree away than make her bend to her brother's wishes. Instead of pointing that out, I grunt something that sounds similar to agreement.

"It'll be good for her to be around a real man," he says.

I guess that's supposed to be a compliment.

"Have her call me tomorrow."

"Will do," I promise before hanging up.

"Thank you," Bree says from behind me.

I turn and find her watching me, eyes still drowsy with sleep. "Did I wake you?"

"No." She lets out a brief yawn and lowers her gaze. "Thank you for defending me. What's he worried about? That I'll drop the charges and go running back to Chad?"

I'm not sure how to answer, since, yeah, that's exactly what her brother thinks.

She takes my silence for a yes. "Of course he does. That's what my mom did with my dad all the time."

Their father was out of the picture by the time I met them, but I remember their mother's penchant for picking up seedy boyfriends and bringing them home. It's one of the reasons Vince and Bree ended up staying over at my house so frequently when they were kids.

"Do you think that too?"

"No," I answer quickly. Although the thought had crossed my mind. Because of what I've seen on the job, not because of Bree.

"Thank you."

"Come on, why don't you go to bed. Get some sleep."

She glances at the bedroom and shakes her head. "I'm not sleepy anymore."

That turns out to be a lie. A few minutes after we're back on the couch, she conks out. "Bree?" She looks so uncomfortable all scrunched up in the corner. "Bree, come on, let's put you to bed."

As I slip my arms under her body and lift her off the couch, she lets out a whimper. Once I have her in my arms, she settles down and I carry her into the bedroom. Only the weak light from the kitchen provides any illumination. I'm careful navigating over the rugs and kick Bree's bags out of the way, worried I'll trip and drop her.

Once she's tucked in, I stop and watch her for a few minutes. The peaceful expression transforms to anxiety. Short, scared cries fall from her lips. Each one breaks me a little more. "Liam?" she whispers.

"I'm here."

"Don't leave me. Please."

Shit. I run my hand through my hair. This is a bad idea. So wrong.

But I crawl into bed with her anyway. Wrap my arms around her soft, warm body and pull her against me. Bury my nose in her long hair and breathe deep. Thankful she's here in my arms and she's okay.

CHAPTER FIVE
LIAM

I SWEAR I only planned to stay with Bree until I was sure she wouldn't have any more nightmares. Bad plan. I'd ended up falling asleep myself.

Pale sunlight filters through the curtains, reminding me that I'm in my best friend's room. In his bed. With his sister. Not quite sure how I'd explain this if he came home right now.

Nor would I be able to explain the morning wood nestled against Bree's ass. While my brain knows she's not ready for a relationship, my body's clearly decided to disregard the memo. I've wanted to wake up this way for years. Thought it would never happen. But now that it has, it's the wrong fucking time to do anything about it.

I push her hair off her cheek and watch her sleep for a few minutes. Her warm breath fanning over my arm and the slight rise and fall of her chest doesn't make the situation in my shorts any less critical.

Carefully, I untangle myself from Bree without waking her and head for the bathroom. I need one long, cold shower.

Brianna

MORNING CHILL WAKES me. Or maybe it's the absence of Liam's solid, warm body behind mine. Each time I woke up during the night, his presence assured me.

I hate myself a little for needing that reassurance.

The shower starts up both informing me of Liam's location and notifying my bladder that I need to pee.

Dammit.

Squirming doesn't make the feeling go away.

Reluctantly I toss the covers back and stand.

Tapping on the door gets me nothing, so I crack it open. "Liam?"

"Shit!" There's a loud rattling and I assume I startled him and he bumped into the shower door.

"Sorry."

"I thought you were asleep."

"I need to use the bathroom."

He doesn't answer right away and I wish I could see him. Between the steam and the frosted shower door, he's nothing more than a flesh-toned blur to me. "Go ahead."

I groan and cross my legs, trying to decide if I can wait. "Fuck it," I mutter before hurrying over and yanking my shorts down. "Don't look."

"I'm not looking."

"Don't listen either."

He chuckles. "What?" A few seconds later he adds, "Are you still there?"

"Don't talk to me. Now I can't go."

His rumbling laughter fills the room and I grit my teeth in frustration and humiliation. "You're the one invading *my* shower," he says. As if I'm not aware.

"Yeah, well tell my brother while he was busy doing all these upgrades he should've added a second bathroom."

He doesn't have a response for that except more laughter. I'm finally able to finish up and run out of the bathroom completely mortified.

LIAM

FEELING LIKE AN absolute creep, I can't even take a normal breath until I hear the bathroom door click shut.

Can't a guy discreetly jerk-off in peace?

Caught dick-in-hand, I was almost *there*. So close. Painfully aware I was using the lingering feeling of Bree snuggled up against my body to beat off to. Then she blew in here using sassy comments to cover her embarrassment, which only made me want her more. Now I'm stuck. My poor dick's so confused. I mean, the woman we want was just in here. Now she's not.

Fuck if I didn't come recklessly close to inviting Bree into the shower.

My body's on edge, in case something interrupts the slow build again. It takes more than the length of a normal shower to *finish*. And when I finally do, I don't feel any less wound up.

When I finally join her in the kitchen, she won't meet my eyes. Christ, did she hear me and figure out what I was up to in there?

"Everything okay?" I ask in a neutral tone.

"Sure, I pee in front of my friends all the time."

Oh, *that*. I can't help laughing. Her eyes blaze with indignation. "It's not funny," she insists.

"I'm pretty sure you've done it before. When we were camping or something."

"That's different."

"I'm sorry. Next time I'll wake you up and ask if you need to use the facilities before I take a shower."

The corners of her mouth twitch and she ducks her head to hide her laughter.

I can't talk her into eating more than a bowl of cereal for breakfast, but at least it's something.

"What are your plans today?" I ask.

She groans. "I have to go down to Empire and give another statement."

"Okay. I'll go with you."

Her eyes widen and she shakes her head. "No, Liam. I can't—"

"Can't what?"

"Come on, I know it's the Empire police not the Sheriff's department, but don't you guys all know each other?"

Not getting her point, I just lift my shoulders. "I know a few guys down there." Spent about an hour conversing with the investigator assigned to her case yesterday too. But that's something I won't share with her right now.

"I'm sure cops gossip."

I snort because, yes that's true. "Still don't understand your point."

She blows out a frustrated breath. "You don't want guys you work with knowing you know someone like me."

Blood rushes through my ears and I sit up, unsure I heard her correctly. "Wait, what?"

"I don't want to embarrass you."

"Embarrass me?" I reach over and slide my hand over hers. "You didn't do anything wrong."

"What if people see you with me?" She touches her cheek. "And someone thinks *you* did this?"

All I want to do is wrap my arms around her. Bree's always been sensitive. And while I'm glad her piece-of-shit boyfriend didn't destroy her sweetness, right now, it's killing me.

"I don't give a fuck what anyone thinks, Bree. I'm not embarrassed to be seen with you or have anyone know you're my friend, and I'm sure as fuck not letting you go down there by yourself."

She blinks a few times. "Wow, I hope you don't kiss your mother with that mouth."

Even though she's teasing me, the relief in her eyes makes me think I might have gotten through to her. "Go on. Get ready. Truck's pulling out of here in twenty minutes."

"Twenty minutes? I need more time than that. And we can take my car. I'll drive."

I almost open my mouth and remind her of our little traffic stop yesterday. Thankfully, I catch myself before the words come out. "I don't think I can fit in your car, Bree. My knees will be under my chin."

"Oh. I'm sorry. I didn't think about…I'm sorry."

"It's fine." I come dangerously close to patting her ass. Jesus, this is bad. "Go get ready," I urge, patting her back instead.

She wasn't kidding about needing time to get ready. Maybe forty-five minutes later she emerges from the bathroom and I freeze. My gaze skims over her bare shoulders and down to her long legs then back up, taking in every inch of the light greenish-blue dress that makes her blue eyes seem even brighter. It's a bit sweet and a bit sexy, just like Bree. "Is that what you're wearing?"

Too busy staring at the fitted top and the gentle way the dress hugs her curves before flaring at the hips—I miss the change in her demeanor. "Excuse me?"

When I meet her eyes, they're snapping fire. "Liam," she says, clearly forcing some patience into her voice. "I spent four years with a guy who was constantly telling me what I could and couldn't wear—"

"Shit, Bree. I'm sorry. I didn't mean it like that. You look beautiful. That's a pretty color on you." Now I feel like an ass and figure I better attempt to explain myself. I lift my hands in the air and curl them into fists, thinking about what she said about her ex. "I know how some of the guys act down there. I don't want to get in any fights if someone says something inappropriate to you."

Her forehead wrinkles. "Why would you get into a fight over me?" she asks. This isn't a flirtatious game she's playing, she genuinely doesn't get it.

"I—" Admitting that I don't want any of the horny fucking cops I know eye-fondling her or asking for her phone number feels like revealing too much. "You're like my little sister, Bree. Can't have guys whistling at you and stuff."

Lie, lie, lie. I don't have a brotherly feeling in my body toward Bree at the moment.

CHAPTER SIX
Brianna

"*Y*OU'RE LIKE MY *little sister.*"

Ouch, that hurt.

It shouldn't. It's not like I don't know Liam has no romantic interest in me. I'm not exactly girlfriend material at the moment anyway. I guess I should be thankful to count him as a friend.

Instead of sleeping or doing whatever he does during the day before he starts the afternoon shift, he's offering to drive me all over Empire County so I don't have to be alone. Even so, I can't take the overbearing *is that what you're wearing* attitude from anyone ever again. Not even Liam.

"Well, I'm not changing. It's supposed to be like ninety-five degrees today. If some degenerate cops can't behave themselves in the presence of a girl in a dress, that's their problem, not mine."

"You're right. Come on, let's go."

I follow him outside to his truck, where he opens my door. The bright sun stabs me in the eyes and I paw through my purse looking for my sunglasses.

Liam's rough fingers brush my cheek. "Your face?"

I force out a laugh that borders on deranged. "Nothing but the best corrective camouflage concealer. Bought a whole goddamn palette," I grumble. I hate wearing makeup. Especially heavy makeup when it's so damn hot. I'm self-conscious about looking like a clown. Having Liam stare at me isn't helping.

"That's what took you so long?"

I lift my chin and meet his concerned gaze. "Yes."

"Bree." He reaches out and takes my hand. "What he did to you. That's *his* shame, not yours."

My mouth opens but no words come out. He leans down and kisses my forehead, then opens the truck door wide, offering me a hand for support.

LIAM

NO MATTER HOW much I try to joke with Bree or get her to talk to me, she's quiet until we leave the town limits.

"How big of an area do you patrol?" she asks.

"Base is in Clarktown, runs up to the Slater County border and down to the Empire City limit, but I can be sent anywhere in the county depending on what the department needs that day. Why? You want to apply for a job?" I toss her a cocky grin. "The academy is rough, but I think you can handle it."

She finally laughs. "No, I'm still set on Psychology."

"No one likes the headshrinker, Bree."

"Yeah, I imagine all you macho-tough-guys have a rough time getting in touch with your feelings."

That hits close to home and I snap my mouth shut.

After a few minutes I ask, "Where do you have to go after we pick up the report?"

She pulls her purse into her lap and digs through it until she finds a yellow slip of paper. "I'm meeting with Magdalene McKay in the Special Victims Unit."

"I know Maggie. She's good."

"How do you know her?" Bree asks in an even voice. I glance over quickly, but can't read her expression.

"From different cases I've worked on."

"Oh. Yeah. Duh." Out of the corner of my eye, I catch her shaking her head.

It takes a few minutes to find a parking spot in front of the station.

"You can drop me off and I'll just run in," Bree says the second time we circle the block.

Not happening. "We're good," I say, slipping into a spot designated for county workers. I toss a card on the dashboard and hustle to open her door.

"I'm fine," she says, brushing off my attempt to help her out of the truck. She runs her hands over her dress, fluffing the skirt a few times and I realize she's nervous. "My hem isn't tucked up in my underwear or anything, is it?" she asks.

The question forces me to look at her perfectly curved backside. "You're covered," I mumble.

"Why are you so cranky?"

"I'm not. Let's get this over with."

My hand fits perfectly into the small of her back as I guide her into the station. The quick smile she flashes when I open the door rocks me, but somehow I keep my cool. We're not on a date for fuck's sake.

"Hollister! How've you been?"

"Hey, Howard." I take his outstretched hand. "I'm good. You still with corrections?"

He pulls a face that most C.O.s make. "Puttin' in my twenty-five. Headin' back there now." His gaze strays to Bree and he raises an eyebrow.

My arm tightens around her waist. "This is my friend Bree."

She stretches out her hand which he takes—briefly—after checking out the look on my face.

"Will you be here for a minute?" I ask.

"Sure."

I lead Bree upstairs to the window where she needs to pick up the police report and an additional incident report. "Hi, Patty, can you take care of my friend? She's picking up a DRI and—"

"I have the incident number," Bree says, cutting me off and handing over the information.

Confident she has it handled, I walk back downstairs to chat with my buddy Howard.

Brianna

I'M A MESS of contradictions. Having Liam with me today makes my situation seem too real. Even so, I miss his strength when he runs downstairs.

The woman at the counter is efficient and hands over what I need quickly. Since there's only one staircase, I figure I can't miss Liam, and head down to meet him as soon as I'm finished.

We nearly collide at the bottom of the staircase. "Sorry," he says, gently gripping my arm to steady me. "I was coming right back."

"I wanted to meet you."

He flashes a tight smile and takes my hand. "Get everything you needed?"

"Yup. They were nice and helpful."

"Good," he says, absently holding open the front door.

"It wasn't as awful as I expected," I confess as soon as we're back in Liam's truck.

"Were you worried?"

"A little."

"I'm sorry I left you."

I reach over and settle my hand on his leg. "Liam, it's fine. Really."

He seems to accept that and gives my hand a quick squeeze.

When we reach the District Attorney's office, he walks me inside there too. I appreciate his company more than I've been able to express today. We're sitting waiting for the attorney when I bump him with my shoulder, drawing his attention to me. "Thank you for everything."

"No problem, sweetness." His gaze flicks to the cubicle farm in front of us and the closed office doors along the outer wall. "Maggie's not going to allow me in there while she's interviewing you. Will you be all right if I run a few errands? I won't be gone more than an hour. Your interview will probably take that long."

"Sure. No problem."

"If I'm not back in time, wait here. I'll come upstairs to get you, okay?"

"Okay. Thank you." I curl my fingers around his and he gives me a gentle squeeze.

"Brianna Avery?"

I shoot up out of my chair so fast, I almost stumble in the high-heeled sandals I'm not used to wearing.

"Hi. I'm Brianna."

"Hi, Miss Avery." The woman can best be described as short and severe. From her no-nonsense brunette bob to her low-heeled comfort flats, she radiates professionalism and confidence. "I'm Assistant District Attorney, Magdalene McKay."

"Thank you for meeting with me today."

She nods as if to say it's no big deal, just part of her job. Her gaze lands on Liam and she scowls. "You're not assigned to her case, Deputy Hollister."

"Bree's a personal friend. I'm escorting her around today."

The attorney cocks her head and studies him for a minute. I like her already.

AN HOUR OF questions later, I'm not so sure I like Maggie—as she insisted I call her—as much as I thought I would. She gave me time to tell her my story without interruption—up to a point. When I wandered off-topic, she gently guided me back. When I had trouble remembering details that I've blocked, she picked out a certain element and asked me to expand on it until I was flooded with memories.

She's incredibly thorough in her questions.

What I'm going through today is only a taste of what will happen if my case goes to trial.

"This is a tough one, but I need to ask. What's the worst thing Chad might say about you?"

That's not tough at all. "That I'm a bitch and a slut. Those two insults were pretty common. He constantly accused me of cheating on him even though he knew where I was every second of the day." The anger I've held down for the past few years bubbles up and my fists tighten. Why did I put up with that for so long? I *know* better.

"That's what these guys do," Maggie says. "Not that it's an excuse, but *did* you cheat on him?"

"Never."

"What's your relationship with Deputy Hollister?"

To be honest, I'm surprised she didn't ask sooner. "We grew up together. He's my brother's best friend."

"Any romantic history?"

"No."

"Anything else Chad might say?"

"About me? I have no idea. The cheating accusation was pretty constant."

"More likely he cheated on *you*."

I swallow hard. "I considered that. Sometimes I hoped he was cheating and he'd leave me, but I wouldn't wish him on my worst enemy. Hell help the next woman who falls for his act."

Maggie chuckles, the first time she's lightened up since she started the interview. "You're going to make a good witness, Bree."

CHAPTER SEVEN

LIAM

I T'S A TWENTY-MINUTE drive from downtown to the Empire County jail. As promised, Howard's on the gate when I arrive and walks me to the unit where Chad's being housed. While his family connections couldn't get him *out* of jail, they did land him in a special unit designated for mentally ill patients.

Since I think you have to be pretty fucked in the head to do what he did, I can't say it's a stretch.

"It was more for his safety," Howard explains. "Throwing around his family name the way he did when he got here put a target on him."

This wing of the jail is a recently-built, gymnasium-size concrete box with two stories of cells lining the walls. Tables fill the center of the box. A couple of small-screen televisions for inmates to watch are bolted to the wall.

"Still too good for him," I mutter.

"Agreed." Howard stops me before we reach Chad's cell. "Go easy. I only have so much control over the cameras." He points to the ceiling.

"That's not what I'm here for."

It's the middle of the day and as long as the inmates behave, they're allowed to roam around the unit. Chad's in his cell reading when I step inside.

He glances up. "Who the fuck are you?"

I stand there waiting for recognition to kick in.

"Shit." He stands and backs up against the wall. "You lay a hand on me and my parents will sue the shit out of you."

Dark, low laughter eases out of me as I stalk farther into the cell.

43

"Just what I figured."

"What's that?"

"You're only a tough guy when you're hitting women."

"My father knows—"

"I don't give a fuck who he knows." I come closer until I'm right in his face. The little shit actually turns his head and whimpers. "In here you're at a bit of a disadvantage. Seems unfair to kick the shit out of you if you can't fight back." I take a step back and run my gaze over his cowering form. "Although, my guess is you don't know how to fight like a man."

"You touch me, and I'll make sure you're fired and prosecuted."

I laugh even harder, then stare him straight in the eye. "You think I'm worried about a *job* more than her?"

"Why are *you* here instead of her brother?"

"Not your concern."

When he's confident he won't be getting a fist to the face, he lifts his chin at me in defiance. "I always suspected there was more going on between you two."

"She's my friend. Nothing else."

He points at his face where there's a faint red scratch. "She tell you she did this to me? Huh? Cops should have arrested both of us."

"Christ, you're even more pathetic than I thought."

"Bree needs me. Who do you think paid all her expenses through college? She loves me." He flashes a smug smile. "Can't get enough. She always comes back."

Although I hadn't asked her directly yet, I suspected that this wasn't the first time Chad hit her. This asshole implying she tolerated the abuse for money makes me sick. The expression on my face doesn't change, though.

"Not this time," I explain slowly. "And if you're released, you better stay the fuck away from her."

"That's up to Bree."

"Forget her name. Forget you ever knew her."

"How can I forget her when she's pressing false charges against me?

Tell her to drop the charges. She's not as sweet and innocent as you think. I have plenty of dirt that will get her kicked out of that fancy psychology program."

Threatening Bree? *Now* some force is necessary. I step closer, placing my forearm across his throat, pinning him to the wall. He sputters and chokes, claws at my arm, but I don't even flinch and I don't back off. "You need to listen and absorb every word of what I'm saying, Chad." I apply more pressure. "Are you listening?"

He can't nod with my arm in his way, but he lets out a strangled noise I take for *yes*.

"Seek professional help. Forget all about Bree and move on with your life, because I'm warning you, if you ever come near her again, I *will* kill you."

CHAPTER EIGHT

Brianna

LIAM'S WAITING FOR me with a patient smile on his handsome face when I emerge from Maggie's office.

After dredging up so much emotional garbage, I can't think of anything to say on the way home, so I stare out the window, willing the tears that have threatened to fall all afternoon to go away.

For some reason Liam's also quiet. Both of his hands grip the steering wheel so tight, it's in danger of snapping.

"Did you run your errands?" I ask because I can't stand the silence any longer.

"Yes." His short, clipped answer stings, so I return to staring out the window.

"Everything go okay with Maggie?" he asks in a tight voice.

"It was…difficult going over all those details." I don't tell him the worst part, that Maggie gave me the number of a therapist she wants me to contact.

His jaw works from side to side. "I know. But you have to do it." He smacks the steering wheel with his palm to emphasis his point.

What the hell? "I did it, didn't I?" I fire back.

"Well, it's only going to be more difficult if it goes to trial." His condescending cop tone makes me want to flip him off, stick my tongue out, or something equally juvenile.

"Yeah, I know. Maggie warned me," I answer calmly instead.

"Good," he says, staring straight ahead.

"Are you mad at me, Liam?"

"What?" He glances over and takes my hand. "No. Why would you ask that?"

"You've seemed angry since you picked me up."

"I…" He hesitates and squeezes my hand. "I hate that you have to go through all this. I wish I could make it easier or do it for you or something."

That I can live with. His admission removes the remaining tension between us and I relax into the seat. "You've already done so much for me. Thank you, Liam."

"I'd do anything for you, Bree." His low hypnotic voice melts me. He glances over. "You look so pretty, let's go out to dinner."

My cheeks heat up from the compliment. "Don't you have to go to work?"

"I switched shifts. I'm working the day shift tomorrow."

"Oh." I hate disappointing him when he's gone to the trouble of changing his schedule for me. "I'm so drained. I don't think I can—"

"Another time." He glances over and gives me a half-smile. "Will you wear that dress for me?"

"If you like it that much, you can borrow it." I cover my mouth with my hand, but it does nothing to cover my giggles.

He snorts and shakes his head. "Wiseass."

LIAM

UNEASE FROM MY "talk" with Chad follows me home. That's the first time I've bent a rule since I was accepted into the Sherriff's academy. Never choked anyone or threatened them on the job either. I fully believe law enforcement should be used to strengthen relationships within the community and protect the public in a fair, respectful way. And I'm well-aware that not all my colleagues have that view.

I behaved in a way I ordinarily despise.

And I felt nothing. No beat-on-my-chest moment when I left the jail. No guilt. Nothing but the grim satisfaction of checking off an item on my to-do list.

There's a remote chance I'll lose my job or worse.

I glance over at Bree and know that I'd do it again, no matter what.

I wasn't bluffing either. He's dead if he comes near her.

The interview must have brought up a lot of painful things she'd rather forget. Mom and Dad's house would be a better place to take her than the two of us sitting around Vince's place all night.

"You want to stop by and see my parents?" I ask as I pull into Vince's driveway. "They'd love for you to visit."

"I don't want to drop in on your mom. That's rude."

"Bree, you pretty much grew up at my house. You're family. Trust me, she won't mind."

I sense she's still unsure. "I'll call and check that they're not busy or something, okay?"

She flashes a brief hint of a smile. "Okay. Let me run in and freshen up."

I watch as she flies into the house, before calling my mother.

"Of course I want to see her," my mother says after I explain most of the situation.

Bree's tugging on the door and throwing herself into the passenger seat by the time I hang up.

"All clear." My voice comes out strained as I run my gaze over the denim shorts, T-shirt, and sneakers she changed into. How can someone look so damn sexy in sneakers?

"I bet now that their nest is empty it's best to call ahead."

It takes a minute for her meaning to sink in. "Thanks, Bree. Now I'm always going to have *that* in my head when I stop by."

She laughs while I make a big show of shaking that mental image out of my head.

My parents have a decent amount of property a little outside the town limits. Not a lot of neighbors. Perfect for target practice and bonfires. Two of my favorite things when I was a kid.

"Man, my legs always got a workout when Vince and I rode our bikes over here," she remarks as I steer the truck onto the narrow mountain road leading to their house. "I was so happy when he finally got his license."

"There's a bus stop at the top of the hill now."

"What? You're kidding," she grumbles, sitting back and folding her arms over her chest.

When Vince and Bree stayed over—which was often when they were younger—the long trek up the hill after school was brutal. Sometimes my mother would be waiting for us at the bus stop to drive us the rest of the way. Other times she told us the fresh air would do us good.

In the spring, Bree would stop to pick so many flowers, the walk took twice as long. Drove Vince crazy, having to stop and wait every five minutes, but I never minded. It was one of the few things that made her smile.

I haven't missed Bree's endless fidgeting the entire way. Without even thinking about, I reach over and settle my hand on her leg. "Relax. They'll be so happy to see you. My mother's always asking about you."

She reaches up and pulls down the visor mirror. "You didn't tell them...about Chad...about what happened to me, did you?"

I'd give anything to take the shame and uncertainty out of her voice.

"No. You asked me not to say anything to anyone, so I didn't."

"Thank you."

"You could talk to my mom. If you need...I know I'm not..."

"I don't think so. It's too embarrassing."

"She wouldn't judge you, Bree. You know she loves you and your brother."

She's silent for a few seconds. "I feel terrible," she finally says. "I love your parents. I haven't called or stopped by to see them in so long. They always treated me so well, and I've been a shit in return."

Anguish colors her words. Reaching over, I capture one of her hands in mine. "Stop. It's normal to get wrapped up in stuff when you leave home for the first time."

Out of the corner of my eye, I catch her shaking her head.

"Hey, you send them cards every Christmas and on their anniversary. They're my parents and I don't always remember their wedding date. But you do."

"I remember because it always amazes me that two people can still be so in love after so many years," she says so quietly, I almost miss the words. "Do you want that eventually?" she asks.

I'm not sure how to answer. Of course I do. Except when I try to picture myself with someone, she always looks like…"Doesn't everyone?"

"No. I don't think my brother does."

"Sure he does. He just hasn't met the right girl."

"If by *right girl*, you mean he hasn't met someone who can tolerate his grumpy butt for more than two weeks, then I guess you're right."

Laughter rolls through me as I park the truck in my parents' driveway. "Ever since he dated the one who chalked "happy one-week anniversary" in front of his house, I try to stay out of it."

"Wow, I never heard that story." She chuckles. Love that I can break through the grim shadows she's wrapped herself in, even if it's only for a few seconds. "Ready?" I ask, tucking a stray wisp of hair behind her ear. "You look beautiful, Brianna."

Her lips part, as if the compliment surprises her.

The sudden urge to kiss her overtakes me, but I pull away.

"Come on. You know Mom hates it when we're late."

"I remember."

I meet her on the other side of the truck and take her hand, surprising both of us, I think.

"Liam," my mother calls out as we step into the foyer.

"Bree," she sings even louder as soon as she spots Brianna hiding behind me.

I bend down to kiss my mom's cheek and allow her a few seconds to run her hand through my unruly hair. "You need a haircut," she *tsks* at me.

"Where's Dad?"

"Out back," she answers, shoving past me to get to Brianna. "Look at you. Beautiful girl, come here." She pulls Bree into a tight hug, which Bree returns. At the last second I catch Bree staring at me with tears shining in her eyes.

"I'm so happy to see you, Mrs. Hollister."

"The house smells amazing, Ma. Are you planning to feed us or make us stand here and drool," I say, hoping to move things along and make Bree a little less uncomfortable.

That does the trick. My mother takes pride in entertaining. Even the suggestion she's not taking care of her guests sends her into a frenzy.

"Let me help, Mrs. Hollister," Bree says, reminding me of when she was younger. She'd always been eager to help my parents do things around the house. As if one wrong move would get her tossed out.

Sounds of chaos erupt from the backyard and my mother sighs. "Please go help your father before he sets the place on fire."

I leave the two of them and hope my mother's able to work some of her magic with Bree.

CHAPTER NINE

Brianna

NOT MUCH HAS changed in the Hollister household. Mrs. Hollister still adores her only son. She still welcomes me into her home with open arms.

"Good grief, young lady. You've known me long enough to call me Amanda by now."

"Thank you, Amanda."

"Or Mom," she suggests with a quick look at her son. Painful longing rolls through me, twisting my stomach. How many times when I was little had I wished this woman *was* my mother? How many times had Vince and I sought refuge under the Hollisters' roof?

Liam disappears out the back door, and Amanda sweeps me into the kitchen where she won't let me do anything. Instead, she directs me to a stool next to the counter where she can pepper me with questions and feed me tidbits.

"Tell me about school."

I spill everything about the last four years of my academic life. As the words flow out of my mouth, it occurs to me that it's a miracle I made it through my program and into graduate school. The fog I've been living in seems to lift.

Even though I've been gone for four years, in this house I feel at home.

When dinner's ready, I help carry everything to the table.

Mr. Hollister gives me a big hug. "You must have gotten lost in the kitchen, since you didn't come out to say hello."

"Sorry."

"Shush. She was helping me," Amanda says, playfully pushing him into his chair. I'm pretty sure he reaches around and pinches her butt. Smothering a smile, I turn and find Liam watching me.

"They're so cute." I silently mouth the words at him, and his lips quirk. He pats the chair next to him, and I take it.

"So Liam says you just graduated," Mr. Hollister says after all of our plates are full. "You'll have to show us some pictures."

He doesn't say it unkindly. Maybe that's why it makes me feel so awful. I duck my head, fiddling with the cloth napkin in my lap. "There aren't any. I didn't bother going."

"Why the heck not, honey?"

"Dad—"

"I just didn't see the point," I answer, cutting Liam's protest off. My shoulders lift. "They give you an empty folder and mail your actual diploma to you later." Not to mention my brother was out of town and Chad said it was a waste of his time to sit through a three-hour ceremony for the whole five minutes I'd walk across the stage.

"We'll have to do something for you to mark the occasion," Amanda says, driving guilt down into my soul. It didn't occur to me to ask them or Liam to attend. I might have gone if I'd known at least one person who gave a shit about me was in the audience.

"It's no big deal."

"Mom, are you still working at the library this summer?" Liam says, thankfully changing the subject.

"Yes." She happily rattles off a bunch of details about the children's literacy program she's taught every summer at the town's local library since I can remember.

Somehow the conversation comes back to me, though.

"What are your plans now, Bree?" Mr. Hollister asks.

"I'm starting graduate school at the end of August."

Next to me, Liam's hand tightens around his fork and he lays it on the table with a thump. He knows I'm going back to school, doesn't he? I can't stay here forever. Although this time I promise myself I won't let anything stop me from staying in touch with Liam and his family.

After dinner, I follow Amanda to the kitchen to help her clean up. As I'm watching her packing leftovers, I realize she plans to send them home with me. "You don't have to do that," I protest.

"Nonsense. Gabe and I can only eat so much. Besides, with the long hours Liam works, I know he doesn't have time to cook for himself."

"True," I say without thinking.

She glances at me with a curious expression.

"I mean. From what he says—"

"I'm not stupid, dear. I know Liam's staying with you at Vinny's."

Wow. How the hell do I respond to that?

"It's not like that."

To my surprise, Amanda's shoulders slump.

"I had a bad break up, and he's just looking out for me."

She reaches out, cupping my chin and turning my head. Under her intense stare, my heart drums. She releases me without commenting.

"That's too bad," she finally says. Her gaze strays to the back door. "Are you and Liam going to light a fire tonight?"

Yikes. My mind goes someplace completely different than I think she intended.

"It's not too late to join the guys for some target practice." She raises an eyebrow. "If you've finally developed a desire to learn." A smile tugs at one corner of her mouth. This has been an inside joke for years.

Mr. Hollister was a weapons instructor for a private company and used to travel a lot. He made sure his wife and son knew how to protect themselves. Mrs. Hollister would have made a great pioneer woman. She handled a shotgun as deftly as she baked a pie. My aversion to guns had always been a bit of a curiosity in this household.

"Maybe Mr. Hollister can give me some lessons this summer."

"Oh, I think if anyone's going to do that, it will be *Deputy* Hollister," she teases. Her laughter stops abruptly and she takes my chin again, angling my head toward the light.

"Amanda," I mumble through the tight hold she has on my face.

"Bad breakup, huh?"

"I'm handling it."

54

"You're done with him?" Her stern voice leaves no room for any answer other than *yes*. Coming from anyone else, that question would raise my hackles. "I left," I whisper. "I was leaving him when this happened," I explain, pointing to my cheek.

She glances at the back door again. "Did you know I was married before Gabe?"

"No. I had no idea."

"Married right out of high school, against my parents' wishes." She rolls her eyes. "Young love, you know."

I'd have to be an idiot not to know where she's taking this story. Still, I'm riveted.

"He was very...volatile. That's how Gabe and I met."

"How?"

She lets out a long, slow breath as if she wishes she hadn't brought this up. "We were at a gas station and Burt slapped me across the face for not topping off the gas tank. It didn't take much to piss him off. Right out in the open. Gabe was at the next pump." She shakes her head and I feel terrible that she's sharing this story with me when it's obvious she doesn't like to think about those times. "Let's just say, he intervened on my behalf. He dropped me off at my parents' house. They were still furious with me, but Gabe sat down alongside me and explained what was happening. They helped me get the marriage annulled and move on."

"And Gabe?"

"I didn't see him for a while. Needed to take care of myself first, otherwise I was no good to him."

"Oh." Is this her way of telling me to stay away from Liam?

"You," she says. "Are a very different woman, yes?"

"What do you mean?"

"You didn't need a man to rescue you. You didn't marry this guy."

My heart squeezes. She's the most amazing woman I've known. Someone I admired very much growing up. How can she blame herself for what happened? "Amanda. It's not your fault."

Her eyes widen as if she's happy I finally understand the point she's trying to make.

"Anyway, Gabe and I always wanted more children."

This doesn't surprise me at all, but I'm not sure why she's sharing that now.

"Even though we were only blessed with Liam, we always thought of you and Vince as our own."

Shame threatens to drown me. When I walked out of town and cut ties with everyone, I'd also cut ties to the family who had been my safe haven.

"You always treated me more like a mother than my own did," I choke out.

Amanda pulls me into a hug. In her arms I feel like a giant. How this tiny woman created Liam defies logic. "I know your mom had problems. But you and Vince turned into wonderful people, so she couldn't be all bad."

Except, I'd ended up no better than my mother.

"I think that had more to do with you and Mr. Hollister than my mother."

"Oh, honey," she soothes. "I wasn't trying to upset you. What I meant was, I always hoped, well, *you know*."

Confused, I just stare at her.

"The way he looks at you is different than any other girl he's ever brought home," she explains.

Just how many women has Liam brought home to meet his parents? Swallowing down a wave of jealousy that I have no right to feel, I shake my head. He can bring whoever he wants home. It's not my business. "I'm nothing more than an annoying kid sister to him."

Amanda blows out a frustrated breath—clearly disagreeing with my assessment of Liam's feelings, but she doesn't press me further.

The back door screeches open and Liam steps into the kitchen. My heart speeds up as soon as his gaze lands on me.

"I've got a handful of sticks ready. Dad wants to know if you've got dough and pudding for him?" he asks without taking his eyes off me.

"Is the fire ready?"

The corner of his mouth tilts up. "Getting there. Dad got side-tracked showing me the newest addition to the family arsenal."

"Why are you pestering me when it's not even ready?" Amanda swats at him with a dish towel. "Get out of my kitchen. Bree and I were having an important discussion."

Liam bites his lip, trying not to laugh, and ducks out of range of the wet terrycloth his mother's still wielding.

"Ooo! Are we making campfire éclairs?" I ask, bouncing up and down on my toes a little. "I haven't had those in forever. No one else knows what the hell they are."

I attempted to make them for Chad once and he acted as if I'd tried to light *him* on fire instead of a few strips of dough. He didn't eat *low class* food he'd informed me. No wonder I hated to cook, I got slapped down—sometimes literally—every time I tried.

"If I'd had more time," Amanda says, giving her son a healthy dose of side-eye. "I would have made everything from scratch."

"That's all Liam," I explain, winking at him.

He raises his eyebrows and taps his chest in a *who me?* gesture, making me laugh.

Amanda's gaze shifts from Liam to me. "I figured." She gives me an affectionate pat on my arm as she moves past me to the refrigerator. "Here," she says, flailing a tub of pudding around in the air. "Liam, dammit, do you want the stuff or not?" she huffs.

"Sorry, Ma." He grins at me as he rushes to grab the tub out of Amanda's hand.

"See what I mean?" she asks after he leaves. "Too busy staring at you to do what he came in here to do."

"Do you read minds now, Amanda?"

"No. I just know my son." She loads my arms down with a bunch of items and pushes me out the back door. "Ask Gabe to come in here, will you, sweetheart?"

Liam and his father have a pretty decent sized fire going when I walk up and set the tubes of crescent roll dough, jar of Nutella, foil, cooking spray, and a bunch of utensils on the table.

"Your presence in the kitchen has been requested," I tell Mr. Hollister. He chuckles and motions me over to where he and Liam have set up a target about ten yards away.

"I was showing Liam this revolver I picked up for Amanda," he explains, offering the gun to me with the cylinder open to show me it's not loaded.

"Wow. It's heavier than I expected." I'm holding it away from my body as if it might explode at any minute.

His dad smiles. "Good instincts already, Bree. Always assume it's loaded and never point it at anyone."

"No problem there," I mutter.

Liam reaches over and pries it from my hands. "I'll take it, sweetheart."

I give it another look. "Your mom really shoots that thing?"

Both Hollister men chuckle at me.

"Yes," Mr. Hollister says. "She wanted this particular one for concealed carry." He slides a finger over the smooth metal. "All the edges have been taken down, nothing to snag when you draw."

"How about throwing a laser grip on it?" Liam suggests.

"Yes." They discuss grips, sights, and other gun stuff that goes right over my head until I hear my name.

"Would this be a good one for Bree to start with?" Liam asks.

His father's already shaking his head before Liam finishes the question. "Not loaded with .357."

"No, no, with defensive thirty-eights."

"Then, yes. It might be harder for a novice to get on target because of the long trigger pull. But for a beginner, a revolver is a lot easier to figure out."

"Right."

"Let me know when you're ready to buy her one and I'll find you a deal."

Apparently Liam's buying me a gun.

"I better check on your mother." Mr. Hollister leaves instructions for Liam on how to man the fire before going inside.

"Have a good talk with my mom?" Liam asks, flipping open the chamber of the gun and spinning it to show me that it's empty.

"Sure. I always love talking to her."

What am I supposed to do, tell him she *strongly* hinted I'm good daughter-in-law material so I can feel like an idiot when he gives me the "you're like a sister to me" speech again? No thanks.

Mr. Hollister has a small wooden table and bench set up and Liam guides me over to it, casually picking up a few bullets and sliding them into the chamber. My gaze strays to the table top where a much larger revolver, two boxes of bullets, ear plugs, and safety glasses rest.

I tap my hand on the table, next to the larger gun, drawing Liam's attention to it. "Is this the big brother to that gun?" I ask, nodding at the one in his hands.

He huffs out a laugh. "No. That's Dad's Colt Anaconda."

"You know that means nothing to me, right?"

The corners of his mouth twitch with amusement. "It's a whole different league of gun."

"Ooo. Fancy."

Another short laugh from him and I enjoy the sound, even if it is directed at me. "It's a little much for your first time."

"You have no idea how much I can handle."

His eyes widen at the comment, making me laugh.

"Smartass," he grumbles.

"Wait a minute. I'm not shooting anything tonight. I don't have a pistol permit."

"You're with a sheriff," he says with a smooth smile and a wink. "I'll let it slide this time." Turning back to the gun, he adds, "I want to see if you're comfortable with this. I can get you a permit application and sign you up for one of the safety classes this week."

"Wait, why? I don't know if I want to do all that."

He narrows his eyes at me as if this isn't up for discussion. "Okay, but think about it. I'd like you to at least know the basics."

Something about his answer leaves me feeling as if he used a lot of restraint in his words, but I appreciate the effort he's making not to seem like he's bossing me around. I know it doesn't come easy for Liam. Especially after...well, everything.

"You really think I can do this?" I ask, nodding at the gun in his hand.

"I think you can do anything you set your mind to, Bree," he answers in a solemn voice.

"Okay. Hand it over, Hollister."

"Yeah? All right." His half-smile spreads into a full-on grin.

I hold out my hand and he shakes his head. "Not so fast." He hands me a pair of safety glasses and earmuffs. I slip the glasses on, and he settles the muffs around my neck before continuing.

"There's no safety on this gun. The double-action trigger *is* the safety."

"Is that good?"

"Yes. You have to purposely pull the trigger back for it to go off.

"Okay."

"It just means there's less chance of an accidental fire."

"Uh, good, I guess."

Sensing my unease, Liam moves a little closer to show me the cylinder. "This takes six bullets, most small revolvers take five."

He hands me three bullets and shows me how to slide them into the empty chambers.

"Ready?" he asks.

Feeling a little more confident, I answer, "I think so."

He takes his time placing the gun in my palm and showing me how to hold it properly with both hands.

"Line up your sights. Really focus on putting that front sight on the target."

It's harder than I thought. He moves behind me, helping to keep my arms steady. The heat of him at my back momentarily distracts me.

Focus. Prove to him you can do this.

"When you're ready, slowly squeeze the trigger. Nice and smooth. All the way until it fires. It will be louder than you expect."

I practice holding it and aiming the way he showed me a few times.

"Ready?" he asks.

"Yes."

He moves closer and slips my earmuffs into place, then stands behind me and to the left.

"When you're ready," he shouts.

I take a few deep breaths, letting each one out slowly. On the third exhale, I pull the trigger back, back, back and when I'm almost out of breath it goes off.

Because Liam warned me, the noise and movement of the gun isn't a surprise. He taps my shoulder and motions for me to lower the earmuffs.

"That was good. Lean into the shot more. Keep your grip tight to minimize muzzle flip."

"Okay. Can I go again?"

He nods and slips the muffs back over my ears.

I face forward and allow my mind to clear of everything but the gun in my hand and the target in front of me. This time, I'm not even worrying about where Liam is or what he thinks of me.

I shoot again and again, until the gun's empty.

I set the gun down on the table and take the earmuffs off.

"You went through all the bullets," Liam says.

"I'm sorry... Was that okay?"

He steps in front of me, placing his hands on my shoulders. "It's fine. How did it feel?"

"Good."

"Let's go see your target."

My shooting isn't impressive, but I *did* hit the paper all six times.

Liam's gaze roams over the holes I punched through the outer circles. "Not bad, Bree. I think if we work on your breathing and trigger control, you'll be damn good."

"It's harder than I thought."

"But you felt comfortable?"

My shoulders lift. "It might take me a while to get used to."

"You weren't afraid though, right?"

"No." The only thing I'm afraid of is the sick, helpless fear that paralyzed me when Chad attacked. I never want to be that vulnerable again.

The proud nod he gives encourages me. "Eventually when you're more comfortable, we'll work on shooting in different situations and conditions."

I glance out at the target. "I guess in real life, the bad guy isn't going to stand still and let you shoot at him, is he?"

His gaze travels over the back yard before he answers. "No."

For a minute he's so quiet and serious. I'm not sure what changed, but I step a little closer, wrapping my arms around his waist, tucking my hands into his back pockets, and leaning against him. "Thank you. For everything today."

His arms band around me, hugging me tight for a few seconds before he speaks. "You don't have to thank me. I love spending time with you again."

My nose stings and my foolish heart pitter-pats. "I like spending time with you, too," I say as I step back and look up at him.

This time, he puts some distance between us and reaches out to give my cheek a soft, brotherly pinch. "Ready for éclairs?"

"Yes."

I follow him back to the table where I laid out all our supplies. Together we work out a system for prepping everything. When we're finished, he hands me a foil-covered stick and I spray it down with cooking spray before wrapping dough around the end and thrusting it over the fire.

"Remember to turn it," Liam instructs. "Otherwise you'll have a burned side and a doughy side."

"I thought you were done giving lessons for the night?" I give him a gentle push away. "Worry about your own stick."

He huffs out a laugh and squats down next to me. I'm not sure what to say, but that's what was always nice about being with Liam. The easy silence. So far it's the best thing about coming home.

LIAM

STUFFED FULL OF campfire éclairs, I sit and watch the fire with Bree. I'm not sure where my parents went off to. I suspect my mother was up to something earlier, but haven't had a chance to question her.

"Are you cold?" I ask Bree, because she's standing closer to the fire than I'd like.

She half-turns, the flickering fire creating a soft halo of light around her. "My front's warm and toasty, but my back's cold."

"Come here." I sit up and reach for her and she takes my hand, allowing me to pull her down into the Adirondack chair with me.

I wrap my arm around her and she snuggles closer. "Better?"

"Yes," she whispers.

"Did you have fun tonight?"

"I did. Thank you for being so patient with me." She slips her hand out of my hold and gestures toward the targets.

"Anytime." I rest my chin on the top of her head and watch the flames licking and darting around. Relishing the feel of Bree so close to me. "Want another éclair?" I ask after a few minutes.

She blinks up at me as if she'd been falling asleep. "Oh no." She rubs her hand over her stomach. "I'm ready to explode as it is."

"Want to go for a walk?

"No, this is nice," she answers in a dreamy voice.

After that we're quiet again. Nothing but the crackling fire and a whole lot of crickets fill the air. She rests her head on my chest. My nose ends up in her hair, inhaling her scent.

"Are you *sniffing* me?" she asks.

"Yeah, you smell like bonfires and vanilla, two of my favorite things."

She chuckles and presses her hand against my chest. "I'll have to remember that."

My heart rate kicks up and I wonder if she can feel it under her hand.

"If Vince were here, this would be just like old times," she says.

Moment killed.

Vince hadn't crossed my mind once tonight. Instead, I seem to be treating this night as some weird bringing-a-girl-home-to-meet-the-parents date night, when that's the *last* thing this is.

She already fits in with my family perfectly.

Yet, she's nowhere near ready for another relationship. Having her in my lap like this is just playing with fire.

I sit up, shifting her body. "We should probably get going."

"Wait, Liam, I didn't—"

"It's late. I have to work in the morning," I explain. It's not nice playing on her guilt, but this cozy cuddling we're doing needs to end. Even if I don't want it to.

CHAPTER TEN

Brianna

A MANDA AND GABE are curled up on the couch watching a movie together when Liam and I come inside. They've always been an affectionate couple and it's comforting that their fondness for one another hasn't waned one bit.

"Mom, we're going to head out," Liam announces.

"Already?" She seems reluctant to let me leave as she ushers me into the kitchen to load me down with leftovers.

"I'll visit," I promise.

"You better," she says as she follows us out the door.

At the truck, she motions me closer. "Come here." She wraps me up in the type of motherly hug I longed for as a child from my own mother, but never received. "It was so good to see you. Don't hesitate to visit. You're welcome here anytime."

I blink rapidly and force a smile. "Thank you."

On the way home, Liam's the first to speak. "My mother didn't—"

"Don't. You know I love your mom." Amanda's words from earlier echo in my head. Does Liam really look at me differently? Hard to believe when he keeps so much distance between us. "So, how many girlfriends have you brought home?"

He stares straight ahead and takes a few seconds to answer my question. "Why are you asking?"

"I'm jealous." I try to force some lightheartedness into my tone, but end up sounding more like a bunny-boiler. "I don't like you sharing my surrogate mom and dad with anyone else." That has to be the biggest lie wrapped around a truth I've ever told.

"They've always had a special spot in their hearts reserved for you, Bree."

"That doesn't answer my original question." Why am I pushing so hard when I probably don't even want to know the answer?

"Why are you *really* asking?"

"You're a bit of a mystery to me these days."

"There's no mystery. I'm the same guy you've always known."

"You're deflecting. Come on. Tell me. How many girls made the cut?"

"What did my mother tell you?"

I can't believe he's avoiding such a simple question. "Nothing."

He's quiet while he navigates the tight turns of the mountain road. Once we're on the main highway he finally answers, "Three."

"In the last four years, you've brought three girls home?"

"In my life," he clarifies. "I've brought three girls home to meet my parents."

I can't decide if that's too many or too few.

I glance over and although he's casually leaning one arm against the window, while he expertly steers the truck with his other hand, he seems tight with tension. "Does that bother you?" he asks.

In my heart, a little green fairy shouts "Yes!"

"Would it matter if it did?" I ask instead.

"It would matter to me."

Is he trying to tell me something more? That he regrets other things in the past or am I just hearing what I want to hear? "Well, I can guess Meredith was the first one."

He flinches at the name of his first serious girlfriend. They'd dated during my junior and senior years of high school. Meredith had pitched a fit when Liam took me to prom—as just friends. "So, who was the last one?"

I don't miss the way his hand holding the steering wheel tightens. "Why?"

"Well, you know all about my last boyfriend. Tell me about your ex."

"What do you want to know?"

"Was she pretty? What does she do? How did you meet? Did you love her? Why'd you break up? The normal stuff."

A pang of remorse tickles me as I watch him struggle to come up with answers. Maybe it didn't end well. Maybe she broke his heart and he's still in love with her.

I shouldn't be this nosy, but I'm sick and tired of being the only one who has her life on display for everyone to dissect and comment on. It's only fair for Liam to share a little piece of himself with me.

"We met through work. She's a nurse."

"Do you still see her?"

"From time to time, yes. But only when I run into her through our jobs. Not socially."

"Why didn't it work out?"

"Why are you doing this, Bree?"

"I thought we were friends, Liam. Friends talk about this kind of stuff. Don't they?"

He pushes out a frustrated breath. "She liked the idea of dating me, but the reality of being in a relationship with someone in law enforcement bothered her."

"Why?"

"With her job, she's seen officers shot, killed. It was too much for her. She got possessive and clingy. Wanted me to change careers. Plus, she's a few years older."

"I didn't know you were into older women," I tease.

He throws a brief glare at me but otherwise ignores the comment. "She wanted to settle down and start a family, and I wasn't ready for that."

"Are you ready for that now?"

"Are you?" he shoots back.

Liam's never used such a harsh tone with me. Not even when we were kids and I did something to annoy him. Confused, I snap back. "We're not talking about me."

He jerks the steering wheel to the right and slams the truck into park. His fingers work his seatbelt loose and he turns to face me. "No, we're not. We haven't *really* talked about you since you came home."

My time with Chad forced me to perfect the ability to hide my emotions. Emotions made him angry.

Liam's ripping all those walls down in one night, forcing me to feel things I'd rather not. "Are you kidding? *All* we've talked about since I came home is how pathetic I am!"

"Bullshit. You haven't told me a damn thing." The anger in his expression sets me on edge. I'm not afraid of Liam. It's the fear of the unknown we're racing toward that terrifies me.

"What more do you need to know?" I shout.

"How'd you get involved with such a lowlife? Why don't we start there?" Before I even open my mouth, he fires off another question I don't want to answer. "How many times did he lay his hands on you? I know damn well this wasn't the first time." He barely pauses for a breath. "Why didn't you call me when he hurt you? You knew Vince was a fucking ocean away. Why'd you call him instead of me?"

"I didn't want to! The hospital made me call him."

He shakes his head as if he's more sad than angry now. "Jesus Christ, Bree. Anytime you need me, all you have to do is call. I'd drop everything to be there for you."

"How was I supposed to know that?" I snap back. "You and I hadn't talked in months."

"Because that's what *you* wanted!" he shouts, frustration rolling off him in waves. "Not me. You shut me, your brother, everyone who cares about you, out. Why? Because Chad told you to?"

I don't want to think about Chad. The things he forced me to do. To give up. All I want to do is block out the horrible memories of the last four years, but everywhere I turn someone wants a recount of every gory detail. I want to pretend Chad doesn't even exist. But I can't. "I left. I was finally leaving."

"Why? What was the final straw?"

Oh God.

The detachment I built as a kid, and still carry to shield myself, starts to crumble. He's trying to see inside to the darkest, most tainted parts of me. He wants to make sense of my actions and he can't. No one can. Not even me.

He turns and slams his palm against the steering wheel. "The *first* time he laid a finger on you, you should've told me. I would have taken care of it, Bree."

The tears I've been desperately trying to hold back explode down my cheeks. Frustrated, angry, humiliating tears. "I didn't want you to know what a mess I turned into!" My words bounce around inside the truck while Liam stares at me with wide eyes. "Do you have any idea how embarrassing this has been? How stupid I feel? I hate him, but I hate myself even more for staying with him."

The last traces of anger evaporate and he reaches over to touch me, but it's too late. "Bree, baby, I don't—"

No. No. No. Pity shines in his eyes and I can't take it. Flinging off my seatbelt, I throw the door open, ready to run into the darkness rather than hear another word.

"Bree, don't you dare!" He lunges across the seat, almost grabbing my arm, but I slip free and jump out of the truck.

Staring up at him, I spit out words that aren't fair. "You're only here out of obligation to Vince. So don't act like my big protector, swooping in to save me. I saved myself. I don't need you taking care of me. I don't need Vince. I don't need anyone!" Done with my idiotic rant, I slam the door shut and stalk down the shoulder of the road.

We're miles from Vince's house, so maybe jumping out of the truck wasn't the best idea. But I'm committed now, dammit. All my thoughts race through my head at an alarming rate. Home. Pack. Leave. Or maybe just lock Liam out.

As if that would ever work.

Tears blur my vision and I stumble over the uneven ground.

Liam's heavy footsteps snap over the gravel behind me.

Oh, hell no. I don't waste time looking over my shoulder. I break into a flat-out run and pray I don't trip.

But god*damn* Liam and his long, muscular legs that catch up to me in no time. He hooks his arms around my waist, lifting me off the ground and slamming my back against his chest. Wild and furious, I kick and struggle to get free.

"Let me go!"

"No." He buries his face in my hair, his lips briefly skimming my ear. "Shh, I'm sorry. I'm so sorry. Please, Bree. I'm sorry."

The raw agony and regret in his voice squelches my fury, and my body sags against him. Liam holds me a few more seconds before loosening his grip and setting me down.

Spinning, I fling my arms around him, crying into his shirt. He wraps me up in his embrace and runs his hands over my hair and down my back. "It's not your fault, Bree." He keeps holding me and speaking sweet, soothing words in my ear.

All the fury, all the fight, melts from my body as he holds me, rocking me from side to side there on the shoulder of the road.

CHAPTER ELEVEN
LIAM

WHAT THE FUCK did I do?

I hadn't realized how riled I was until Bree started firing off question after question about my love life.

Mentioning Meredith only made it worse.

A ball of dread landed in the pit of my stomach earlier, when Bree casually told my parents about starting graduate school at the end of August. I can't stand her leaving again, even though I know I have to let her go.

Then there's the shit Chad said about Bree always coming back to him. Haven't stopped thinking about that either. Yeah, I'll admit, the fucker hit a nerve there and I hate myself for entertaining the thought. Bree's strong. She's a survivor. She's not going back to him. I shouldn't doubt her.

Ultimately, I'm furious because I can't express how I feel about her. Not now.

Slowly other sounds of the night filter in over the blood pounding through my ears and Bree's soft sobs. Her arms tighten around my waist and her cheek rests over my heart. My hand moves in circles over her back, her silky hair tickling my fingers. Eventually her body stops shaking and her tears subside.

A car slows behind us and comes to a stop. A short sharp blast of the horn makes me groan.

"Everything all right?" a man calls out.

I turn, my movement stiff because Brianna clings to me even harder, hiding her face from the good Samaritan who I recognize as one of my

71

dad's bowling buddies. Before I can answer, he asks, "What're you doing out here, Hollister?"

"Hey, Henry. Nothing. We're fine. Thanks for stopping and checking."

He stares at us a few minutes longer. "All right. See ya later."

Once he's gone, Bree lifts her head. "I'm sorry. I'm sure this will get back to your parents now."

"I don't care about that. I care about you."

"I know you do. I shouldn't have...I didn't mean it."

"I know, baby girl."

After a few more minutes, I take her hand and walk her back to the truck.

The silence is awkward at first. We've never fought before. I've never been angry with Bree in my life. How could I be?

This has bothered me for so long and now seems like the right time to apologize. "That night, Bree. I'm so sorry I didn't stand up for us."

She doesn't ask which night I'm referring to. "Vince is your best friend. Of course you'd take his side." She lets out a dry laugh. "You were just humoring me anyway."

I slide my hand over her leg and gently squeeze. "I wasn't humoring you."

"You gave me my first real kiss that night, so thank you."

"That was your first kiss? How is that possible?"

"I don't know. You and Vince scared any guy who looked at me away."

"You had a boyfriend for a while there. Robbie Whats-his-face."

"Robbie Norton? He gave me a kiss on the cheek once. It was awkward as hell and he smelled like onions."

It's time I tell her the truth. "I broke up with Meredith before your graduation because all I thought about was you and I couldn't stand it anymore."

She sucks in a sharp breath. "What? No you didn't."

"Yes, I did. I wanted to talk to your brother first. But then you so sweetly ambushed me outside."

"Ugh. Don't remind me. That was so embarrassing."

I pull into Vince's driveway and shut off the engine. "Why? I loved every minute, until your brother ruined it."

She whips her head around and nails me with a hard stare. "What a load of shit. You did nothing. You went home. Didn't call me. Didn't even say goodbye."

My blood boils at her words. She's partially right. "Well, you got even, didn't you? You left for college early and never looked back."

She returns to staring out the window. "I didn't see the point in sticking around all summer and having you ignore me. Why didn't you say something?"

"The next I knew you were hooked up with Chad. You seemed happy. I didn't want to mess with that." I drop my gaze to my fists resting in my lap. "I really wish I had, though."

"Don't take this on, Liam. It's not your fault. I'm responsible for my own mistakes." She jerks her door open and jumps down, racing over the lawn to the front door. Part of me wants to go home, but I can't stand the thought of leaving her alone.

"Hey," I call out when I enter the house and find her in the living room. "Are we all right?"

Her wide eyes stare at me for a few seconds. "Why are you still here?"

Now, more than ever, I can't leave her. Not after the fight we just had. The things we said to each other. Even if she won't speak to me for the rest of the night, I don't want her all alone. "Vince asked me to look after you until he comes home." It's a weak answer and doesn't come close to the full truth.

Her jaw tightens. "Right." She glances down at the couch. "Do you need blankets to make this up?"

The meaning is clear. "Sure. I'll sleep out here tonight."

"I think that's for the best."

CHAPTER TWELVE

Brianna

AS IF LAST night's argument with Liam didn't leave enough emotional scars, this morning I'm supposed to meet with a therapist. I hurry and dress, eager to leave the house before Liam wakes up.

Am I really doing this?

"Where are you going?" Liam's gruff words from somewhere in the vicinity of the couch stop me in my tracks.

Shadows surround him, but I can still make out his wide, male form as he sits up, shoving blankets to the foot of the couch.

Even though I helped him fix the temporary bed last night, part of me is surprised he's still here. I'd certainly been a big enough bitch to him.

All night I thought about the implications of the things he admitted to me on the way home.

"Bree?"

The muscles of my throat work hard to swallow, but I can't.

Oh, good God.

Liam. Shirtless.

I'm itching to flip on the overhead light so I can take a better look.

"Bree, where are you going?" he asks in a sterner voice.

I don't like answering to anyone. Not even Liam. No, *especially* Liam.

"Out."

He blows out an irritated breath. "The purse. The keys. I get that. *Where* are you going?"

My tongue sticks to the roof of my mouth as I watch him stand up.

"Bree?" he prompts again. A little softer this time.

I'm still embarrassed to tell him about the therapist Maggie referred me to.

Straightening my spine, I lift my chin. "If you must know, I have an appointment with a therapist."

His shoulders drop and he seems to relax. "Do you want me to go with you?" he asks gently.

Hell no. I can't think of anything I want less.

What a contradiction too. Being with Liam makes me feel safer than I have in a long time. But having him drive me to therapy like I'm a child? Nope. Not happening.

"No. I'll be fine. The first session is one on one and then there's a support group I might stick around for." It's not easy to tear my gaze away from his beautiful bare chest.

"That's great. Did Maggie suggest it?" he asks.

"Yes. I guess she works with this therapist and…" My voice trails off as he moves closer, and I struggle not to stare at his boxers, which are ever-so-slightly tented in front.

I can't meet his eyes or finish my sentence and after a second I think he realizes why. It's hard to tell in the dim light, but a slight flush seems to stain his cheeks.

"I'll be right back. Don't leave yet."

God, why can't I pretend none of this ever happened? Why in a moment of extreme pain and loneliness did I cave to my brother's demand that I come home? And why did he have to call Liam to come babysit me?

Logically, I know I *have* to talk to someone. I'm tired of the fear that cripples me every time I hear a floorboard creak or an unfamiliar car drives by.

The only time I can relax is around Liam.

Unacceptable.

I'm working so hard to be more independent. I can't throw that away to wind up needing a man to feel safe.

So therapy it is.

Worse, *safe* isn't the only thing he makes me feel. For a moment last night, I thought he might admit real feelings for me.

He steps out of the bathroom, pulling a shirt over his head, giving me one last glimpse of abs and skin.

Sigh.

Sharing space with him has me so tied up in knots, I'll never unwind. But he's made it clear he's not interested in me as anything other than a friend. Maybe not even that after I'd been such an ungrateful brat.

"You're sure you don't want a ride?" he asks from a few feet away.

"I'll be fine."

Having him take me to my therapist? No. That's a cherry I don't need topping off the shit-sundae my life has turned into.

THE SMALL WAITING room looks nothing like I expected.

Diana Ford, LCSW, keeps a homey office with over-stuffed armchairs and a fireplace that give the place a living room feel. Anxious, I pick up a magazine and flip through it. I can't concentrate on any of the pages, but at least it keeps my fingers busy.

"Brianna?" A soft, feminine voice jolts me from the magazine.

"Yes." Should I stand or stay put?

"Diana Ford." She holds out her hand and we shake. "I'm so sorry to keep you waiting. Follow me."

With an extended arm, she directs me to the largest office at the end of the hall. There's a desk in the corner with neat stacks of folders and charts, but she takes a seat in one of the comfy chairs and indicates I should do the same.

Deciding between the loveseat or a chair feels like a test I'm not in the mood for. Finally, I pick a chair covered with decorative pillows and sink into it, clutching one of the fringed cushions to my lap.

"Ms. Ford—"

"Please, you can call me Diana."

"I'm really nervous."

Sympathy shines in the woman's eyes, and I think I already like her. I sink farther into the chair while my fingers tug at the lose edges of the pillow clutched to my chest.

"That's completely normal. Why don't I tell you what I want to accomplish today, so there are no surprises. Then you can give me your thoughts."

Not what I expected. "Okay."

"First, I want to do a general risk assessment. Then I'd like a little more detail and we can go from there."

I nod. Okay, no different than some of my coursework where I'd drafted these types of questions. Dry air ghosts over my lips, distracting me. Shifting, I pull out a tube of lip balm and smooth some on.

"Do you want some water?" Diana asks.

"No. I just want to get started."

She gives me a slight nod and picks up a folder full of forms. "On the phone you indicated that you just separated from your boyfriend?"

"Chad. Yes." I can't stand having him referred to as my boyfriend.

"What prompted the separation?"

I take a deep breath and meet her gaze. My bruises are still visible. I didn't bother wearing makeup today. "He's very controlling. I had a light bulb moment at the end of the semester that I needed to get out."

"And?" she prompts.

"I packed up my stuff first. I planned to leave him a note and take off, because I knew he'd lose his shit. But he came home early. Flipped out when he saw the boxes. He went after me..." Good God, how many times am I going to have to tell this story? "Thankfully our neighbors heard and I guess someone called the police. I blacked out during the...and I woke up in the hospital."

Diana doesn't blink. "This wasn't the first time, then?"

"No."

"Was it the first time you had to go to the hospital?"

The muscles in my throat constrict. "Once," I whisper. After a few heartbeats, I find my voice and continue. "When we were first dating, he smashed my hand in the car door after he saw me talking to a male friend on campus. He swore it was an accident, and at the time I believed him."

"It could have been an accident. Did you see a doctor?"

"Yes. The ring and pinky fingers on my right hand were broken." Wiggling the fingers brings on the faint, familiar ache. "I had to be creative that semester."

"When was the next time he hurt you?"

"The night we moved into our apartment. My brother helped us move in and he expressed some disapproval. After he left, Chad and I got into a fight. I thought we resolved it, but later he wanted to have sex. I was exhausted and he got pissed. He slapped my face, but claimed it was an accident in his sleep."

"Lot of accidents?"

I let out a snort. "No. That was the last one. Every time after that was deliberate. I used to think that he finally had me where he wanted me, locked into a lease, all my stuff in that apartment, financially dependent on him, my family an hour away so I couldn't easily leave him."

"Are your parents supportive?"

"They're both dead."

My bluntness leaves Diana staring at me for a second. She recovers quickly, though.

"So just your brother? And you said he didn't get along with Chad?"

"Not so much."

My brother called him a pretty boy. Not to Chad's face, but on the phone with me. *So are you and pretty boy coming home for Christmas?*

The answer, of course, was always *not this year*, because Chad expected me to spend Christmas with his family. He and his well-mannered family reeked of money. For a girl who'd grown up in a run-down house and frequently wore her brother's hand-me-downs, Chad impressed me. He seemed safe.

"What about friends?"

"They think he's wonderful. He comes from a wealthy, well-respected family. He's exceptional at playing the loving boyfriend. But over time, he tried to restrict my contact with my closest friends."

"Did he succeed?"

"In some ways, yes." Eventually they got tired of my excuses and stopped inviting me places. "I found ways around his restrictions until it got too complicated."

Diana nods knowingly. "You're a very strong-willed woman."

I swear there's a touch of admiration in the woman's voice. My vision blurs with unshed tears. "I don't feel very strong."

"Well, you're away from him. You're here. It takes strength to do both."

When I don't answer, she continues her questions.

"Is there a current Order of Protection?"

"Yes. He's still in jail too."

Diana raises an eyebrow. "That's excellent. Has bail been set?"

"No. The judge took one look at my face and heard the threats Chad made to me after his arrest and said no."

"Is there a chance that could change?"

I lift my shoulders in a casual shrug, but inside my heart's pounding. "His parents were mortified. It was in the papers, so I think they're trying to distance themselves."

She seems to be going through a standard checklist of questions. Oddly, that seems to relax me. "Have they contacted you?"

"No. Well, just his brother. He's been relentless."

"Have you reported it to the police?"

Does Liam count? "Not yet."

"Where are you staying now?"

"At my brother's house."

"Good. You should be with family. Is he supportive?"

"He's away for work. But a childhood friend of ours is staying with me."

"I'm glad to hear that." She shuffles through her papers before continuing. "You don't have children, correct?"

"Correct."

"Good. Often the violence only escalates when the woman gets pregnant."

I'm aware of the statistics. I'd diligently taken birth control since I was a teenager. At one point, I was pretty sure Chad tried to tamper with them, so I hid them in my car. No way would I let him dictate when I brought a child into this world. Not after the way I'd grown up.

I let out a breath, relieved the conversation shifted away from anything to do with Liam. Guilt tugs at me. Something tells me Diana wouldn't approve of my feelings for Liam.

She'd be right too. One thing is painfully clear after this session. I'm a mess. No good for Liam.

Not that he wants me, anyway.

CHAPTER THIRTEEN
LIAM

I RUB THE back of my neck, feeling slightly claustrophobic in the cab of my own damn truck. Both of us still pretending our argument and the conversation afterward the other night never happened.

It's my day off and as a peace offering, I asked Bree if she wanted to go fishing with me. Her enthusiastic yes gave me hope we'd moved past the awkward spot in our friendship. But she hasn't spoken more than a few words on the hour-long drive.

I pull into the small convenience/tackle store near the reservoir and shut off the truck.

"Stay put. I'm going to grab some worms."

The tension in the truck melts as Bree scrunches up her face into the same *yuck* expression she made as a kid. "You *still* haven't made your peace with live bait?" I tease.

"It's gross. Can't we use lures?" she asks.

"Yeah, if the bait doesn't work."

As I stride over the asphalt, a truck door slams behind me. I glance back and find Bree hurrying to catch up with me.

"You don't have to come in."

"I want to use the bathroom. Unlike you, I don't like to pee in the woods."

"One time, Bree. Once." I hold out my hand and relief spreads through me when her soft fingers curl around mine.

The small shop has minnows and worms. Bree doesn't care for either, but I buy some of both anyway. I want her to have fun today. Best way to do it will be keeping her fishing line in the water.

"What's the bucket for?" Bree asks as she joins me at the register.

"Minnows need something."

"Poor fish."

I nudge her with my elbow. "Go grab some waters and whatever snacks you want."

She ambles over to the candy display and goes right for the chocolate. At least some things haven't changed. "Do you still like peanut M&M's?" she asks, waving the yellow packet at me.

"Sure."

At the last minute, I remember she needs a fishing license. We take care of that at a different counter.

Finally, we return to the truck.

"I haven't been here in years," she comments as I drive us through the park's front gate.

I take one dirt road after another until I find the right spot and park.

"The water's low," she shouts from the other side of the truck.

"We're in a drought."

"Think we'll catch anything?" she asks, coming around to my side.

"Hope so. Or we're not eating tonight."

"That doesn't sound very encouraging."

She helps me carry our gear, and we hike down to a spot not a lot of people know about.

"You didn't warn me we'd be hiking," she grumbles as we trudge through the woods. I peer over my shoulder and slow my pace so she can catch up.

"Your brother and I found this spot last year. Caught a lot of trout, and no one bothered us all day."

When we finally find the spot, I mutter a curse at all the discarded fishing line, beer cans, and other garbage littering the shore. So much for it being a spot no one knows about. Bree pulls an extra plastic bag out her pocket and helps me pick up the area. Once it's tidier, I rig the poles up.

I can't seem to stop watching Bree. Her long periods of silence bother me. I'm not sure if she's still angry with me or it's a sign of something else.

The words I want to say to her ping-pong in my head before I line them up the way I want. "How's therapy going?"

Without turning around, she answers, "Okay."

Well that's not very informative. Should I probe for more information, or leave her alone?

I choose to probe. "Do you like the person you're seeing?"

Finally she turns around. Her lips push into a curious pout. "Why do you want to know so bad?"

Every answer I come up with is bound to insult her. I want to be sure she's comfortable with the person so she keeps going. "Just making sure you're okay."

Her lips curve up. "Oh. I thought you wanted to report back to Vince or something."

To be honest, she has a point. Vince will bug me for an update soon. Even though I know Bree's spoken to her brother a bunch of times, Vince counts on me to give him the "real deal," as he so tactfully puts it.

"No. You can talk to him about that yourself."

"I haven't talked to him in a few days."

I hide my surprise by casting my line out again. My mouth quirks when the bait lands exactly where I'd been aiming.

"Still got it," Bree says. The crunch of gravel makes me turn my head. She drops down onto a rock next to me.

"You watching your rod tip?"

She points to her pole, which is nestled in some rocks. "You've been asking me that for close to fifteen years."

"Nah. We haven't even been here an hour."

She doesn't laugh at my lame joke. Instead, she picks up a rock and drags it through the dirt in intricate patterns. "You're going to mess up your pretty nails," I caution without thinking.

The rock falls from her hand and she stares at her fingertips as if noticing the sparkling polish for the first time. "Chad hated when I wore any color but pink. Said it made me look cheap and trashy."

Anger beats against my forehead. Chad better pray he never gets out of jail. "You could never be anything but sweet and beautiful," I say as calmly as possible.

She wiggles her fingers in the sunlight, flashes of blue and silver dancing on the tips.

"It's pretty."

My opinion doesn't seem to register. She wraps her arms around her legs and lays her cheek against her knees. "She wants me to take an antidepressant," she murmurs so softly I almost miss the words.

Bracing my pole against the same rocks Bree used, I lower myself to the ground next to her. "There's nothing wrong with that."

She picks her head up and finally looks at me. Tears sparkle in her eyes, shredding me inside. "You don't think it makes me weak?"

It's impossible to keep my distance any longer.

I slip my arm around her shoulders and pull her closer. "No. Never. It's okay to get help if you need it."

While she ponders that, I consider whether I should share something with her I've never even told her brother.

"I took one for a while."

She pulls back and studies me for a second. "Why?"

I blow out a breath, considering if I'm really going to talk about this with Bree. "My second year on the job, I shot someone." Memories rush back and a chill expands in my chest.

"What? How come you never told me?"

I'm not sure if she realizes it but she takes my hand, pulling it into her lap. That's the Bree I know. The girl who always wanted to comfort everyone around her. "I couldn't talk about it. It was in the local papers. Masked guy held up the liquor store downtown. He had a gun on the owner when we arrived. Ignored me when I asked him to put the gun down. He swung it my way, and I shot him. That's what we're trained to do with an armed suspect."

Stunned silence stretches between us for a few beats. "Liam, I'm so sorry," she whispers. "You did what you had to do, though. You probably saved the store owner."

"Sometimes I still see his face after we took the mask off. He was just a kid. Barely eighteen—"

"Old enough to know better," she insists.

"He was tweaked out on meth."

"Doesn't sound like he gave you much of a choice."

"The gun wasn't loaded." There it is. What's bugged me ever since. What would've gotten me kicked out of the department if it hadn't been for the numerous witnesses and the video proving the kid turned his gun on me first.

"How could you know that?"

"I couldn't. But the thought of how young he was wouldn't leave my head. He could've straightened himself out. Gotten help. Something."

"Unlikely." She pauses and squeezes my hand. "So, you talked to someone?"

"I'm sure it seems obvious, but cops don't like talking about their feelings. They don't like to admit that they can't handle the ugly stuff. So, the department requires mandatory counseling after a shooting."

A soft smile turns her mouth up. "That's a good thing."

"I didn't see it that way at the time."

"What happened?"

Damn, I hate reliving that period of my life. But the eagerness on her face is the first strong emotion she's shown since our fight, so I continue. "I couldn't sleep or eat. I was a miserable dick to everyone around me."

"You weren't…in trouble or anything, were you?"

"At first. There was an investigation."

"That's ridiculous."

Her outrage on my behalf lifts some of the lingering bitterness in my chest. "A kid lost his life."

"But it wasn't your fault."

"It didn't matter. I didn't do myself any favors by acting like a jerk to everyone who tried to help me."

Her cheeks flush and she drops her eyes to the ground. "So, how did you get back to yourself?"

"My parents. Dad dragged my ass out of bed. Mom found a doctor.

I couldn't go back to work until a psychologist cleared me. But I didn't dare go to the department doc until I had my head on straight."

"It's a good thing your mom and dad were there for you." Her voice cracks and a few tears roll down her cheeks.

I cup her face with my hand and she leans into my touch, briefly closing her eyes. "*I'm* here for you. Whatever you need, Bree. You just have to ask."

"God, Liam. Don't you ever get tired of helping me out? I've been a mess since we met."

"What the hell are you talking about?"

"Come on. Vince and I always needed a place to stay when things went to shit at home."

"That wasn't your fault."

"No. But look where I am. I haven't turned out much better."

My fingers drop to her chin and I turn her to face me. "Listen to me. You're amazing. Don't let this one guy define you."

She shakes out of my hold.

"Bree, eyes on me," I snap, using my sharp cop voice. Her eyes meet mine, and I search for the right words to get through to her. "I've seen enough of these guys. They're smooth. Good at convincing a woman it's all her fault. It's not. You didn't do anything wrong."

"I feel so stupid."

This time, I pull her into my arms and kiss the top of her head. "You're such a sweet, smart, loving beautiful woman. There's nothing wrong with you."

"Easy for you to say. You're a hometown hero." A quick smile brightens her face.

"I'm no hero, Bree."

"You're *my* hero," she insists.

"Br—"

One of our poles clatters against the rocks, startling us apart.

"Fish on!" Bree yelps, wriggling out of my embrace. She jumps up and races over to her pole.

The second she grabs her rod and starts reeling it in, my rod tip dips down.

Bree's hoots of joy are contagious, and I also yell "Fish on" even though we're the only ones in the area.

We reel them in side-by-side.

Bree's trout dwarfs mine. By a lot.

"Aw, it looks like we caught a mama fish and her baby," she teases.

Laughter bursts out of me, and she smiles even wider. "Yup. I think you caught yourself a trophy there." The only thing that matters to me is that she's having fun. This is what I wanted today to be about. Bree doing something she's good at and enjoying herself.

"You're going to be delicious with lemon and garlic," she says to her fish.

"For a girl who was worried about the worms and minnows, that's awfully mean." I bend down, releasing the smaller fish back into the water.

"Did you have another recipe in mind?" she asks innocently.

"Hold it up. Let me snap a picture for Vince." She flashes a wide smile and then makes a kissy face at the fish.

After I fire the pics off to her brother, I stuff my phone in my pocket. Bree pushes the fish in my direction.

"Seriously? You still won't take your own fish off the hook?"

"Hell no. Hurry up. Let's catch another one. Otherwise you're going to starve tonight."

"Yours is big enough for two," I point out.

She gives me an exaggerated head shake and her shoulders jiggle with laughter. "I'm not sharing."

"Ingrate," I mutter, wriggling the hook out of the fish's mouth and slipping it into the cooler. As I stand up, Bree surprises me by pressing her body up against mine and wrapping her arms around my waist. Her cheek rests against my chest. "Thank you for today." She tips her head up and smiles so sweetly, I can't help but kiss her.

Is it the curve of her full, pink lips that invites me to take a taste, or something else? Doesn't matter. The urge overwhelms me. I cradle her jaw with one hand and capture her mouth with a gentle kiss. It's soft and tender at first.

How had I never noticed how perfectly we fit together? Her smaller, softer body conforms to every hard and hot part of mine.

She pulls back, staring up at me. "I think you got fish scales on my cheek," she whispers.

I touch my forehead to hers and breathe out, "Sorry."

She reaches up, and I meet her halfway. Once again the dizzying sweetness of her lips on mine. Our lips meet over and over. Simple kisses. Her fingers dig into my shoulders as she tries to get closer. My hands drop to her hips, pulling her in tight.

Her lips part and I stroke my tongue against hers. She tastes sweet, like chocolate and cinnamon.

For the rest of my life those will be my favorite flavors.

She moans into my mouth and I open my eyes briefly.

Whether it's from the heat or activity, some of her makeup has smudged, leaving the bluish-green bruising visible this close up.

What the fuck am I doing?

I squeeze her hips and gently push her back. "Stop, Bree. Baby, stop." My voice is so hoarse I barely recognize it.

She blinks up at me.

I don't let go of my hold on her hips. My thumb sweeps under the hem of her shirt, brushing warm, bare skin.

Her big blue eyes pin me in place and she opens her mouth, but no words come out.

Rocks tumbling down the hill and the *snick-snick* of snapping twigs enters my consciousness. Stuck in this moment with Bree, I don't recognize what those sounds mean until someone clears their throat.

Tamping down a string of curses, I pull away from Bree. Disappointment, then embarrassment, passes over her face.

I turn to find a DEC officer behind us. "Can I help you?" I ask in the gruffest tone I can call up.

The guy isn't deterred. He doesn't blink, apologize, or acknowledge what he interrupted. Another officer stumbles down the rocky incline, landing next to his partner. "We're checking fishing licenses today, sir," the first officer says.

Silently, I'm cursing the intrusion, but I yank my wallet out and hand over both our licenses. One of the officers accepts the documents while the other one circles around our cooler.

"Care to open this for me, sir? We need to check—"

"Yeah. Here," I say, cutting him off, while leaning over to flip the lid open.

"Nice Rainbow Trout. Probably a trophy."

"My friend caught it," I say, nodding at Bree. So far she hasn't uttered a word or moved from my side. I'll admit, I like having her up against me. Especially when the officer spends a little too much time running his gaze over her legs.

My arm tightens around her waist, making it clear who she belongs to.

Hoping to move them along, I accidentally flash my badge when the officer hands our papers back.

"Oh, sorry. I didn't realize—"

"No problem."

Mercifully, the officers finally leave. Bree moves away, picking up our stuff.

"Bree?"

"That's never happened before."

The kiss or the license check?

"They're always patrolling around here," I answer.

She nods and walks to the water's edge to pick up the dropped pole.

Shit, I'm not sure what to do here. Every instinct says to spin her around and kiss her some more. But she's obviously uncomfortable.

I made her uncomfortable.

I did the right thing, stopping the kiss. In the future I'll need to be more careful around her.

Today was supposed to be about her relaxing and having fun, not getting mauled by me, and I fucked it up.

I can't let that happen again.

Brianna

MY LIPS STILL tingling from our kiss, I can't concentrate on the fishing pole in my hands.

Liam kissed me!

The scent of fish still lingers from where he touched my cheek and I inhale deeply, remembering how it felt to have his fingers pressed against my face. His mouth on mine.

"Hey, the bait doesn't seem to be working anymore. Want to switch to lures?" Liam asks, pulling me out of my fish-scented daydreams.

I force a smile onto my lips. "Sure."

He props his sunglasses on his head and pulls a sparkling lure out of his backpack. He concentrates on rigging up the pole way more than seems necessary. Obviously trying to pretend our kiss never happened.

I'm tired of pretending with Liam.

"Liam. What was that?"

"What?" he mutters without looking up.

"Liam, look at me." A trembling ball of want tumbles in my stomach while I wait for him to glance up.

And when he does, something that resembles regret flashes in his dark brown eyes. "I'm sorry."

Wow. His apology shouldn't hurt, but it does. It hits me in the ribs, crushing me.

"It's fine," I mumble, turning to stare out over the water.

After a few seconds, he casts the line and pushes the pole into my hands.

"Bree, what I meant was, I shouldn't have kissed you. Taken advantage of you."

"Taken advantage?" Doesn't he realize how insulting that is? "Did it seem like I didn't want to kiss you?"

My pole jerks down before he answers and I want to chuck the damn thing in the water and demand he answer my question.

"Fish on!" Liam cheers. "You got it?"

"Sure." I put all my anger into reeling it in. This fish is a feisty one and puts up a good fight. "I'm a little scared to see what's on the other end," I joke.

He settles one of his big hands over mine, guiding me. "You got it," he encourages.

When the fish is close enough, he splashes into the water's edge and scoops it up with a net.

"Good size smallmouth bass," he says. "Probably four or five pounds. Nice job."

I lean over to get a better look while he works the hook out of the fish.

Thoroughly pissed-off with his current situation, the bass flips and flops, still fighting hard.

"Ow! Fuck!" Liam bellows, staggering backward a few feet.

"What happened?"

"Hook went through my finger. Shit that hurts."

"Let me see." I take a few steps closer.

Mistake. Blood pours through the wound, small rivers traveling down his hand. So much worse than I thought, considering how calm Liam is. "Can we pull it out?"

"No." He sucks in a deep breath. "Treble hook. Barbs." Each word comes out clipped and laced with pain.

"What are we going to do?" I ask, unable to hide the panic in my voice.

"First," he says after taking a deep breath. "Cut him loose and put him in the water. Every time he flops around, it's making it worse."

Fingers shaking—hell, my whole body won't stop trembling—I dig out a pair of mini-scissors from Liam's backpack and snip the line.

"Now what?"

"Can you pack up our stuff?" he asks a whole lot calmer than I'm feeling.

"Yes." I'm grabbing stuff before he's even done with the question. Catching sight of the two DEC officers who'd interrupted us earlier, I call out to them. "Hey! Help!"

"Bree stop, what are you doing?"

"Getting help."

"They're not going to be able to do anything for me. Come on. Hand me the cooler."

"You can't carry—"

"My other hand is fine. Hurry up, this hurts like a bitch."

He's cradling his hand against his chest. My eyes zero in on the hook—lure still attached—sticking up obscenely while blood continues to drip down his finger. "Liam, it's bad," I whisper.

His mouth twitches into a quick smile. "I'm fine."

"What's wrong, miss?" one of the officers asks from the ledge above.

"He's hurt. Hook through his middle finger."

Liam's right, the two officers are no help. One offers us a first-aid kit and recommends wrapping gauze around it to keep it clean.

Even I realize that gauze around the pointed hook will only make things worse.

Liam stares them down. "No, thanks. How far is the hospital from here?"

"Oh, you don't want to go to the ER. You'll be there all night," the officer says. "There's an urgent care center right over the Empire county line."

Liam grinds his teeth and glances at me. "Yeah, I know it."

At the truck, I turn and hold out my hand to Liam. "Keys."

He has the nerve to look at me and then the truck. "I can drive, Bree. I'm fine."

"Seriously?"

"I can drive with one hand."

"No, Officer Caveman, you can't. Hand them over."

His mouth curls into a half-smirk. "They're in my pocket."

Carefully, I slide my hand into his side pocket.

"I can't even enjoy this," he says, making me laugh.

He directs me to the urgent care clinic.

"You know the place?"

"I've been there once or twice," he mumbles.

It's dusk by the time we arrive. Not many cars fill up the parking lot, but I still struggle to pull his big truck into one of the tight spaces.

"Good job," he says when I finally straighten out. There's no mocking in the words, but I stick my tongue out at him anyway.

"You don't have to come in if you don't want to," he offers.

"Of course I'm not letting you go in by yourself." I'm surprised he'd even suggest it.

He slides out of the truck and meets me on my side. "Okay, let's get this done so we can grab dinner. I'm starving."

"You're awfully calm for a guy with a jagged piece of metal through his finger."

"Trust me, it hurts. I'm trying not to dwell on it too much"

No one's in the waiting room, and Liam saunters right up to the counter.

"I guess I don't need to ask," the receptionist says, greeting him with a sympathetic smile.

She fires off a round of questions. Liam answers everything calmly, while slipping an arm around my waist and drawing me closer.

He's the one who's hurt yet he's trying to comfort me. Great.

"Hey, Linda, can you check if there's an open room?" the receptionist asks.

Liam's entire body stiffens. I can't figure out why until I glance up at the pretty nurse standing in front of us.

Of all the urgent care clinics in the world—seriously, universe?

Because there's no doubt in my mind this is Liam's ex.

Especially when the receptionist hands him a clipboard full of forms to fill out. "I can do that for you, Liam. I still remember all your details," she says with a flirty smile.

Unprofessional much?

Awkward, actually. The receptionist stares, her gaze darting between Linda and Liam.

"That's okay. I've got it." I snatch the clipboard off the counter and tug Liam over to one of the waiting room chairs by his uninjured hand.

"I take it that's your ex?" I mutter as I start scribbling down his information.

He grunts out an affirmative sound.

I tap the pen against the clipboard a few times to get his attention, and he helps me fill in the few details I don't know.

Linda returns and shows us into a room. "So besides the hook in the finger, how've you been?" she asks.

"Fine. You?"

Clearly I have no claim on Liam. The irrational side of me doesn't see it that way, though.

Liam said she was older, but she doesn't look it. She's dainty. Almost doll-like. Idly I wonder if it makes her job harder. If people take her seriously.

"My friend, Bree."

Hearing my name snaps me out of my fog and I raise an eyebrow at Liam.

"Oh, you're Vince's little sister. Right. I've heard all about you," she says, instantly dismissing me and focusing her lovesick gaze on Liam.

"Uh," I answer lamely.

Brilliant.

At least she finally helps Liam. She sets up his hand for the doctor, then gently disinfects the area around the wound while subtly shoving her boobs in his face.

"How's work?" she asks him.

"Fine," he answers in a clipped tone that doesn't invite follow-up questions.

Liam winces and I lose it. "Can't you give him some Advil or something?" I snap, since it doesn't seem like Nurse-Can't-Take-A-Hint plans to do anything other than stare at Liam and give her push-up bra a workout.

"Sure." She settles her hand on his shoulder. "Unless you want something stronger?" she asks.

He reaches up with his good hand and removes her hand from his shoulder before answering. "Can you see how much longer the doctor will be?"

That seems to be enough to remind her to do her damn job and she hurries out of the room.

"Did you know she worked here?" I ask as soon as she's gone.

Liam's eyes close briefly. "Yes."

"That's why you didn't want to come here?"

"I was hoping she wouldn't be working tonight."

"She was working it all right."

He huffs out a laugh, but otherwise ignores my comment. "Come here," he says, holding out his uninjured hand to me.

I step closer and wrap my hand around his. "How's your finger?" I ask because there really isn't much more to say.

"Hurts."

The door swings open. "How are you, Mr. Hollister?" the doctor greets.

Finally.

Liam grits through the shots to numb his hand, barely flinching. When the doctor pulls on the hook, trying to determine the best way to remove it, I sway on my feet.

"Bree? You all right?" Liam squeezes my hand, forcing me to concentrate on his face. "I'm okay, baby. I can't feel a thing."

"Are you sure?"

"Go sit down. You look pale."

For once I'm thankful for his bossiness and take a seat.

I MANAGE NOT to embarrass myself by passing out and we don't run into Nurse Linda again before leaving the clinic.

"I'm sorry our day was ruined," Liam says when we're on our way home.

"You're sorry?" I nod at his finger wrapped tight in gauze. "You took a hook through your flesh and you're apologizing to me?"

"Let me make it up to you."

Another kiss would be a good start but there's no way I'm suggesting it.

"The ice cream shop near Vince's is open. Want to stop there for a cone?" he asks.

"I'm not five anymore, Liam. You can't cheer me up with an ice cream cone."

"Well, it will cheer me up," he says, wiggling his injured hand at me.

I take the exit that leads to the small ice cream shack and we pull into the parking lot right before closing. After stepping out of the truck and swatting away a swarm of mosquitos, I'm taken back to when Vince and I used to scrounge for enough change at the bottom of my mother's purse to walk down here to buy ice cream on the hottest summer nights.

"Are you all right?" Liam asks, brushing hair off my face.

I force out a laugh. "Just remembering all the times Vince and I came here when we were kids."

"You still like chocolate sprinkles on yours?"

"Nah. I'm too old for sprinkles."

"You're never too old for sprinkles."

I trail behind him to the window, where a bored teenager slides the glass open and taps her pencil against her green notepad. "We're about to close," she informs us.

"Two small twist cones," Liam orders.

She rattles off a total much higher than the change Vince and I used to carry here would've ever covered. "Pricey," I say after the girl closes the window to go fill our order.

Liam shrugs.

"Bree, is that you?" A high-pitched voice calls out. I barely have a chance to turn when a girl barrels into me and squeals. "I thought so. How are you?"

"Lucy? Oh my God. I'm fine. How are you?"

Her gaze ping-pongs between Liam and me. "I always knew you two would end up together."

I almost choke and we haven't even been handed our ice cream cones yet.

"We're not…we're hanging out. I just came home from college."

"Oh, that's right. Weren't you dating…" Her voice trails off as recognition sinks in. Great. Someone else who read about Chad's arrest in the paper. Even though they didn't use my name in any of the articles, it's not that difficult to figure out who the "live-in girlfriend" he pummeled is.

"We broke up."

"Good…I mean. Oh. Well, have fun." She smiles nervously and tosses a bunch of napkins in the garbage before jogging back to her car.

Liam hands me my ice cream, but I've lost my interest. He seems to understand my shift in mood and steers me over to one of the picnic benches near his truck.

We eat our cones in silence. When I can't finish mine, Liam takes it and chucks it in the trash can. I'm shaking and on the verge of tears when he returns.

When are these feelings going to go away?

"Talk to me, Bree," he says quietly.

Across the parking lot there's a family with two small children who have more ice cream in their hair than in their mouths. Otherwise we're alone.

"I'm so ashamed," I whisper, unable to keep the words inside for another second.

He wraps his arms around me, pulling my body against his and rests his chin on the top of my head. One of his big hands strokes over my back in a calming gesture. "You have nothing to be ashamed of."

I pull back enough to tip my head and search his face for the truth. "I let it happen."

A stony hardness enters his eyes. "You didn't let it happen, Bree."

"But I did." I bury my face against his shirt again. "You were right. This wasn't the first time. I made excuses for him. He swore he was sorry and he'd never do it again. Said he loved me so much…" My voice trails off because I realize how stupid and gullible I sound.

LIAM

BREE'S ANGUISH SCRAPES over my heart, leaving me raw and ready to explode. "He's a manipulator. I'm sure in his twisted head he thought he loved you, Bree." The words burn like ground glass in my throat, but they're probably true and I think she needs to hear them.

"I hated it here so much. Growing up. Everyone always looked down on us."

My body stiffens with her words. I remember how all she used to talk about was getting out of this town and never coming back. "I didn't."

"No. You were always a good friend. *Are* a good friend. To Vince. And to me." She adds that last part almost as an afterthought.

"I wish I'd been a better friend to you."

She shakes her head. "I believed him when he said he wouldn't do it again. He always made me feel like somehow it was my fault because I made him so crazy and jealous." She stops and looks up at me. "I know how stupid that sounds."

"It's not stupid at all. You're going to be a psychologist. You know how these things work."

"Exactly!" she explodes and I realize too late that was the wrong thing to say. "I should've recognized the signs, the cycles we went through. The tension, the blowups, the apologies and promises. And the whole time I just kept telling myself it wasn't that bad, or he didn't mean it or if I was a better girlfriend it wouldn't have happened."

Listening to her describe what she's been through leaves me somewhere between anger and anguish. Between wanting to comfort her and wanting to kill Chad. She may have glossed over the details, but I've taken enough classes on how to handle domestic violence situations to know what each of those phases entails.

"I can't stand being here," she says in a harsh whisper. "Did you see how Lucy couldn't wait to get away from me?"

"Do you think you stayed with Chad so you wouldn't have to come home?" I ask and brace myself for her answer.

"Maybe there was part of me that thought coming home meant I was a failure. Besides, Vince and I don't seem to get along anymore."

Something I'm afraid is my fault. After the night he caught us kissing, things were tense in our friendship until Bree left for school. Then we never spoke about the incident again. "I'm sorry." I don't know what else to say.

She ignores the apology. "Lucy won't be the only one. People always judge the woman. 'Why'd she stay for so long? Maybe she liked it. The first time a man hit me, I'd leave. You can't help someone who won't help herself.' I've heard them all. Hell, I've had those same thoughts."

Guilt threatens to crush me. "Bree, that's not what I...I'm sorry about the stuff I said the other night...about everything. I'd never judge you like that. I don't judge you at all."

"Not even a little?"

"No. I'm mad at myself. I wish I'd known. I hate that you went through any of that by yourself."

"One of the first cops who questioned me asked what *I* did to piss Chad off so badly."

My blood boils. "Who?" I snap.

She gives me a small smile. "I can't remember his name."

"I'm not surprised that happened. I encounter guys in the department all the time who have zero empathy or compassion for the people they're supposed to serve and protect." I'm hesitant to use the word victim, because I don't want her to think that's how I see her. "But it doesn't matter. No one has the right to judge you. You dealt with something horrible no one should have to go through. You're out."

I wish she'd nod or say something more reassuring than *mmhmm*.

"Chad's in jail where he belongs. There is no reason you can't go anywhere you want with your head held high."

Finally, she nods slowly, trying to take in my words.

"I should've left sooner."

"*Should'ves* do us no good, Bree."

"My mother always said I was so stubborn, and I'd end up hurting myself more in the long run because of it."

Her mother cared more about her boyfriends than her children, but I keep that observation to myself. "I think what she meant was you're tenacious."

"I doubt that." Her mouth pulls into a half-smile. "She didn't hand out many compliments."

We're quiet for a few minutes and she seems to shake off the seriousness of our conversation. She pokes a finger in my side. "So, your ex is pretty."

At first I'm thrown by the change in conversation. Ex-who? What?

"Did you love her?" she asks.

Linda, right. Yeah, because the metal stabbing through my finger wasn't enough of a pain. I needed to run into my ex to really cap off the evening. I don't know what I did to piss off the universe today, but Karma sure did have fun kicking my ass. "I cared about her," I finally answer.

"She's obviously still interested in you."

"I'm not interested in her," I answer quietly.

Her mouth opens as if she wants to ask more questions, but instead she tilts her head toward the truck. "Let's get you home and get some Advil in you. That anesthesia will start to wear off any second now."

"It already is."

"Why didn't you say something?"

"Because you're more important."

She leans up and presses a soft kiss to my cheek. "Thank you."

CHAPTER FOURTEEN

Brianna

FOR THE FIRST time in days, a sense of accomplishment fills me as I leave my support group. I wish I felt as confident about the prescription rattling at the bottom of my purse. Encouraged by Liam's story and our talk last night, I gave in and let the psychiatrist my therapist works with write me a script for an antidepressant.

The support group gives me hope. Sure, the stories of the other women are different from mine. Lots of them have children to provide for. Many of them don't have friends or family to turn to. It doesn't matter, though. Everyone was so supportive. No one treats me different-ly. I kept my shit together and didn't break down in tears once.

With a lighter heart, I stop in town to explore some shops. The area seems much more built up than I remember it being when I was little. There's even a small shop that serves and sells specialty teas.

As I walk out of the teashop, I'm so wrapped up in my own thoughts, I slam into someone on the sidewalk. Big hands settle on my shoulders to steady me. Startled, I jump back, heart hammering. I'm so freaked out I can barely focus on the two guys in front of me.

"Sorry, darlin.'"

Something about the voice brings on a flood of happy memories and I dare to glance up into a familiar pair of teal-blue eyes. "Marcel?" My gaze darts to his friend, who I also recognize. "Blake? Oh my God, I haven't seen you two in *forever*."

"Little Bree, you're all grown up," Marcel says as his gaze travels down my body.

My skin heats at the appreciative way Marcel takes me in. He's no longer the teenage heartbreaker full of attitude who lived down the street from me. Now, he's a man. At least six feet of lean muscle, thick blond hair, broad shoulders and enough confidence to stare me straight in the eyes without a lick of hesitation.

Wow. I haven't had a reaction to anyone other than Liam in too damn long. Marcel's best friend, Blake, isn't looking too bad either. Far from the chubby ginger I remember as a teenager, he's bulky, muscled, bearded, and *manly* now.

"What are you two doing in town?"

"Taking care of a few things," Marcel answers.

"I heard about your grandmother. I'm so sorry."

He shrugs, reminding me the two of them weren't close. "Thanks."

"How's Heidi?" His little sister had been his constant shadow and I've wondered about her a lot over the last few years.

"Raising hell like always."

Blake laughs. "True story."

"If I remember correctly, *you two* were the hell raisers."

"Nah." Marcel glances away with an exaggerated sort of false modesty.

Blake lifts his chin at me. "What're you doing here? Thought you left for Empire U and didn't come back?"

"I'm back." My hand strays to my sunglasses, pushing them up on my face. Marcel's eyes narrow and he looks me over more carefully.

"Everything okay?"

My shoulders lift and like an idiot, I blurt out, "Bad breakup. I'm home to lick my wounds and then I'll start graduate school in the fall."

"What are you studying?"

From what I remember, Marcel hated school, so I'm surprised he cares.

"Psychology."

"Heidi might be interested in transferring to Empire. If you have time over the summer, would you mind talking to her?"

"No, not at all."

"Appreciate it." He pulls out a phone and flips it open. "Let me give you my number. You need anything while you're home, call me."

My gaze drops to his muscled forearms covered in full-sleeve tattoos. *That's new.*

Guys with tattoos never attracted me before. But I find my eyes following the bright, intricate designs that disappear under the sleeves of his blue T-shirt.

He catches me staring and I clear my throat. "Sure, I'll give you my number too. So, uh, you can have Heidi call me whenever."

We exchange numbers and he gives me a sly smile. Hell, he'd been waiting for me to offer up my number.

"Still riding motorcycles?" I ask.

"Hell yeah." He taps the patch on his leather vest. *Treasurer.* The patch below it says *Lost Kings MC.* I peek at Blake's vest. *Road Captain. Lost Kings MC.*

"Sounds like fun."

Both of them smirk at me as if I might have accidentally insulted them.

"You should come to a party at our clubhouse some weekend," Blake offers. Marcel shoots him a weird look. Maybe he's not keen on having me crash one of their clubhouse parties.

Clubhouse? Party? Am I ready for socializing? "Maybe."

"Still scared to ride on the back?" Marcel nods at two intimidating Harleys parked across the street.

"Yours?"

"Yup."

After everything I've been through, a ride on the back of a motorcycle doesn't seem as scary as it used to. "I might be willing to give it a try."

Marcel chuckles and runs his hand over the back of his neck. "All right, Bree. Give me a call when you think you're ready." His gaze strays to Blake, who lifts his chin ever-so-slightly. "I'll come pick you up."

Somehow that sounded more like an invitation into his *bed*, than an offer to attend a party.

I'm not insulted. Instead, their attention gives me the boost I desperately need these days. Between Chad crushing my spirit for the last couple years, and Liam keeping our relationship firmly planted in the *brotherly concern zone*, I've been questioning myself a lot lately. At least someone finds me desirable.

Someone? Two hot bikers, you idiot!

"Brianna!"

My eyes briefly shut as mortification sets in. I recognize that voice.

I fake a smile at Marcel, but his entire demeanor has changed. He steps in front of me, shielding me from the street. I peek around him and follow his line of sight.

Right to Liam's patrol car.

Liam had been extra-overbearing this morning, asking me for every little detail of my plans for the day. It'd been a relief when he finally left for work. Now, he's back to full overprotective-big-brother mode. He's also probably five seconds from jumping out and, judging by the look on his face, shooting Marcel.

"That your man?" Marcel asks without taking his eyes off Liam.

"No." I sigh and tug on his arm to draw his attention away, but he doesn't budge. "That's Liam. My brother's friend."

They're like two dogs glaring at each other before an attack.

"Yeah," he says slowly. "Officer Do-gooder. How could I forget." Marcel ducks down to get a better look at Liam and gives him a cocky wave. "'Sup, officer?"

Liam ignores the obvious challenge. "Bree. Get in the car," he barks at me.

"You in trouble, darlin'?" Blake asks.

Marcel shakes his head. "Wow, little Bree, in trouble with the law. And here I always thought you were such a *good girl*."

"Shut up. He thinks he's taking my brother's place while my brother's away. He's so far up my ass, it's absurd. And not in the fun way."

Blake's eyes twinkle with mischief. "Wanna go for that ride now?"

I run my gaze over the two hot bikers in front of me. "I better not. He's taking this babysitting job very seriously."

They both glance over at Liam, whose car is blocking traffic now.

"Guess so," Marcel says. When he turns my way again, he grabs my hand. "No joke, sweetheart. You need something, don't be afraid to call."

"Thanks. I appreciate it."

Both of them give me hugs before they leave. Marcel's hand strays to my ass, but I'm sure that was more about pissing Liam off than feeling me up. The idea makes me laugh.

On my way to his car, I count to ten.

Something tells me I'm in for a lecture.

LIAM

BLOOD BOILING, I don't say anything until Bree's tucked into the passenger side and we're moving down the road.

"Did you have to embarrass me like that?" she finally asks.

"Weren't you supposed to be at the doctor? Not out flirting with thugs?"

Damn. I did *not* mean for that to come out so harsh.

"Are you serious right now?" she asks in a low voice.

"I'm sorry. I shouldn't have said that." She sits there with her arms crossed over her chest, staring straight ahead. "Where's your car?"

"The parking lot on Front Street."

Instead of scolding her, I should have asked that question when she first climbed into the car. I execute a U-Turn and head the other way.

"Why do you care who I talk to?" she questions.

"I worry about you."

"I can take care of myself."

I bite back the *that's debatable* retort forming in my mouth. "Their motorcycle club's mixed up in stuff I don't want you around."

She makes a *pfft* sound. "Please. I've known Marcel since I was a kid."

"Yeah, well, he's not a kid anymore."

"He's too old for me anyway."

"He's *my* age."

Out of the corner of my eye, I catch her trying not to laugh. "You're a little brat."

"So I hear," she answers dryly.

Too soon, I pull up behind her car. "Where are you headed now?"

She rolls her eyes at me. "Home."

"I won't be back until nine or nine-thirty. Will you be all right?"

She huffs and wraps her fingers around her bag tightly. "I'll be fine."

"Call me if you need anything."

Without answering, she steps out of the car, but before she slams it shut, she pokes her head inside. "Be careful, Liam."

"Always, baby girl."

She shuts the door, and I'm left staring at her.

After following her car a few miles to make sure she's headed home, I'm no less wound up. Fact is, I'm feeling even more possessive of her. Not romantic—at least that's what I keep telling myself—but *protective*. She's mine to take care of until Vince returns home.

I can't stand the thought of her being hurt again.

Guys like Marcel—or *Teller*, as his gang buddies call him—Whelan would do nothing *but* hurt her.

Because this is such a small town, not even five minutes later, I come up on Marcel and his bro on their bikes, heading east. Before I realize what I'm doing, I flick on the lights and siren.

Unprofessional? Probably.

Do I care? Not really. Not when it comes to Bree's safety.

Marcel taps his fingers against the side of his leg as I approach. His buddy straight-up ignores me, which is fine. He's not the one who put his hands on Bree.

"Afternoon, Officer," Marcel greets me in a smug way that says he'd been expecting a confrontation.

I'd hate to disappoint him.

This is another first for me. I've never let my personal life interfere with my professional life so much.

"We're in a bit of a hurry, so unless you're gonna write me a ticket—

”

"Where you headed?" Standard cop question.

"Home."

"Where you coming from?"

He slips his helmet off and swings his leg over the bike. I don't step back, place my hand on my gun, or anything else to indicate I think he's a threat. Because he's not, as far as I'm concerned.

Not to me.

Bree? Definitely.

"Do we really need to do the cop and criminal routine? Just say what you want to say, Liam." He stands there with a bored look stretched across his face and his hands at his sides.

"Fine. I know what your motorcycle club's into, Marcel. Stay the fuck away from Bree."

He cocks his head and his mouth settles into a smirk. "Funny, she told me she was single."

"That's not the point."

"Yeah, she mentioned you've been babysitting her while Vince is out of town."

After the talk we had the other night, is that how Bree thinks of me? As her babysitter? "Not your concern. Stay away from her."

The punk has the nerve to snicker. "Chill the fuck out, *officer*. She's a friend from high school. That's all."

"Yeah, I know all about how you guys treat your female friends." I spent time in gang task force, and even though Marcel's MC doesn't have the *worst* reputation in the area, they're certainly not the innocent, motorcycle-loving, good guys they want you to believe they are. I don't need her deciding to spice up her life by attending one of their club-house parties. Bree shouldn't be anywhere near them.

His eyes darken and he pushes into my space, but I stay right where I am and stare him down. "You don't know fuck about me or my club," he says through clenched teeth. "I asked Bree to talk to my little sister about college. So back the fuck off."

Sister. That's right. Now I remember he has a much younger sister he's crazy protective of. My gaze flicks to his buddy, who's standing next to his bike silently watching us. "I forgot about your sister. Heidi, right? Bree used to babysit her?" Maybe I don't have to rip his arms off today.

He takes a few steps back. "Yeah. She's thinking of switching majors or transferring and I thought Bree could help her out."

"She's in college? Jesus, I feel old."

Marcel lets out a short humorless laugh. "Tell me about it." He tilts his head to the side, studying me for a second. "You two together or not?"

And just like that, I'm ready to kick his ass again. "Not your business."

Marcel rolls his eyes while Blake walks over to join our conversation.

"What's up with Bree? She seemed kinda timid," Blake says. Unlike his friend, he doesn't say it to rile me up. He seems genuinely concerned about her.

Should I spill Bree's personal business? *No.*

Would I feel better if more people were looking out for her? *Yes.*

Marcel straightens up. "She said she had a bad breakup. Some guy hassling her?"

"I have it covered."

"I'm sure you do, *Officer.*" He glances at his buddy, who gives him a subtle nod. "Bree was always really good to my sister. If handling this guy's *out*side your jurisdiction, let us know. We'll be happy to help."

I know exactly what the two outlaws mean by *handling* him.

"Thanks. I'll keep it in mind."

CHAPTER FIFTEEN

Brianna

THE SCOLDING LIAM gave me for talking to two old friends was enough to confirm his lack of romantic interest. The sooner I accept he'll never see me as anything other than Vince's little sister, the better. I'd rather have him as a friend than nothing at all.

Pulling into the driveway knowing Liam won't be home for hours is a drag. I glance at my bag of tea, remembering my idea to make homemade iced tea this afternoon and the simple plan cheers me up.

Celebrate the little victories.

That was one of the pieces of advice we received in group therapy today. I wanted to stamp it on my arm, so I wouldn't forget.

I keep myself busy until eight when I finally plop down to watch television. Every little creak and noise in the house freaks me out, so I crank the volume way up.

"Bree!"

Heart pounding I turn my head and find Liam in the entryway. I grab the remote and mute the television. "Shit, you scared me."

"Sorry, baby girl."

"You're home early."

He finishes taking off his boots before answering. "I missed you."

"Really?"

"Yes," he says, dropping into the opposite corner of the couch. "I'm sorry I gave you a hard time today."

Wow. I never expected to hear an apology from Liam. I shift a little closer to him. "You embarrassed me and made me feel like a little kid."

His eyes close briefly and for a few seconds I'm lost staring at the face that is still one of the most beautiful I've ever known. Not perfect. But perfect to me. Familiar. He opens his eyes and there's a hardness burning in the deep brown depths that I don't remember being there when we were younger.

My heart thuds as a slow slide of awareness shimmers over my skin. Why do I have to want this man who doesn't want me? Never has.

"I didn't mean to embarrass you. I was…worried."

Whoa. I expected another reprimand. "Thank you. Just so you know, if they were two strangers I wouldn't have stopped to talk to them."

"Good."

"How's your finger?"

A smile kicks up at the corners of his mouth. He holds his hand up, waving it for me to see he's replaced the big gauze wrap with a normal-sized Band-Aid. "Honestly, better than I thought it would be."

He drapes his other arm over the back of the couch, leaving his fingers a few inches from my face. I tilt my head, resting my cheek against the back of his hand.

"Tired, baby girl?" he asks.

"A little."

"How was group?"

"Intense."

"Hmm," he murmurs as he slides his hand out from under my cheek and runs his fingers through my hair.

"I think I might get my hair cut."

"Why? It's so beautiful."

That snaps me out of my sleepy trance. I sit up straighter. "You think my hair's beautiful?"

He slides his gaze over me. From my bare toes, up my legs, and I swear heat sears my skin everywhere until he stops at my eyes.

"Yes, Bree. Everything about you is beautiful."

I grab a bunch of my hair, combing my fingers through it to hide the way my body's trembling. "It's so hot and heavy."

"You'll be just as pretty with it shorter."

I risk glancing into his eyes again. "Do you want me to move so you can go to bed?"

"No. You're fine."

"You can always take Vince's room and I'll sleep out here."

He's shaking his head before I finish the sentence. "Absolutely not."

My phone buzzes and I reach behind me to grab it. "Ugh, another voicemail."

He leans forward and takes the phone out of my hand. "Chad's brother?"

"Yup. What a jerk."

"I'm sorry. Blocking it only means it goes straight to voicemail. I'll listen to it after you go to bed."

"Thank you."

He stares at the phone but doesn't listen to the message. "Might need you to sign some papers when we file the restraining order."

"Okay. Whatever you need me to do, Liam." I let out a yawn and, as much as I want to keep talking to him, I decide it's safer to go to bed.

LIAM

AS SOON AS Bree shuts the bedroom door, I listen to the message Chad's brother left.

"Listen, Bree, my parents are willing to pay if you drop the charges. Let's meet up—"

"Hell-fucking-no," I mutter as I forward the message to my phone and delete it from Bree's.

I tap out a text to my buddy, Sully, then head into the bathroom for a quick shower. Before returning to the living room, I stop and listen for any sounds of distress. She's been sleeping better since the first night, but every time she gets one of those messages I worry about it stirring stuff up in her head.

She left the door slightly open and I push it wider to steal a glance at her.

Christ, I'm turning into a creeper.

It's a king-size bed. Plenty of room.

Before my mind wanders any further down that path, I shut the door.

CHAPTER SIXTEEN

Brianna

M Y BEDROOM DOOR'S shut the next morning.

One of us can't take a damn hint. I'm just not sure if it's him or me.

After breakfast, Liam places his hand over mine, so I don't leave the table.

"Come take a ride with me?"

"Where?"

"It's a surprise."

I nod at his hand. "I don't think you're ready for another fishing adventure."

He chuckles and squeezes my hand. "Not yet."

I glance down at my leggings and fitted T-shirt. "Let me change."

"No. You're perfect like that. Grab some sneakers." He runs his gaze over my shirt again, lingering on my breasts. "Maybe a hoodie."

Curiosity has me following his instruction. I jam my feet into a pair of Skechers and tug on one of Vince's sweatshirts that's so big, I have to roll up the sleeves.

Liam's waiting for me on the porch and his mouth turns up when he sees me. "Perfect," he says, taking my hand and leading me to the truck.

Do *just friends* hold hands?

After our kiss—that we never talked about again—it weird to have him touch me more than necessary.

Once we're on the road, it's time to pry more information out of him. "Will you tell me now?"

"Nope."

I glance over. He's straining to keep the corners of his mouth from turning up.

"What are you up to, Hollister?"

"You'll see, Avery."

I let out an aggrieved huff of air and force my own lips to stay in a firm line. This is much better than the awkwardness of the past couple days. It was beginning to wear me down.

He pulls the truck behind a gym with an attached martial arts studio, kills the engine, and turns to face me. All the questions fade from my mind when I see how serious he is. "I want you to meet a friend of mine."

I hesitate before answering. "Okay. Why didn't you say so?"

"He owns the studio and works with the department from time to time, teaching self-defense classes."

"Oh." What am I supposed to say?

"I asked him to give you some lessons." He pauses and glances out the window. "I gave him a few details about your situation."

Clearly, Liam's worried I'll be mad at him. And yes, I don't want my business spread around. But how could I ever fault him for worrying about my safety? "Thank you, Liam. This is a really sweet thing to do."

He arches an eyebrow. "You're not mad?"

"No. Not at all." Unless he plans on leaving me here by myself. "You're going to stay, though, right?"

He exhales and seems to relax. "Of course."

"One of the counselors for the group suggested self-defense classes."

"I know," he says in a low voice.

Right. Because he works in law enforcement and deals with victims like me all the time.

That certainly tamps down my enthusiasm.

He leads me to the back entrance and knocks on one of the office doors.

"Open," someone shouts.

Liam pushes the door wide. "We're here."

"Hey, Hollister!" The guy inside greets us in a booming voice that seems bigger than it should, considering he's only a few inches taller than me.

He comes closer and slaps palms with Liam. "Sully, this is my friend, Brianna Avery. Bree this is Sullivan Wallace. Biggest badass I know."

Shaking his head, Sullivan chuckles. "This one's the biggest bull shitter *I* know." He holds out his hand. "Vince's little sister, right?"

I take his hand, impressed with his firm grip. "Yup."

"He's a good guy."

Wondering how he knows my brother, I follow Sullivan and Liam to the main floor. It's an impressive studio. Light, shining hardwood floors cover one half of the space and blue plastic gym mats cover the other half. Full-length mirrors run along three walls.

Feeling too self-conscious to stare in the mirrors, I turn away. Liam gives me a reassuring smile and squeezes my hand.

I'm trying so hard to remember the positives in my life. Sure, I'd been in a bad relationship. I'm out. I'm taking charge of my life and moving on. There's nothing to be ashamed of.

Now, I just need to repeat those statements a thousand more times and maybe I'll actually believe them.

Sully clears his throat, capturing my attention. "So, first I like to tell my civilian clients a few things before I teach them how to be danger-ous." His mouth quirks into an irresistible grin.

I like this guy.

My gaze drifts to Liam, who's standing a few feet away, arms crossed over his chest, watching our every move.

"Every place is safe, until it isn't," Sullivan says, drawing my atten-tion back to him.

Isn't that the truth. Including my own home.

Between my overprotective brother and Liam's own fierce protective streak, I spent my teenage years feeling a bit bulletproof.

Dangerous thinking once I went out into the world on my own.

Sully watches as I work through my emotional epiphany. When I give him a quick nod, he continues. "The most important thing you can do is be aware. Keep a clear head. Pay attention to your surroundings."

"Gotcha."

He takes on a more serious expression. "Now, the next thing a lot of women don't like to hear. Avoid danger when possible. Think about it, do you really need to put yourself in potentially dangerous situations?"

I cock my head, inviting him to elaborate.

"Do you need that late-night run to the drug store? Do you need to go jogging at night? Keep yourself out of dangerous situations like dark alleys, parking garages, bad areas of town. Be wise when making your plans and consider going out with friends so you're not alone."

"Okay." His warning had been appropriate. It helps me keep an open mind instead of saying, "Fuck that, I'll go where I damn well want."

"Please don't think I'm victim-blaming. Bad people are solely responsible for their bad actions."

"No, I understand what you're saying."

"Good. I also like to tell women to prepare themselves for a fight. Consider different scenarios. 'What would I do if someone were following me? Try to get into my car? Run?' Visualize yourself escaping danger."

My mind immediately flashes to an image of kneeing Chad in the groin and ramming the heel of my palm into his nose.

I wish.

But God dammit, if anyone ever comes at me again, I *will* be ready to defend myself.

"We can talk about weapons at a later time." He glances at Liam. "But I should probably let the good sheriff or his dad handle your weapons training."

Liam chuckles. "Already started."

Sully nods his approval and then turns back to me. "Okay, Bree," Sully says.

I drag my gaze from Liam to Sully.

"Come closer," he says, waving me over.

I take a few steps toward him. His arm shoots out, wrapping around my bicep. He turns and pulls me tight to his chest in a bear hug. A startled scream rips from my throat.

Liam drops his arms and pushes off the wall.

"Now, we're not strangers, Brianna." Sully's hot breath wafts over my ear, tickling my skin. "But if a stranger asked you to come closer, would you do it?"

While he keeps his arms around me, I consider the question. "Yeah, I probably would."

"Okay. Good," he says, releasing me. "You're being honest. Most women are conditioned to be nice, polite, and obedient. I want you to retrain yourself to always listen to your gut. If a man approaches you and you even think he means to do you harm, use a loud, strong voice to tell him to *stop.*"

My eyes widen, not sure if I can just yell at strangers on the street.

Sully seems to understand my hesitation.

"Better to be safe and a little embarrassed than sorry, right?"

"Right."

"Make it known you're not an easy victim."

His words sink in, hitting me on a deeper level. Chad must have sensed I was an easy target. My gaze goes to Liam. Maybe that's why he's not attracted to me. A man like him needs a strong woman by his side. Someone more like his mother who's not afraid of anything.

Sully pulls me against him again. "Now, if you're grabbed like this." He squeezes me tighter for emphasis. "The easiest thing to do is lift your arms up and out to the sides, while at the same time dropping to the ground."

I don't wait for him to finish speaking. I jam my arms up, breaking his hold, while at the same time going boneless, melting to the floor.

Sully smiles down at me. "Good job. Since you're down there, it's the perfect opportunity to jam your elbow into the attacker's groin." He takes a step back. "I'm going to ask you *not* to try that at the moment."

Pressing my palms into the mat, I power up off the floor and chuckle.

"Quick reflexes. Nice," he says with an appreciative nod.

This is fun. The subject matter unnerves me, but Sully's easy demeanor pushes my negative feelings aside. A quick glance at Liam confirms he's watching every move. He hasn't gone back to his casual pose since I yelped earlier.

"Let's try that again," Sully suggests.

He steps up behind me, wrapping his arms over my chest, pinning my arms to my sides.

Panic stirs in my belly, but I suck in a deep breath, lift my arms and slide down.

"Good. Now you could use your elbow. You could also pivot and ram the heel of your hand into his groin. No matter what, you want to disable him so you can either get away or get to a weapon."

Sweat trickles down the side of my face, and I flick it away. I haven't done enough to be sweaty. I peel off my sweatshirt and toss it in Liam's general direction. Sparks fire in his eyes as his hungry gaze roams over my newly bared skin. For a moment I can't move.

"The bear hug escape is one thing, but what if an attacker knocked you to the ground?" Sully asks, breaking the spell.

An unpleasant shudder works through me at the thought.

"You're flexible and have good reflexes. But if you can't get back on your feet, the best thing is to maneuver onto your back."

"Isn't that worse?"

He nods, understanding. "I know why it seems that way. But from your back you're in a position to use your legs as weapons."

With caution, he flips me onto the mat. I roll to my back and wait for instructions. Sully kneels over me. "Tuck your knees in and kick out hard to keep him off you. Kick the crotch, shins, knees, head, whatever you can get at. If you're wearing heels, jab them into his shins. Then get up and run."

I kick out at half-power, catching Sully in the chest and knocking him backward.

He falls back, laughing. "Good job."

I stay down, staring up at the ceiling to catch my breath and absorb what I've learned. As my heart rate slows, I sense the matt shifting under me. Both Sully and Liam appear, smiling down.

"Think you'll come back?" Sully asks.

Liam holds out his hand and I grab it, but instead of letting him pull me up off the mat, I try to tug him down.

No such luck.

Too strong for me, he keeps his feet under him. But he does squat down next to me.

His eyes soften as they search my face. "Are you okay?" he asks in his smooth, rumbling voice that always makes my stomach twirl.

"I think so." I stand and Liam pops up next to me, graceful as a panther. He pats my back before striding over to pick up my sweatshirt.

"I'm impressed, Brianna. For a first timer, you did well," Sully says.

I cock my head. "I bet you say that to all the distressed damsels Liam brings you."

He bursts out laughing and shakes his head. "No, you're the first. You're no damsel in distress either. You're a strong girl, Bree."

He moves in a little closer. "I give a longer class every Thursday night and on weekend mornings if you want to try one out. I even wear the protective gear so you can kick and jab at me as hard as you want." The corners of his mouth twist into an irresistible grin.

Is he flirting with me? Would he really do that if he thought Liam had a smidge of interest in me?

"How can I say no?"

LIAM

UNEASE—OR ANNOYANCE—weaves through my chest as I watch Bree and Sully eye-fondle each other much too long for my liking.

Maybe the unease is from Sully's lecture. Sure, I've listened to his speech dozens of times. Today was different, though. The words punched me right in the gut. How could Vince and I have been so damn stupid with Bree? I should have taught her some of these things years ago. Instead, we treated her like a little princess. Someone bothered her at school—Vince or I would go have a word with them. Bree didn't want to learn how to use the most basic of shotguns—we thought it was cute. Vince scared away any guy who wanted to date his sister, so of course that's the first thing she did when she got away from him.

More annoyance floods through me as I stand to the side, watching Bree flirt with my buddy. Even though I hate it, I don't say anything. I *want* her to feel more confident about herself. I trust Sully. He's a good guy. Would treat her like gold.

They seem to like each other.

Yup, that's what's bothering me.

In the truck on the way home, Bree's quiet. "Did you have fun?" I ask to break the silence and keep my mind off the jealousy that settled in my gut.

No, I didn't like Bree batting her long lashes at another guy. Not even someone I consider a friend.

She's mine.

Except, I can't have her.

She gives me a sideways glance and a knowing smirk tugs at the corners of her mouth. "Yeah. He's a babe. Is he single?"

Busted.

"Last I knew, yes. Why? Are you interested?" I was aiming for a neutral tone, but fail miserably, especially the way I choke on the last word.

She doesn't respond right away. Instead, she keeps her head turned away from me, watching the town speed by. When we pull into the driveway, she finally turns her big blue eyes on me.

"Maybe. I can't keep pining for you forever, Liam."

With those words, she shoves the truck door open, jumps down, and stomps into the house without a backward glance.

Well, I guess I deserve that. Should have kept my mouth shut.

I should go home.

Chad's still safely behind bars.

Bree seems to be almost back to normal.

The longer I stay, the more my iron control crumbles. She doesn't need me here.

Fuck it.

Brianna

STUPID.

Yanking off my workout clothes, I toss them in the hamper harder than necessary.

Why'd I bait Liam like that?

I slip into a pair of shorts and fresh T-shirt and fling myself down on the bed.

I'd never, ever date one of Liam's friends.

Date. I have to be out of my damn mind to be worried about dating.

The front door opens. There's a pause and then it clicks shut.

The thud of Liam kicking off his shoes.

I exhale hard and realize I'd been holding my breath. Afraid I'd chased Liam away.

Scooting off the bed, I work out an apology in my mind. I stop and pull my hair out of its ponytail and brush it until it's not as ratty.

I open the door and find Liam standing across the hall, leaning against the wall. Both arms crossed over his chest. The same way he'd watched me at the gym, except here in the house, he seems so much larger. His biceps and forearms bulge in a way that sends heat zipping through me.

"Hey," he says.

My mouth's too dry to answer. I run my tongue over my lower lip, and Liam's gaze follows the movement.

"What are you doing? Holding up the wall?"

Except for a tiny quirk at the corners of his mouth, his expression doesn't change.

His silence flips my annoyed switch.

"What is this, Liam? Some sort of cop interrogation technique?"

That gets his attention. He crosses the short distance, invading my space. Making me aware of his size and strength.

"Maybe. Want to tell me what you meant out there?" He jerks his head to the side.

I don't answer. Instead I study his expression. His eyes seem to simmer with desire. But lord knows I've been wrong before.

"Shouldn't I get a warning, Deputy Hollister?"

That finally makes him chuckle. "Sure. Anything you say, can and will be held against you."

Game on.

I lift an eyebrow in silent challenge.

"In that case, *Liam,*" I say, using my huskiest voice.

I'm rewarded with a sharp intake of breath.

My heart thumps as he comes closer, leaning down to whisper in my ear. "Baby girl, you are playing with fire."

He settles his hands on my hips and pulls me closer. Taking a chance, I wrap my arms around his neck. "I can handle the burn."

Everything fades away the second his lips brush against mine. His cinnamon taste tingles over my lips. The slow slide of his tongue against mine sends heat boiling through my body.

Finally.

That's right. Finally. He's been rejecting me for days. Bracing my hands on his shoulders, I push him back.

"Wait a second. I showed some interest in your friend, so now you kiss me?" Anger and desire won't stop warring inside me. I try to shove past him to go outside and clear my head, but he's impossible to move.

He watches me for a moment then takes a step back.

"That's not it, Bree. You're Vince's sister. I'm supposed to be watching out for you."

"I appreciate that, Liam. I do. Thank you for everything you've done for me." My throat tightens. "But I can take care of myself."

"I know you can, baby girl."

My gaze drops to the floor. "Why can't you ever see me as Brianna? Not baby girl. Not Vince's little sister. Just me."

He steps closer, and runs the back of his hand over my cheek. "I see you."

"I don't think you do."

"I've cared about you since we were kids."

Ugh. "So you do think of me like a sister?"

He blinks and averts his gaze. "No. God help me. I wish I did."

"You're really frustrating."

"I've been told that once or twice." He stops and leans in for another kiss. This one quick and on my cheek. "If you're really interested in Sully, I'll give him your number."

Doesn't that knock the wind out of me?

Too shocked to come up with a meaningful response, I mutter, "Thank you," and head back into the bedroom.

CHAPTER SEVENTEEN
LIAM

FROM THE DARKEST corner of the bar I'm able to watch the door for my buddy Keegan. The oppressive summer heat has people seeking shelter in the bar's frigid AC. Loud music pounds from unseen speakers, and I question why we still meet up here on Friday afternoons.

Although, after the week I've had I think I deserve to knock back a few beers with my buddies. Even so, I can't stop thinking about Bree. About kissing her. About the stupid way I implied it was okay for her to date my friend when it is absolutely, one-hundred-percent, never happening.

Keegan enters, and a lot of heads turn. A few inches taller than me and a lot broader, heads pretty much turn wherever he goes. Ignoring everyone in his path, he shoulders his way to the back of the room.

"Antisocial much?" he asks, dropping into the booth across from me.

I point a discreet finger at the pool table where I've watched a young couple hustle a couple college-age guys. "As a sheriff, I'm trying not to notice the illegal gambling going on over there."

Keegan glances at the couple for a few seconds before turning back to me. "Why do we keep meeting here?" he asks.

"Blame Sully." I signal our waitress to our table. I shouldn't be drinking to forget what's waiting for me at Vince's house. I'll have a full-blown habit in no time.

He shrugs. "At least it's better than it used to be. A little harmless gambling's better than the drug deals that used to go down." Our waitress takes our orders and after she leaves, he lifts his chin. "Where is that fucker?"

"Sully? On his way. Had to pick up his brother."

Keegan's not a big fan of Jake and rolls his eyes at the mention of Sully's brother.

"Still avoiding Bree?" he asks.

Wishing I'd never spilled any of the story to my friend, I prolong answering the question by draining the last of my beer. "I wouldn't call it avoiding."

He snorts and grabs our drinks from the waitress before she even has a chance to set them down.

"Christ, you've had it bad for her for as long as I can remember. What's your fucking problem?"

"What are you talking about?"

"Seriously? You're gonna play it that way? I get why you steered clear of her before. But she's what, twenty-four now?"

"Twenty-three. And that's not the point."

"Vince know about some freaky shit you're into?"

"What? No. She just got out of a bad relationship. Seems like a shitty time to make a move on her."

"Didn't you tell me *she* made a move on *you*?"

I pick up my beer, tipping it to my lips, so I can think about the question. "She was mad at me."

"That makes no sense."

"I took her to Sully's place, so he could go over some self-defense moves with her."

Keegan tilts his head, and I realize he has no idea why that was so important. When I hesitate, his face hardens.

"Fuck me. This guy hurt her? Where is he? Can we go kill him?"

"Can you keep your mouth shut? She doesn't want anyone to know."

"I understand. Seriously, though, where is he?"

"Lock-up down in Empire."

He lets out a low whistle and throws himself against the back of the booth. "Had to be pretty bad. You pay him a visit."

"Yup. Not sure the message sunk in though."

"I got plenty of shovels. Just say the word."

And this is why Keegan and I have been friends since we met at an arson scene a few years back. A loyal friend. Always ready to help bury a body.

"What's new with you?" I ask to take the attention off my Bree situation.

He lets out an annoyed grunt. "Tyson got this dog to train for search and rescue and it's not working out. She needs surgery, so now I gotta hold out my hand for donations."

"I thought S and R dogs were usually male?"

"They are. She's a rescue. Ty's heart was in the right place, but—"

"Well, let me know. I'll donate."

"Thanks." He cocks his head. "Your parents looking for a watch dog?"

"I can ask."

"Aw, you two look like you're on the most awkward date ever," Jake hollers as he approaches our table.

"Make sure you hit this asshole up for money too," I grumble and Keegan laughs.

Without looking up, I flip Jake off and he snorts. "So unprofessional, Sheriff."

"Where's your keeper?" I ask, slapping his outstretched hand.

"He got distracted by a butterfly."

Keegan's brow wrinkles. "What?"

Jake waves for Keegan to move over and slides in next to him. Not-so-discreetly he points to the pool table. "Butterfly tramp stamp. Gets him every time."

"You're both degenerates," Keegan mutters. "Why do Liam and I still hang out with you?"

"For street cred."

Sully ends up joining us a few minutes later. "Strike out?" Jake asks. "Need me to show you how it's done?"

"Fuck off." Sully takes the space Jake just vacated. "What up?"

"Just trying to avoid the heat."

"How's Bree doing?"

"All right."

"She's such a sweetheart." He shakes his head. "She did well. I hope she comes back."

I eye my friend carefully and manage not to crack my beer bottle over his head. "I think she will."

He glances at Keegan. "He told me," Keegan says. "Figure we need to go kick this kid's ass."

"Fine by me," Sully grumbles. "I get a lot of girls like her in my classes. Gonna take her forever to trust someone else. If she doesn't end up back with him."

"Fuck that," I mutter.

Sully shrugs. "I've seen it over and over. At least I hope I've taught them something useful."

"She liked you." Why the fuck did I have to say that?

Sully's slightly more refined than his younger brother. He shakes his head and laughs. "She's cute. I wouldn't mind helping her get back in the game."

I've known Sully for a long time. Never wanted to kill him until today.

He must read the murderous intention in my expression because he throws his hands in the air. "Not trying to step on your toes."

Jake calls his brother over for a game of pool, leaving me with Keegan, and I can tell by the smirk on the big bastard's face that he can't wait to needle me.

"Got some competition?"

"Shut up."

"What's the problem?"

"You heard him. She's not going to be able to trust anyone for a long time."

"You're not just *anyone*. But if you really feel that way, let her ride Sully's dick for a while. Then you can swoop in and play hero when he dumps her."

He's deliberately trying to piss me off. So instead of reaching over the table and choking him, I sit back.

"Or maybe," he continues, having way too much fun at my expense. "She'll be the one to tame him, and you can be the best man at their wedding."

"You're an asshole."

Keegan, fucker that he is, sits back and laughs. "Settle down. I'm jerking your chain because you're being stupid."

"Vince would have a stroke if I got together with his sister."

"Fuck him." Keegan takes an exaggerated look around the bar. "I don't see his ass here, taking care of her."

Vince is my best friend. Has been for most of my life. But I can't deny that Keegan's words get under my skin.

"He's working." Even to me, the excuse sounds lame.

"Bullshit. Some punk beat my sister up, nothing would keep me away."

"He knew I was here."

"Then obviously," he says with exaggerated slowness, "he trusts you with her."

"You don't date your friend's sister. That's basic bro—"

Keegan cuts me off by leaning over the table and growling in my face. "I swear to fuck if you say any variation of *bro code*, I'm gonna punch you in the throat. You're too old for that shit."

I hold in my laughter, even though I know Keegan's threat is very real. "Come on, there are rules to that sort of thing."

He grunts at me and I decide to be more serious. "It's not just Vince. She's returning to school at the end of the summer. I don't want to interfere with that. She's worked really hard."

"Is her school on the other side of the moon?"

"Empire. Don't be a dick."

"You seen Jenson lately?"

Not sure why he cares if I've seen one of my dad's old cop buddies, I answer with caution. "No, why?"

"He asks about you a lot. You should transfer to Empire PD."

"My parents are *here*. And I happen to like my job."

"You'd earn more money down there."

Yes, I know that, because the lack of competitive pay was one of the reasons we had so many deputies leave the job within their first two years. "This area is running thin as it is."

"That's not your problem."

"It has to be someone's problem. We need experienced deputies."

"You sound like a recruitment ad."

When I don't answer, he sits back against the booth and in a lower voice says, "You've known her since she was a kid. You have history."

I should've known he wouldn't let this go. "You trying to tell me she's *the one*?"

"Come on, Liam. You're not some rebound guy for her."

The words click in my brain, but I refuse to acknowledge why. "Since when do you say things like 'rebound guy'?"

Whatever half-ass answer he was about to spew at me dies in his throat as his attention is drawn to the door. Following his line of sight, I groan when *she* steps farther into the bar. Giant bag slung over her shoulder, weaving her way through the crowd, Bree's wearing a loose green sundress that does nothing to hide her curvy body. She tosses her hair over her shoulder and zeroes in on our table. A brief smile lights up her face and she hurries over.

"Speaking of our little dark-haired devil," he says and I shoot a glare at him.

"I was hoping you'd still be here," she says to me after waving a quick hello to Keegan.

"Is everything okay?"

I stand so she can slide into the booth next to me, but not before I catch the corners of her mouth turn down.

"I'm fine."

She probably didn't want to be alone, jackass.

Keegan gives me a raised-brow-smirk face that I'm pretty sure is saying the same thing.

"How you been, sweetheart?" he asks her, settling his hand over hers and turning on enough charm to make me want to drill my fork through his other hand.

"Not bad," she answers. "Still putting out fires?"

I tune them out and consider Keegan's words.

Or at least I try to.

"Hi, Bree. Good to see you again," Sully says, motioning for Keegan to shove over. Jake follows him over and slips into the booth next to his brother.

Jake eyes her in a way I don't care for. I've only met him a handful of times, and each time he's gone home with a different girl. Thinks he's the goddamn pussy whisperer.

I don't want him anywhere near Bree.

I wrap my arm around her shoulders and tuck her against me, making it clear she's not to be whispered to or anything else Jake might come up with.

Keegan ducks his head, his body shaking with laughter. Under the table I kick him, but he just laughs harder.

Bree's gaze shifts between us, but she doesn't move out of my hold or ask me what the hell I'm doing.

Brianna

THERE'S SO MUCH weirdness going on here tonight.

Keegan and Liam seem to be challenging each other. Sully and Jake seem to be afraid to even look at me.

And let's not forget Liam has his arm around my shoulders.

Even so, I'm enjoying hanging out with Liam and his friends. It's like catching a rare glimpse into his world. The guys are obviously close and know how to walk a fine line between entertaining and irritating each other. I'm happy to be a part of it, even if only for a short while.

Liam leans over and whispers in my ear. "Do you want to go somewhere else for dinner?"

His all-consuming heat gives me a jolt. I turn and our lips almost collide.

My mouth twitches into a shaky smile. It's hard to concentrate with him studying me so closely. "I'm okay. This is fun."

"You trying to get away from us, Hollister?" Jake asks, pulling Liam's attention away and giving me a chance to breathe.

"Yeah, I don't want Bree exposed to your deviance."

"Are you always this mean to your friends?" I tease.

"Only Jake."

"He considers me more of an *obligation* than a friend," Jake explains, jerking his thumb in Sully's direction. "'Cause he's friends with my brother."

"Ohh, I'm familiar with *that* situation. We should compare notes." Nervous laughter follows my words. But I'm the only one who seems to think it's funny.

Liam's whole body tenses and his hold on me tightens. His silent way of telling me he doesn't see me as a chore?

"Our waitress looks overloaded, I'm gonna go up to the bar. Anyone need anything?" Keegan asks as he slides out of the booth. Jake gives him an absurdly long list, which Keegan ignores. Sully slaps his brother on the arm and follows Keegan to the bar.

Liam leans down, his lips brushing my ear again. "Let's be clear, you'll never be an *obligation* to me."

If only that was true.

Jake waves his arm in the air, signaling to someone by the door. With Liam blocking my way, I don't see who it is until he's almost at our table.

"Teller! You're early. Where's Murphy?" Jake asks, half-standing and reaching across the table for a fist-bump.

Jake tries to introduce us, but I wave him off. "I've known Marcel since I was a kid. Teller, huh? I didn't know you had a secret identity."

Marcel shrugs off my comment with a smirk. His gaze slides to Liam and they each give each other a subtle chin lift that's...almost friendly.

Weird. Since the last time they saw each other, they acted like two Pit Bulls about to lock jaws around each other's necks.

"Evening, *Officer*."

131

Liam nods at Marcel's leather vest. "You supposed to be wearing your colors in here, *Teller?*"

Okay. So much for friendly.

Marcel's not offended though. "I'm here to see Oscar. I think he's okay with it." He turns, dismissing Liam. He nods at Jake and jerks his head toward the kitchen.

"I'll be right back," Jake says, sliding out of the booth.

"Did you have to be so rude?" I ask after they're gone.

Liam's eyes widen, all country-boy charm—a look he hasn't been able to pull off since ninth grade. "He's probably here to shake the owner down for money."

"Oh, stop it." I playfully smack his arm and he leans in closer.

"I'm glad you came and found me." His low-spoken words trigger goose bumps along my arms.

"I was worried I'd be interrupting guys' night out or..." I drop my gaze to the side. A blush burns up my neck, landing on my cheeks.

"Never."

Keegan and Sully return with two pitchers of beer and extra glasses. "Are we interrupting?" Keegan asks.

"Yes," Liam answers in a bored tone.

I spot one of the girls from my support group and nudge Liam. "Can you let me out? I want to go say hello to someone."

He actually hesitates and I wait for him to question me. Then he slides out of the booth and I hurry over to catch Emily before she leaves.

"Hey, Em."

She turns and smiles when she sees me. "Hey, I thought I saw you over at Hot Guy Island."

I let out a snort. "Overprotective Island maybe."

"Is tall, dark, and staring holes in your back the guy you told me about? Your brother's friend?"

"That's him."

LIAM

MY EYES FOLLOW Bree to the bar, where she stops to talk to a red-haired girl about her age.

"You scare Bree away already?" Keegan asks.

When I don't respond, he and Sully resume whatever they were talking about.

Jake returns without Teller. "Where'd your buddy go?" I ask.

"He's here somewhere," he answers with the evasiveness I expect from Jake.

While the guys continue their discussion, my gaze strays to Bree, still talking to the redhead.

My diverted attention doesn't go unnoticed by Jake. "So, is Bree single or not?"

Silence descends on the table while the guys wait for my answer.

"Not as far as you're concerned."

Keegan snorts.

"Dude, just piss a circle around her," Jake suggests.

Hostility lights me up inside. "Fuck off."

He's not intimidated by my outburst. "Obviously you're into her."

"She's special. She's not one of your hit-it-and-quit-it chicks, so don't even think about it."

"Does she get a say?" Sully asks.

I cock my head, disappointed in my friend. "You too?"

"Nah. I hate seeing you so twisted up."

"He'll be fine," Keegan says. "Can we discuss something else? I feel like I'm on an episode of Oprah listening to you three."

Jake rolls his shoulders. "Just trying to get our boy laid."

"Thanks for the concern."

"It's been what?" Sully asks. "Five or six months since you broke it off with Nurse-stick-up-her-ass?"

Guess I'll never live down the night I brought Linda here to hang with my friends. It'd been an unpleasant night for everyone involved.

"Something like that," I grumble, hating that my friend knows I don't do one-night hookups.

I spot Teller coming out of the back hallway and stand. Jake follows my line of sight. "Christ, Hollister, aren't you off the clock? You really need to hassle him now?"

"Mind your own business."

I intercept Teller before he reaches the bar area and tap his arm, gesturing for him to follow me outside. He's naturally suspicious of me and keeps his distance.

"What do you want?" he asks when we're alone.

I hold up my hands, wanting him to understand this is personal. "Easy. You said if I needed anything for Bree, you'd help."

That snags his attention and he drops his scowl. "What's wrong?"

"Are you going to be around Sunday?"

"I can be. Why?" His gaze never stops moving, assessing everything around us while he waits for my answer.

Am I really asking this thug to look out for Bree?

"I have to work a double. I'm worried about Bree being alone so long."

He runs his hand over the back of his neck and gives me a crooked smile. "I feel like you warned me to stay *away* from her last time we spoke."

"Yeah, and then you fed me that line about her treating your sister nice and being a friend. Were you full of shit?"

His cocky act disappears and he glares at me. "No."

"Can you come up with an excuse to drop by? Maybe mid-afternoon, early evening?"

"Am I staying for dinner or just checking on her?"

"Just checking on her," I growl.

"Do I get more information?"

"What more do you need?"

He folds his arms over his chest. "Even with all the spackle she's got caked on, it's obvious someone cracked her in the face recently." He stares me directly in the eyes. "Since I assume *you* didn't do it, who did and where is he?"

"Her ex and he's down in Empire County Jail."

"Ahh, okay."

"Satisfied?"

"I just like to know what I'm walking into."

Fair enough. I still have an urge to punch him, though.

"If he's in lock-up, what are you worried about?"

"His family. Specifically his brother. I'm having him served with a restraining order for continuing to harass her."

"This douche have a name?"

"Chad Joseph. The brother's name is Christopher."

"Why you asking me?" He lifts his chin toward the bar. "Why not one of your more *upstanding* friends?"

"Because Bree doesn't know them that well. It would be obvious I asked them to check on her." I hesitate before adding. "And I don't trust Jake around her."

Teller snorts. "Can't blame you there."

"I can ask one of the other guys in my department to drive by, but I don't want to freak her out."

"Yeah, I hear you."

"Thank you."

"No problem." He cocks his head, studying me for a minute. "You have any connections in Slater County?"

And *this* is why I didn't want to ask for Teller's help. Now he'll want something in return.

"Not really. Their department's a fucking mess. Word is that they're under investigation for corruption."

He nods slowly as if that wasn't new information.

"Sunday afternoon," he confirms.

I hold out my hand and he shakes it. "Thanks."

Inside, Bree's finishing her conversation and meets me at the table. Feeling territorial, I take her hand and she smiles up at me. "Emily said a group of her friends are going dancing at the Lantern and asked if we wanted to go."

Christ, that's the last thing I feel like doing. But I want her to feel more comfortable to go out and do things. I guess I can suck it up for one night if it makes her happy. "Do you want to?" I ask.

She glances down at her dress. "I do, but maybe another time."

Can't say I'm not relieved.

"Who's the hot redhead?" Jake shouts to Bree.

She giggles and slides into the booth. "You stay away from her. She's getting out of a bad relationship."

The jerk has the nerve to raise his eyebrows. "You know what they say, right, Bree? The best way to get over a guy is to get under a new one."

"No, I've never heard that before," she deadpans. "That's brilliant." Her tone makes it clear she finds it anything but. The guys crack up. Even Jake.

Keegan leans in. "So when do you start graduate school, Bree?"

"End of August."

"Moving back to Empire or you going to commute?"

"I..." For some reason her gaze lands on me. "I haven't decided yet."

I'm not sure where Keegan's going with his questions, but given his earlier interest in my career, I sense the sneaky bastard's up to something.

"Vince is away so much, you'd have the house to yourself most of the time," Keegan says.

Bree tosses her hair in a vigorous headshake. "No way. It's bad enough I need to stay there now. I don't want to make it permanent."

I raise an eyebrow and give Keegan a pointed look that he ignores.

"Going to live on campus?" Keegan asks.

"I guess I could. I liked my apartment..." her voice trails off. "I really need to look for a job."

Jake jerks his thumb toward the bar. "Oscar's always looking for pretty girls to serve drinks."

"No," immediately pops out of my mouth.

All heads turn and stare at me. Mistake. Telling Bree 'no' is as good as laying down a challenge.

Under the table, I squeeze her hand. "You don't want to be on your feet all night long, dealing with drunks. Can't the school find you an internship or something?"

My explanation seems to relax her. "I'll ask around Monday."

While I want what's best for her, I know if she takes a job near campus, it's one more thing that will pull her away from me.

CHAPTER EIGHTEEN
Brianna

LIAM AND I had such a fun evening. Even with his friends hassling each other. He may have wrapped his arm around me, but I think that had more to do with keeping his friends away from me than any romantic feelings on his part. It still felt good to be included, let go and feel normal.

I want to repay him by making breakfast before he leaves for work.

"What's this?" he asks, walking into the kitchen and rubbing his face.

"Breakfast."

"You don't have to—"

"I want to. You've been doing so much for me. I should at least send you to work with a full belly."

He chuckles and drops a kiss on the top of my head. "Thank you. I told you I have to work a double tomorrow right?"

The smile slides off my face. Whoa. That's a lot of hours alone in this house. Not that my loneliness is Liam's problem. "I should probably pack a lunch for you then."

"You don't have to. I usually grab something at Stewart's."

My nose wrinkles. "That's gas station food. What if you get food poisoning?"

He slaps his hand over his stomach, the gesture moving the material of his faded green T-shirt up enough to provide me with a glimpse of abs. "I can handle it," he says.

"What?" I mumble, distracted by muscle and happy trail.

His finger brushes under my chin, lifting my face. "You all right?"

"Uh, yeah. Are you ready to eat?"

"Bring it on."

Even though I protest, he grabs plates and utensils for both of us.

"I'm not messing up your morning routine, am I?" I ask, once we're seated.

"Not at all. This is nice. Usually I just rush around and grab whatever."

"Figured," I mumble.

"Have any plans for today?"

I glance up. "Not really. Why?"

"You could always go up to my parents' if you wanted," he suggests.

I gather up my patience before answering. "I'm not some lonely charity case, Liam. I'll be fine."

"Hey." He reaches out and touches my face. "I didn't say you were. I just feel bad for leaving you alone so long."

"I can entertain myself."

He stares at me for a few beats before taking his hand away. "I have to get ready. Thank you for breakfast."

LIAM

FOR A SATURDAY, our little town is surprisingly quiet. That'll probably change later tonight, but since I'm off the clock in a few, I'm not going to worry about it. Tomorrow I'm sure there'll be plenty for me to do.

As I climb into my truck, my phone buzzes and I groan. If it's someone calling me back into work I'm going to be pissed.

It's Keegan.

"What's up?" I answer.

"Were you able to talk to your parents?"

My mind blanks. "About what?"

"The dog I need to find a home for."

"Shit. No. I didn't realize it was urgent."

He sighs. "We can't get her in for the surgery until next week. She

139

needs to be supervised and be somewhere calm so she's not making the injury worse."

An idea forms and I wonder if Bree will go for it.

"How bad is it?"

"She's mobile. Great guard dog. You don't need to carry her around or anything. Just figured your parents are home and—"

"I'll take her."

"How? You work more hours than I do."

"You heard Bree last night. She needs something to do. I'd feel better if she's not home all alone when I'm working."

"Okay, but what about when she goes back to school? I don't want to keep re-homing the poor dog every couple months."

Inside I'm laughing at the way my big, intimidating friend worries about animals more than people.

"I understand. We'll work something out. I'll talk to my parents too. Bring her over tonight so Bree can meet her."

"Yeah, all right. At least Vince's place doesn't have any stairs."

"Just the front porch, but we can take her in and out the back door."

"Thanks, bud."

We work out a time for him to stop by, and inside I'm excited about this plan. Bree's wanted a pet for as long as I've known her.

Or at least she did. Am I overstepping?

If nothing else, at least I'm helping Keegan out.

BREE'S IN DOG heaven a few hours later. As soon as Keegan brought the dog in the house, Bree knelt down on the living room floor and the oversized Rottweiler immediately plopped down next to her and rolled onto her back. Bree's been rubbing the dog's tummy and humming to her ever since.

"So, I think this will work out," Keegen comments with a smile on his face.

"She needs a more dignified name," Bree says without looking up at us.

"What's not dignified about Waffles?"

Bree shoots a glare at us. "She's not some weenie dog."

"How about Kimber?" I suggest.

Keegan raises a brow. "Like the guns?"

I tip my head in Bree's direction. "First gun she ever shot."

"I like it," Bree says.

"Fine by me. Now, I need you two to keep her meals light. Haven't been able to exercise her much, so she's gotten chubby," Keegan explains, earning another glare from Bree.

"You're not chubby," she croons to the dog.

I doubt Kimber cares what anyone thinks of her waistline as long as Bree keeps rubbing her belly.

Keegan leaves us with the medical instructions, which aren't much. Keep her off her feet as much as possible. Pain meds as needed. Light meals. Easy enough.

Bree unfolds herself from the floor and plucks the list out of my hands.

"Will you be all right with her tomorrow?" I ask. "Sorry I sprung this on you."

"We'll be fine." She hesitates and glances down at the dog. "Now that I have some protection, I guess you don't need to keep staying here with me."

Shit. I hadn't even considered leaving. I hate when I have to go to work. Can't imagine going back to my apartment knowing she's a few streets away.

Even I have to admit, my reluctance to leave has little to do with her safety.

"That's not why I told Keegan we'd take her." Bree raises an eyebrow at "we" and I rush to finish my thought. "He was in a bind."

"So, you won't be gracing the couch anymore?"

Does she *want* me to leave? Or is she daring me to leave?

Kimber struggles to sit up and then stand, unsteady with her injured back leg.

"I'm not leaving. You can't pick her up by yourself if something happens," I answer, feeling only a twinge of guilt for using the dog as an excuse.

A look of what I want to believe is relief washes over Bree's face. "Think Vince will be mad?"

"Nah. He'd love to have a dog. Just can't do it since he's never home."

"What about when I go back to school?" she asks softly.

The question hits me hard and all the points Keegan made at the bar last night flip through my mind.

"We'll worry about it then. I might see if my parents want her." I take a step closer and brush a few loose strands of hair off her cheek.

She glances down at Kimber, who's watching us closely. "Looks like we're both homeless, girl."

My chest tightens from the pain in her voice. "No, you're not."

She lets out a huff of air. "You know what I meant."

CHAPTER NINETEEN

Brianna

WITH KIMBER TO keep me occupied, Liam's long hours don't seem so daunting. Besides, at a certain point I need to learn I can't lean on him forever, right?

We spent last night helping Kimber adjust to her new surroundings. With Liam sleeping in the living room and me in Vince's room, Kimber picked out a spot halfway between the two locations and made it hers by dragging over her bed and flopping down.

This morning she glued herself to my side once Liam left for work.

"Maybe you'll come live with me," I mutter out loud. Kimber turns her head, her fat pink tongue hanging out. She's belly up, all four feet in the air while I rub my hand in circles over her short fur. So far we've discovered she *really* likes the belly rubs.

Knowing that my job is to keep the dog calm seems to calm *me*. For the first time since I came home, I feel settled and able to concentrate. I unearth my laptop and plop down on the floor next to Kimber. Opening my email jolts me into action. So many unanswered messages from people at school. I work through them steadily, ignoring the ones who must've read about Chad's arrest in the paper and clearly want the gossip.

I also find a number of ranting emails from Chad's brother. Once I realize the content is all pretty much the same, I set them aside in a special folder for Liam to go through.

A few hours later I've done some research on student housing—no dogs allowed—and glanced at a few *for rent* ads. One thing becomes clear—I need to find a job. Chad covered our bills while I was in school.

My job at the college bookstore barely paid for our groceries. I have a lead on a Teaching Assistant position, but I'm not the only one applying for it.

"Okay, that's enough depressing stuff for the day. Let's go get some sunshine." Kimber rolls onto her side at the sound of my voice. Alert and waiting for my next move.

Slowly, I pick myself up off the floor and set my laptop on the couch then help Kimber up. She waits at the back door patiently while I attach her leash, her black nubby tail twitching from side to side.

Outside, she keeps her head down, sniffing everything in the yard and I follow her lead, happy to be in the sunshine, even though it's already in the high eighties.

Kimber halts and lifts her head, focusing her attention on the street. A low growl eases out of her a few seconds before the rumble of a motorcycle registers in my brain. Not an uncommon sound around here, but not usually on this street.

Kimber keeps herself a few steps ahead of me as I circle the house to the front yard.

The dark blue Harley Davidson rolling into the driveway startles me and my hand tightens around the leash. Kimber's ears go up, her entire body stiff and alert. When the bike shuts down and the rider slips his helmet off, I relax.

"What are you doing here, Marcel?" I call out.

Still unsure of the intruder, Kimber stays between me and what she obviously sees as a threat while Marcel approaches.

"Whoa," he says, stopping in his tracks.

"It's okay," I try to reassure Kimber. "Sit." She sits but doesn't take her eyes off Marcel or relax her posture.

Keeping one eye on the dog, Marcel advances carefully. "I didn't realize you had a dog."

"We're watching her for a friend. What are you doing here?"

He lifts his broad shoulders and jams his hands into the front pockets of his jeans. "I was in the area and thought I'd say hi. See how you're doing. If you needed anything."

I swallow my surprise and try to ignore the warmth spreading through my chest. "I'm doing okay." The glowy feeling abruptly ends. "Wait a second. Did Liam ask you to check on me?"

Marcel's crooked smile is the only answer I need. He takes his hands out of his pockets. Without making eye contact, he offers his hand, palm down for Kimber to sniff. "I would have stopped by anyway eventually."

"Yeah, right," I tease and he laughs with me.

Having decided he's not a threat, Kimber moves closer to Marcel, leaning on him and allowing him to scratch her rump.

"I guess she likes you."

"She's a good girl."

I nod down the street in the direction of his old house. "Did you come by to check on it?"

"Nah. Not in the family anymore," he answers, clearly not wanting to discuss it.

"Do you want to come in for something to drink?"

"I don't think your Sheriff would approve," he answers with a teasing smile.

"We're not together," I blurt out for some stupid reason.

"Does *he* know that?"

"Of course he does. He doesn't see me in that way."

"Sure." He turns his head to the side and snort-laughs. "Okay."

"Seriously. He's my brother's best friend, so he thinks I'm off-limits or he's following some stupid bro code, you know?"

He laughs even harder. "Yeah. I'm familiar with the concept."

I place my hands on my hips and narrow my eyes. "I feel like you're making fun of me."

"I'm not." He holds up his hands. "Swear it."

We end up sitting on the front porch steps, catching up on the last few years of our lives. Well, I end up doing most of the talking. Marcel's pretty evasive beyond the basics. I can't deny I'm a little annoyed with Liam for asking someone to check up on me, but it's also really sweet, especially since I know he doesn't like Marcel all that much.

We're interrupted by a red sedan slowly moving down the street. It's a small neighborhood, so after a few days back home, I already know all the vehicles that belong on our road. I definitely don't recognize this one. Marcel notices my interest and his gaze narrows on the unfamiliar car. "Someone you know?"

"I don't think so."

The car speeds up and makes a sharp right at the end of the street. For some reason my heart won't settle down. Marcel seems to sense my unease and offers to take me for a ride on his bike.

"Is it safe?"

He gives me a crooked smile in return. "I won't let anything happen to you."

Feeling brave, I stand, giving Kimber's leash a gentle tug.

"Where you going?" Marcel asks when I head toward the back of the house.

"I need to take her in the back door. She can't do steps."

"Here." He leans down and pats Kimber's head. "Don't eat my face off," he mutters to the dog before slipping his arms under her big body and lifting her up. Kimber's big, amber eyes widen. She seems as surprised as I am and doesn't move a muscle. He gently sets her down by the front door and I scurry up the steps to let us in the house.

"I think if Liam trusted you to check on me, you can come in," I say to Marcel, waving him through the front door.

His hands go back in his pockets and he follows me inside. "Holy shit. Your brother's been busy fixing up the place."

"Right? Doesn't look anything like it used to."

He drops down onto the couch and Kimber plants herself between his legs, sitting on his feet. "Lap dog, huh?" he says, scratching behind her ears. He glances up at me. "You got some jeans? A pair of boots?"

When I give him a blank look, he jerks his head toward the door. "For the ride."

"Oh, yes. Give me a second."

Having another guy in the house makes me feel like I'm doing something wrong, but I shake it off. He's just a friend. I might appreciate his impressive male beauty, but no one's as impressive as Liam.

Not to me, anyway.

When I return, Marcel's in the same spot. Kimber's slid to the floor, and given him her belly to rub.

"What a hussy," I tease as I bend down to pet the dog.

She sneezes at me and rolls to her side.

"Ready?" Marcel asks, extracting himself from between Kimber and the couch.

I nod and stand. Kimber watches us leave with a passive expression. I feel bad leaving her alone, but we'll only be gone for a few seconds.

Outside, Marcel goes over a few basics about riding on the back of the bike. "Once around the block?" Marcel asks as he hands me a helmet.

"Sounds good."

He grins and flips me a thumb's up. I climb on the way he explained and settle behind him. The first time, Marcel turns right at the end of the street and cruises slowly through the neighborhood.

"How you doing back there?" he shouts when we're close to Vince's house.

"Good!"

He nods and keeps going. This time we turn left at the end of the street and he does a lazy loop through the neighborhood. When we turn onto my street, what looks like the same red car from before is passing Vince's house again. Slowly.

Marcel doesn't say anything, but decreases our speed to a crawl.

When the car disappears around the corner, Marcel accelerates and pulls into the driveway.

"Who do you think that was?" I ask once I'm on solid ground.

He takes in my nervous expression and forces a smile. "Probably someone visiting relatives in the area. It's summer. Lots of people visiting, right?"

I huff out a laugh. "True."

"Did you have fun?"

"Yes." Laughter follows my answer. "I expected you to pull some macho-guy thing and go a hundred miles an hour."

The corners of his mouth turn up. "Nah. I wouldn't do that to you."

"Thank you for stopping by. I'm sure you had much more exciting things to do today."

He shrugs. "No problem." He lifts his chin toward the house. "Let me watch you go inside," he says.

When I'm safely tucked behind the screen door, I wave and Marcel revs his engine a few times. He takes off way faster than he did with me. Kimber barks at the noise and hurries over to greet me by the door.

Shutting the door behind me, I realize how much I miss Liam.

LIAM

THIS EVENING, MY patrol car's tucked into a spot off the road. Strategically placed facing the downward slope of a hill where drivers always forget to watch their speed. So far I've written three tickets. Almost enough to fill the quota the department denies it has for the day. Overall, an uneventful afternoon and evening for me.

For Chad's brother, today was very eventful. I received the call around dinnertime that he was located hiding out at his parents' house and served with the order forbidding him from contacting Bree again. It sounded like the parents weren't too pleased to find out what their other son had been up to. And I hope that's the last we hear from the Joseph brothers until the court case proceeds.

The deafening roar of an engine makes me sit up. Lucky me. Maybe I'll write a fourth ticket before sunset.

When I realize the noise belongs to Marcel's Harley, I push open my door and step out.

He shuts the bike down and swaggers over. Running his gaze over my car and radar gun, his mouth quirks. "You ever feel like a douche sitting here waiting for speeding citizens to write up?" he asks.

The answer is actually *yes*, but I'm not going to admit that to him. "Are you here for a reason?"

He drops the attitude. "Just left Bree's place."

"Everything okay?"

"She figured it out within five seconds, you know."

"Great," I mutter, surprised I haven't received a pissed-off text from her.

"Thanks for warning me about the guard dog."

I snort, realizing it never occurred to me. "We just got her last night. Did she try to eat you?" I ask, trying not to sound too hopeful.

He rolls his eyes. "No. She's good, though. Real protective of Bree already."

"Good."

"One thing *did* happen." He slips his hand inside his leather vest and pulls out a scrap of paper. "This car drove by while we were talking outside. Seemed to pay a lot of attention to the house."

"She recognize it?"

"No. I took her for a short ride to see if it belonged somewhere in the neighborhood—"

"Wait. You did what?"

"Relax. It's not like I tucked her in and read her a bedtime story. Don't worry, I saved that for you," he answers in the cockiest way possible.

"How do you not get punched in the mouth on a regular basis?"

His eyes widen and he touches his chest. "Most people think I'm charming."

"Yeah, right."

"Can I finish?" he asks.

When I don't object, he continues. "The car was on the street again when we came back. I'm almost positive it was the same vehicle." He hands over the scrap of paper. "It's probably nothing, but figured you'd want to run the plate."

I'm impressed by his quick thinking, but keep that thought to myself because I doubt he cares one way or another about my opinion. "Thanks."

"No problem." He hesitates for a second. "The car seemed to freak her out. I'd go back, but I need to be somewhere tonight."

No doubt a drug deal or something else I'd rather not know about.

"That's okay. I'm going to ask one of the guys in that zone to check it out."

"Good." He throws his leg over his bike. "If you need anything else, let me know. Bree has my number." He's smirking by the last word and I barely resist the urge to flip him off.

Before I have a chance to respond, he twists the throttle and takes off.

CHAPTER TWENTY

LIAM

THE TEXT FROM Bree I'd been waiting for comes a few minutes after Marcel leaves.

Interesting choice for a babysitter.

In spite of the situation, I laugh.

Figured Keegan or Sully would be too obvious.

When she doesn't respond, I take a second to call her.

"You mad at me?" I ask as soon as she answers.

Her sigh and a hint of laughter come through the phone. "No. I should be, but I know you're just worried."

"He behave himself?"

She snorts. "Yes. Kimber pulled a Cujo act at first—"

"Good dog."

Her laughter makes me smile and she continues as if I hadn't interrupted. "But then she warmed up to him. Even let him rub her belly."

"*Hmm.* No more cookies for her."

More laughter and I take it as a good sign. She doesn't bring up the car that drove by and that's encouraging too. I'd hate it if she was home alone freaking out.

It was probably nothing. A tourist whose GPS took them the wrong way. Happens all the time.

Even so, the fact that it went by twice unnerves me.

"I'll be home late. You don't have to wait up for me." *Home.* Right. I wish it were our home. That we weren't just playing house.

Her voice turns serious. "Be careful, Liam."

"Always."

The red car turns out to be a rental and I can't obtain much more information without turning it into an official inquiry. I place a call to Brady, a fellow deputy and friend. I trust him and feel comfortable asking him to check out Vince's neighborhood. I even give him the vehicle information.

It's probably nothing, but just to be sure.

I receive a call to assist with a D.W.I. and after that my night is full of taking statements and filing reports.

It's much later than I planned when I finally pull into the driveway. Brady's sitting across the street and I jog over. "What are you doing here?"

He shrugs. "You seemed worried and it's been a quiet night in my area." He lifts an eyebrow. "Heard *you* had some excitement."

I fill him in on the details of the drunk who shot his own toes off, then tried to drive himself to the hospital.

"You always have all the fun," Brady jokes.

"Yeah, real riot."

We say goodnight and I watch him drive off before heading toward the house.

Lights flicker behind the curtains.

Bree's still up.

Waiting for me?

Shit, I missed her tonight. Worried about her. Can't wait to see her.

As much as I try to handle myself around her, it's becoming impossible.

That she might have stayed up waiting for me, even though I told her not to bother, causes the corners of my mouth to curve up.

I make sure my heavy boots thud over the porch, so I don't startle her when I open the door.

It takes a few seconds to make out her small form curled up in a ball at one end of the couch. Burrowed under a pile of blankets. Kimber's on the floor right next to the couch, her alert gaze trained on the front door.

"It's just me girl," I say in a hushed voice in case Bree's asleep.

"Hey," Bree calls out, her voice raspy, making my mind wander where it shouldn't. She aims the remote at the TV, pausing whatever she's watching. "I'll get out of your bed."

If only.

If she were in my bed, I'd never let her leave.

She tosses the blankets back and swings her feet to the floor, stopping to pet Kimber.

"No. Stay." She raises an eyebrow at the note of desperation in my voice, but fuck, I've wanted to see her all damn night. "I won't be able to go to sleep for a while. Finish your movie," I say, gesturing at the television.

Kimber's apparently decided I'm not a threat and puts her head back down.

Sparks of satisfaction light up inside me when Bree eases back against the couch. My eyes are drawn down her long, bare legs, to the thick wooly socks pooled around her ankles. Some sort of loose tank top barely keeps her covered up top.

My gear lands on the floor with a thud, and she turns her head. Busying myself with unlacing my boots keeps my mind off of speculating about what else she's wearing. When I'm done, she pushes the blankets aside and pats the couch.

Cautiously, I lower myself next to her. Close enough not to offend, but far enough away that none of our parts touch.

"What are we watching?"

I can barely make out the blue of her eyes when she turns my way, but I definitely catch the teasing smile playing over her lips. "First, how was your day?"

"Long."

"Nothing exciting happened?"

Her gentle voice lifts the darkness that followed me home. I could get used to this. Floating in her sweetness night after night.

Except she's leaving at the end of the summer.

And once Vince gets home, there's no reason for me to stay.

"Nothing exciting until now," I finally answer.

She twists her mouth in a way that suggests she doesn't believe me.

"Honestly, this is the best part of my night."

"That's sweet, Liam."

It is sweet. Sappy even. But so damn true. "What are we watching?" I ask her again.

She rattles off a story about the action drama, which centers around two British intelligence officers who alternate between screwing anything that moves and blowing shit up.

"Sounds right up my alley," I tease.

With deliberate slowness, she inches toward me—as if she's afraid I'll deny her. I lift my arm and she eagerly cuddles against my side.

"I missed you today," she says softly.

"Even with your visitor?"

She tips her head back. "Yes, even with."

"You mad at me for asking him to stop by?"

"No." She lays her head back on my chest and my fingers stroke through her soft tangle of hair for a few seconds.

"Missed you too."

"Do you mean that?" she murmurs.

"Yes, Bree."

Not sure what else to say, I keep stroking her hair. She tucks her feet up under her until she's a little package nestled next to me.

"Do you have your phone?"

Without answering, she leans over and picks it up off the end table and hands it to me.

"No more calls. But I found a bunch of emails from Chris."

"Fuck." Did that asshole already violate the restraining order? "From when?"

"Looked like he's been sending them since I left, but I didn't see them until this morning when I went through my email."

"You didn't delete them, did you?"

"No, Sheriff Serious." She picks her head up and I feel the weight of her gaze over my skin. "Can we not talk about that right now? Can we just be Bree and Liam? Friends binge-watching some kick-ass television tonight?"

Nothing has ever sounded better.

"You've got it."

She places a kiss quick on my cheek and settles back into my hold.

Against my better judgment, I curl my arm around her, my hand resting on her hip.

Christ, she must have on another pair of those micro-shorts she seems to own in abundance, because I'm acutely aware that my fingertips brush bare skin.

On screen, agent number two is busy getting *busy* and things start to get uncomfortable behind my fly.

I clear my throat and glance away from the screen. "Uh, I guess this is on cable?"

Her head moves up and down against my chest as she nods. The sweet friction combined with her fresh clean scent tickling my nose doesn't help the situation below my belt. Should I grab one of the blankets and throw it over my lap?

Fuck, I'm so hot, beads of sweat break out along my hairline. How can she stand all these blankets in this heat? Why isn't the AC on?

Her fingers splay over my chest, her touch searing me through my cotton T-shirt. "Your heart's pounding. Are you okay?"

On the surface, her question is all innocent concern. The way she peers up at me, though, is anything but innocent.

This is getting a little too intense.

My hand gently squeezes her hip before I unwrap my arm from around her body. I attempt to push myself off the couch, but her hand still resting on my chest stops me.

"Bree," I warn.

No. Oh, shit. If she drops her gaze, she'll definitely know where all my blood went. She pulls her hand away only to do something even worse. Pressing one knee into the couch cushion, she flings her other leg over me, straddling my lap.

Bad idea. Fuck me. Bad idea.

My body recoils as far back into the couch as the cushions allow. Unruffled by my reaction, she settles her hands over my shoulders, staring into my eyes.

"What's wrong?" she asks. "Are you mad at me?"

"No."

"I really did miss you tonight."

Her low voice, her searing eyes, the weight of her in my lap—all of it hypnotizes me, leaving me powerless to do the right thing.

"We shouldn't be doing this."

She cocks her head to the side. Another gesture meant to be innocent that isn't. "What are we doing?"

Over her shoulder, the couple onscreen are still fucking frantically. The woman's happily bouncing away on top of the guy. Lusty moans and orgasmic shrieks from the surround-sound speakers fill the air.

Desire slams into me swift and furious.

Fuck me, but I want to carry her into the bedroom and copy every single position on the screen right this second.

"Do you want to watch something else?" she asks in a light, teasing tone.

No, I want to do everything they're doing and then some. But it'd be a huge mistake.

"I think we should."

With the room still bathed in shadows, I don't see her hand approaching until her fingers trace the line of my jaw. At first my body flinches away from her touch.

"Brianna, don't." The warning comes out with zero authority.

Then I give in and close my eyes.

She shifts in my lap. Nope. No. Can't think about all of her heat pressing against me. Even so, I slide down a little, placing my hands on her hips to keep her steady.

"Why?"

"We can't."

"Why?" she insists.

Can't she understand I'm trying to do the right thing here?

"Vince is my best friend and you're his little sister." My gaze roams over her face, stopping at her plump lips that I really want to taste again.

She tilts her head. "I'm an adult. What does my brother have to do with anything?"

Nope. She doesn't get it at all. Or if she does, she's not buying it. "Bro code, Bree. Guys don't mess with their friend's sisters." Jesus Christ, that has to be the lamest thing that's ever come out of my mouth. Right about now I could use a punch from Keegan to shut me up.

She squints and laughs at the same time. "Did you really just say *bro code?*"

Any other time, I'd love Brianna calling bullshit on me.

Not tonight.

"Do you like Vince?"

I shake my head in confusion. "Of course."

"If you had a sister, would you let him date her?"

"That's not the point." The words come out sharp. I so desperately need to gain control of this situation. My hands move to her thighs in an attempt to remove her from my lap.

Her smooth skin distracts me and instead of pushing her *off* my lap, I run my hands up her legs, under her shorts and grip the globes of her ass.

Not a single scrap of underwear obstructs my exploration. Soft, silky, hot skin glides under my fingertips.

Her head lolls back, her heavy-lidded stare the sexiest damn thing.

Any words I planned to say leave my brain in a puff of smoke.

"Jesus, the things I want to do to you aren't right," I murmur. The words rush out before I consider their implication.

Her head snaps back up, her eyes stinging me with sharp curiosity.

"Tell me anyway," she insists.

My hands knead her ass harder, forcing her against the hard ridge of my erection. A low groan slips from her throat and she swivels her hips just enough to make me lose my damn mind.

She swoops in, brushing her lips against my ear. "Do you want to spank me, Liam?"

"Fuck!" I jerk back as if she'd slapped me.

She nods in a maddening way. Both teasing and knowing. "You'd like that, wouldn't you?"

"Stop. I couldn't. With you. Not after." Christ, she's fried my brain, and I can't get any words out.

"You can admit it, Liam."

My dirty mind conjures up a whole list of things I want to do to her. This conversation needs to end. I'm confused, pissed off, and so goddamn aroused I'm dangerously close to losing it and fucking her on Vince's living room floor.

Grasping at something to stop this insanity, I blurt out what's been bothering me since she came home and I realized how much I still want her. "You're not thinking clearly. Even if I—you're not ready to be in another relationship."

She sucks in a deep breath, her blue eyes simmering with anger.

Well, that worked.

With deft movements, she plucks one of my hands off her thigh, guiding it to the *V* between her legs.

My brain says *No. Pull back.* But I can't. No fucking way. I *have* to explore.

She presses my hand up against her hot center. The sensations take a second to infiltrate my foggy brain. Her shorts are wet.

My nostrils flare, and I sit up straighter, pressing my hand against her harder. Her nipples tease me through the flimsy material of her top. Does she ever wear a damn bra?

Heat pours from her. Those tiny shorts would be so easy to shove to the side. I press my thumb against her, seeking. I trace her slit through the damp material with several firm strokes. She leans back, bracing her hands on my knees, arching her back.

So beautiful. Perfect in every way.

She lets out a soft moan.

Her body trembles.

I'm completely powerless to stop even though the timing is so, so wrong.

Suddenly, she snaps her head forward, almost colliding with mine.

Pressing her fists into my thighs for leverage, she jumps out of my lap with the grace and quickness of a cat.

"Do you have any idea how insulting that is?"

My brain scrambles to sort out her words while my body struggles with the loss of her heat.

"Does that feel like I'm not ready?" she snaps.

No. She felt fucking amazing and I want to shove my face between her thighs and taste her next.

Before I can squeeze out an answer, she turns and stalks off to the bedroom.

Follow her.

She's pissed. I should let her cool off. Hell, *I* need to cool off. I handled that like a complete asshole.

Kimber lifts her head and chuffs as if to say she has a stronger word than *asshole* in mind for me.

After a few minutes, I'm no calmer.

Bree's end of the house is quiet. I duck into the bathroom. Like a creep, I listen against the door that opens into the bedroom.

Nothing.

I contemplate going in and apologizing, but I know if I step foot in that room we're going to finish what we started on the couch.

The last time I was this crazed over a woman, it was Bree. Back when she was finishing high school and I was barely in my twenties. That was nothing compared to what I feel for her now. After the time we've spent together. The things we've confided in each other. We've created a bond different from any we've shared before.

And I don't want to destroy it.

I turn to splash water over my face.

Bree's little bag of personal items sits on the counter.

Open.

Toothpaste, comb, unidentifiable makeup items, hair ties. My lips twitch into a smile. There's something sweet about all her girly stuff taking up space in Vince's minimalist bathroom.

The smile dies on my face when I notice the little round plastic package.

Birth control pills.

A sharp ache twists in my chest. Bree's not a little girl anymore.

Back then, pushing her away had been the right thing to do. I kept my friendship with her brother intact and allowed her to escape our small town to make something of herself. Now, she's finished her degree and has a plan to continue. I'm so damn proud of her.

Denying myself back then made sense.

Now, it doesn't.

The asshole in me pipes up. *You could go bareback.*

Shame slams into me, and I whip open the shower door, yanking on the hot water harder than necessary.

Tomorrow, I'll fix everything.

Tonight I'm hard enough to pound nails and need to relieve some tension.

Brianna

DEEP HUMILIATION KEEPS me from sleeping. Not only do I now have absolute proof Liam doesn't care about me the way I care about him, I also managed to ruin our friendship. Let's be honest, there's no way to come back from what happened on the couch. Rubbing myself against him like I was in heat. Practically begging him.

Liam rejecting me.

Telling me I'm not ready.

That stung. My stomach twists with indignation. I'm so tired of having Liam treat me like a kid who doesn't know what she wants.

In the darkest hours, I form a plan. I can't stay here. Not after last night. I can't be in the same house with Liam any longer. It's slowly killing me.

Since he's duty-bound, in more ways than one apparently, he won't leave until my brother returns. Not even last night's disaster will pry his stubborn ass out of the house.

I'll have to be the one to leave.

Once I make the decision, I set my alarm. Sleep finally finds me for a few blissful hours.

I'm up, dressed, and have a week's worth of clothes packed before seven. As soon as I open the bedroom door, Liam's voice reaches me, and I freeze.

Sounds like he's on the phone.

I scurry out of the bedroom and stop short at Kimber's bed.

Shit. How can I leave her?

Her deep whiskey eyes peer up at me.

Crouching down, I run my hand over her fur. "I'll be back for you."

Liam's voice sounds like he's coming closer, so I give Kimber a final pat.

Ignore him. Keep moving.

Hang on to what little dignity remains. March out there and announce you're leaving. Don't ask. *Tell* him your plans.

Actually, fuck it, just grab the damn keys and go.

"Thanks, Keegan, I owe you." Great, maybe Liam's asking his big, burly firefighter buddy to come babysit me next.

No way.

"Bree?"

I turn and face Liam but can't look him in the eye. "Where are you going?" he asks. His low, concerned voice sends shivers over my skin.

Ignore it. He doesn't want you.

"I can't stay here. I'm uh, going back to Empire to stay with a friend of mine." This is actually a lie. I don't know where I'm going. I just know I'm not staying here.

"No."

"Excuse me?"

"You're not leaving."

Chin up. "Watch me."

"Bree," he says, following me to the front door. "Bree, look at me."

"No. I can't."

His hand closes over my shoulder, and I shriek, ducking out of his grasp. "Don't touch me!"

"Shit." He holds his hands up in a gesture of surrender. "I'm sorry, Bree."

My skin burns with embarrassment from my over-reaction. Another gift from Chad. I know no matter what, Liam would never ever hurt me.

"Stop and talk to me for a second," he pleads.

I want to so badly. I want to talk to Liam. I want to rewind the clock and not have acted like a horny slut last night. But I'm too ashamed to even look at him.

Nope.

One look and he'll know I'm in love with him. He'll see how deep his rejection cut me. Again.

I yank on the doorknob, but it won't budge. Too late, I realize Liam's palm is flat against the door, keeping it closed. Blocking my escape from Humiliation Island.

"*Move*," I demand, proud my voice comes out strong and steady even though I feel anything but.

"Not until we talk."

I spin around so fast, he jumps back, but he's quick and maneuvers himself in front of the door.

"Why are you doing this? Last night wasn't humiliating enough? You need to rub my nose in your rejection a little more?"

"Bree, I'm sorry."

"Not as sorry as I am."

His hand slides under the strap of my backpack and he slides it off my shoulder, dropping it on the floor. Humiliated—*again*—and powerless, I can't believe this shit.

Liam's strong arms wrap around me, holding me close to his warm, strong body. The comfort I take from him only makes me angrier with myself.

"I don't know where to start, Bree. I'm so sorry about last night."

Backing away, I glare at him. "About what? Making me feel like a tramp?"

"Jesus Christ. I don't think that. Bree, I love you. I never wanted to make you feel bad. I'm so sorry."

His body was definitely attracted to me last night. But something about *me*, about who I am, obviously repels him. "I can't do this anymore, Liam. I'm sorry. It's too much."

Because I'm a glutton for more blows to my ego, I have to know what it is about *me* that he finds so repulsive. Maybe I can work on it. "You keep using Vince as an excuse. Just be honest. What's wrong with *me?*"

That has to be the most pitiful thing I've ever said.

Gentle, loving Liam disappears. Fierce Liam takes his place. His arms tighten around me and he spins us, pressing me to the door. My back hits the wood with a soft thump. I let out a startled gasp and meet his burning brown eyes.

"You want honesty, baby girl? Buckle up, because here comes a big dose of it."

Startled by the change in his tone, I try to wriggle away from him, but he keeps me pinned to the door. His hands hold mine at my sides, his huge body enveloping my smaller one. He's quick to wedge his knee between my legs, forcing them apart.

My heart thumps with excitement and a little bit of fear. The exhilarating kind. Like right before the drop on a roller coaster.

He brushes his lips against my ear. "You think I don't want you? You're all I fucking want, Bree. Everything I want."

I gasp from his admission. "Then why—"

"No," he says, placing one hand over my mouth. "Time you listen." He waits to see if I'll cooperate before continuing. "You're right. You're an adult now. If Vince has a problem with us, that's too fucking bad. I'll deal with him."

Oh my God. Did he just say *us?*

He moves in closer, skimming his lips along my neck, gently pulling on my earlobe with his teeth. His next words are low and rough. "I'm sorry I couldn't explain myself better last night. Your hot pussy in my lap scrambled my brain."

I moan into his hand, loving dirty-talking Liam.

His eyes widen, taking in my response.

His thigh. Between my legs. Pressing just enough. Pleasure coils tight and hot inside me.

"Listen to me and hear what I'm saying before your fiery temper goes off. Can you do that? Nod once."

Jesus Christ. I think I could come from just the friction of his leg and his low, demanding voice right now.

I nod.

"You have been through hell."

I start to shake my head, but he stops me.

"No," he says dragging the word out. "*Listening*, remember?"

When I don't move, he continues.

"You need to feel safe and trust again. And I can give you that. I *will* give you that. What I can*not* do is be your rebound guy, Bree. Once I have you, you're mine and that's it."

Ohmygod.

"So as much as I wanted to fuck you on the couch last night—and trust me I did—I can't do it without you understanding what it means to me. What it will mean for us."

There it is again. Us.

"Okay," he says, taking his hand away from my mouth. "Let me have it."

LIAM

BREE BLINKS AND stares up at me. Her big blue eyes swimming with questions.

All the weight that had settled in my chest over the last few weeks disappears.

"What does this mean?" she asks, averting her eyes.

Gently placing a finger under her chin, I tip her head back so I can see her eyes. "What do you want it to mean?"

She ducks her head and wriggles out of my grasp. "I'm afraid to say."

I stop her with a hand on her arm. "You're my friend. But that's not enough anymore."

"I want to be more than friends." She hesitates, eyelids fluttering closed. "But what if it doesn't work out?"

"Impossible."

She doesn't seem convinced. Can't say I blame her. I've done nothing but push her away since she came home. She peeks up at me again. So much need simmering in her eyes.

"Were you really going to leave?" I ask, furious with myself for making her feel running away was her best option.

She nods once, then shakes her head. "I can't be here with you anymore. Not like this."

"I'm sorry. You've been through so much. I thought I was doing the right thing by letting you deal with everything first. By—hell, Bree. I don't know." The slippery slope I'm headed down gets steeper with each word out of my mouth.

Reaching out, she grips my arm. "I appreciate it. I know it doesn't seem like it, but I do. And just so you know. You're—" She stops to take a deep breath. "You're so important to me. You could never be...some stopgap until the next guy. I couldn't use you like that."

She might think that now, but what about later? I care way too much about her to ever let her go.

Then show her, jackass.

Curling my hand around the back of her neck, I pull her closer. Her lips part. To protest? Question me?

Her lower lip trembles. "You want me? Really want me?" she asks, so timid I ache.

"Yes, I want you." I brush my fingers against her temple and down her cheek. "I want your mind, your heart, your soul, your body. You already have every part of me."

Tears fill her eyes. "That's what I want."

All I can think about is kissing her. She reaches up, placing her hands on my chest, sliding them up around my neck. I lean down and kiss her with my heart and soul, showing her with every breath, every brush of my lips how much I want her. Need her.

Her body falls into me and I pull her as close as possible.

A thousand ideas demand attention in my overheated brain. *Closer. Get her closer. Her scent. Her taste. Her heat.*

We break away and I touch my forehead to hers as we catch our breath.

I slip one arm behind her knees and the other against her back, lifting her into my arms.

Her fingers trail down the side of my face and she presses her lips against my jaw. "Please don't stop this time."

Pain squeezes my chest. "Never again, Bree. I need you more than air."

I carry her down the hall and have a brief moment of remorse for what we're about to do under Vince's roof.

But there's no way we can wait another second.

In the bedroom, I set her down. She keeps her arms around me, staring up into my eyes.

"Next time we have to go to my place," I say.

She cocks her head. "Next time? Next time what? What do you think is about to happen?"

That freezes me in place for a second, until her mouth quirks up, and I realize she's teasing me.

"I guess I deserve that." I reach out, brushing her hair back from her face.

Without thinking, I kick backward, slamming the door shut. Bree jumps, but a playful smile curves her lips. "Did you say something about spanking me last night?"

"No. *You* did."

I pull her against me and hook my fingers into the strap of her tank top, slowly sliding it down her shoulder. She gasps. A sweet little noise because of something as simple as lowering a strap. Imagine what she'll do when I put my mouth on her.

My hand slides down her back, squeezing her ass with just enough pressure that she meets my eyes. "I probably should, though, since you were about to leave me."

"Your own fault." Her tone is gentle, not mean.

Deciding I need to see more of her a hell of a lot faster, my fingers skim along the bottom of her shirt. My knuckles brush against soft skin and she jerks away. "You're tickling me."

I grip the shirt and strip her out of it. "That's better."

"Now you," she says, fisting her hands in my shirt and yanking it up. I help her by taking it off the rest of the way and tossing it on the dresser.

"Wow." She sighs and rakes her gaze over me from shoulders to shorts. My skin heats at the way she appreciates what she sees. She hooks her fingers in the front of my shorts, but doesn't yank them down the way I expected.

No, she tortures me first. Skimming her finger under the waistband, stopping on my hip.

"What're you doing, baby girl?"

"Exploring. I've waited this long. I want to savor every second."

My hands cup her cheeks, tilting her head back. "You're the sweetest person I've ever known."

"Kiss me."

"With pleasure."

Our lips meet, gentle at first, then I take possession of her mouth. She sighs and presses her body against mine. My heart pounds while my hands touch her everywhere, cupping her jaw, the back of her neck, the slope of her shoulder, curve of her breast, down to her waist. Not about to waste another second, I push her shorts down her legs. If I strip her down completely, we won't make it to the bed.

How long have I been dying to do this?

Too long.

We don't break our kiss as I back her up to the bed. She falls against the mattress and I follow her down, covering her with my body. Each one of her kisses burns me up. Her blue eyes are hazy and unfocused. She flicks her tongue at the corner of her mouth, and I almost lose it.

"Up," I grunt at her, raising myself off her just enough to give her room to scoot into the center of the bed.

"Better." God, she's reduced me to one-word demands.

I take a second to absorb how beautiful she is before descending on her like a ravenous beast.

Hooking my thumbs in her underwear, I drag them down her legs. She's shy, bringing her knees together. I let her have the second of modesty, laying kisses around one ankle, then the other. I trail my lips over her calf, stopping to lick the inside of her knee, before wrapping my hands around her legs and pushing them wide, making room for my big body.

She sucks in a breath. Fear? Or surprise? "Liam?" Her throaty rasp makes it hard to stop.

I meet her eyes. "I'm here." She props herself up on her elbows, watching me.

"What're you doing?" she whispers.

"Staring at your beautiful pussy." I run my fingers over her skin.

She sucks in jerky breath.

I lean in and rub my chin over her inner thigh, tickling her with three days' worth of scruff. My mouth waters to taste her.

"Uh," she reaches down, covering herself.

"Don't." I grab her hands and pin them at her sides. When I'm sure she won't move, I release her and rest my cheek against her leg. With lazy slowness, I drag my thumb over her impossibly soft skin. Teasing and exploring.

She whimpers when my thumb flicks near her clit. Slowly, I press a finger inside her, exploring wet, velvet heat. She gasps and raises her hips when I graze her G-spot.

I want to do everything to her. Pleasure her. Comfort her.

Lose myself in her.

My tongue darts out, licking, sucking, and kissing.

She tenses up, gasps, sighs, squeals. All sorts of delicious noises. Her heels dig into the mattress, lifting her pussy to my mouth. I grunt out a few encouraging sounds because I can't take my mouth off her to form any words.

Spreading her even wider with my shoulders, I keep tonguing her, licking and tasting her. Kissing her lips, flicking my tongue over her clit, and finally sucking it into my mouth. Her legs quiver and she cries out. Her hands fist in my hair, tugging to the point of pain. A rough sound leaves me, my dick hardens.

Her body twists. Trying to get more or get away from me. She pushes me back, then grinds herself against my face. Soft noises work out of her throat, growing louder by the second.

"Liam!"

She trembles and shatters around me.

"Oh. Oh God."

I rub my face against her thigh, smearing her wetness on her skin. When I look up, she's covering her face with her hands.

"That was quick." She misses my pussy-licking grin because she's still hiding.

She peeks out at me. "You've had me wound up for days."

Laughter rumbles out of me. Her giggles are muffled by her hands, but she shifts and squirms as I kiss her hip, then drag my tongue over her stomach. My teeth nip at her bra, pulling at it until the cups slip down, exposing her nipples. I can't decide which one to suck first.

She lightly touches my face. "That was so…"

"Good?"

"Better."

She leans up to kiss me, and I slip my arms under her body, rolling us so she's on top. She slides down, her pussy bumping against my rock-hard dick. "God, Liam. I still want you so much."

"I'm here."

Slowly, she inches down my body.

"What're you doing?"

"Returning the favor."

I open my mouth to say something, not sure what, but her hand squeezes me through my shorts and I'm struck mute. She strips my shorts off and kneels on the bed next to me, her gaze running up my legs and stopping on my cock. "Impressive."

"Why thank you."

She laughs at my brass, reaching out to wrap her hand around me. She squeezes and slides her soft palm up. "Hmm, looks like I need both hands," she teases. "And my mouth."

She says that last one right before sweeping her tongue over the head of my cock.

"Fuck. Brianna…Bree…fuck." I'm not sure what I want to say. I completely forget how to speak when she strokes me with her mouth and hands. I palm the sides of her head, needing to touch her face.

Pleasure and heat tingle along my spine. "Bree. Baby. Stop." My fingers tangle in her hair, pulling her off. "Need your pussy."

She flashes a lopsided grin and plants her fists in the mattress, crawling up the bed. "I like dirty-talking Liam."

"Good. Get on my dick." I even point at it so there's no confusion.

She wiggles her eyebrows, and I reach out, tracing my fingers over her cheek and over her lips.

"Come on."

For some reason she hesitates. "Condom?"

Fuck. I don't want to tell her I snooped through her stuff and know she's on the pill.

I sit up and reach around to unhook her bra, throwing it to the floor. "I just had my department physical. Healthy as a stallion."

"Big as one too," she teases.

"Thanks."

The smile slides off her face. "They tested me in the hospital…"

Shit. I never considered—*fuck*, I'm a selfish asshole.

"I'm fine," she says, reading my concern correctly. "I'm on the pill."

"Then what are you waiting for? Get on top of me."

"Feeling lazy, Liam?" she taunts.

"That's it." I power up and take her down to the bed, pinning her hands above her head. "Guess you'll ride me some other time."

One of my hands slides under her ass, tilting her hips for better access. Even though I'm aching to finally squeeze my cock inside of her, I take it slow. Tormenting us both. Staring into her eyes, I press against her opening. I hiss as I meet nothing but slick, tight, heat. Her eyes widen and she gasps as I slowly slide in. "Are you mine?"

She nods.

"No, baby girl. I need you to say it."

Without hesitating, she gives me the words I've wanted to hear for so long. "I'm all yours, Liam."

I circle my hips, pushing into her and sliding out. "Liam, please," she whispers.

"Please what? Tell me."

"Harder."

I pick up my speed a bit. "Like this?" I ask, brushing my lips over hers. I slam into her harder. "Or this?"

"More."

"You lost your chance to be on top, bossy girl."

She snorts and wraps her legs around my waist. Reaching back, I hook her legs over my arms. She lets out a startled gasp at the different angle. "Too much?"

"No."

It's the last word she speaks. After that it's just the sounds of our bodies crashing together. Breathless grunts mixed with whimpering cries of pleasure.

Her cries increase in volume just as my control snaps, and I hammer into her.

Everything's so intense. Her husky moaning, our sweaty bodies sliding together, the bliss gathering at the base of my spine.

"Bree, come for me."

"I…" She presses her head back against the bed, her mouth falling open, sharp little noises filling the air as I make her come.

I'm done. Pleasure fires through me, and I slam my hips into her one last time, fusing us together.

A few seconds pass, and her body relaxes. Her eyes flutter open. I'm still breathing hard, shaking from my orgasm.

She sighs as I slip free from her body. A satisfied smile curves her lips.

Bree is finally mine.

Brianna

IT'S MUCH LATER in the day when we finally take a break.

"So, you're done fighting this?" I ask, tracing my fingers over Liam's chest. He captures my hand, bringing it to his lips.

"Yeah, I'm done. Well done. Done for. Done in." He tickles his fingers over my ribs, and I yelp.

"Stop! Stop, that tickles."

"That's the point."

He doesn't stop until I'm out of breath from laughing so hard.

"Which one of us gets to tell my brother?" I ask after catching my breath.

"I'll talk to him." He turns his head, glancing around. "I'll probably leave out the part about how we defiled his bedroom."

"At least we didn't use his condoms."

He lifts his shoulders and fake-shudders in horror.

His hand finds his way to my hip, then strokes lower. "No, we didn't." His face turns serious. "I've never done that with anyone else, Bree."

I stare at him unsure of his meaning.

"No condom," he clarifies.

"Oh." I'm not sure how to respond. I don't want to picture him with anyone else. "Yeah, Nurse Linda seemed like she might be a germaphobe."

The shock on his face is quite comical.

To me, anyway. Liam doesn't even chuckle.

"Nothing before you even exists for me anymore, Bree."

Before I can catch the breath he knocked out of me with that statement, he rolls to his side and runs the back of his hand over my cheek. "Are you all right?"

"I'm well-fucked if that's what you mean."

He dips his head, shoulders shaking with laughter. "No. That's not what I meant."

When he settles down, he captures my arm, running his gaze over my wrist. "I didn't hurt you, did I?"

"Don't start."

"I'm sorry I've been such a prick."

I place my hand over his mouth—much like he did to me earlier—and I tingle from the memory. "No more apologies."

He sucks one of my fingers into his mouth. "You taste good." He runs his gaze down my naked body. "Everywhere."

Heat races over my exposed skin. "Careful, I don't think you can handle another round."

"You throwing down a challenge, baby girl?" He moves over me. "I'll show you exactly how many rounds I have in me."

Wailing sirens scream through the air, scaring the crap out of me. He drops his head, muttering, "Fuck."

"What the hell is that?" I ask as the same pattern of sirens repeats.

"My phone. Not good," he explains, launching himself off the bed, hurrying into the living room.

"What?" he barks.

Liam listens carefully, curses under his breath a couple times. "Okay. I'll be there in twenty."

I slide out of bed and tug on shorts and a T-shirt. Liam groans when he comes back into the bedroom. "Why are you dressed? I wanted to burn the image of your naked body into my brain for the night."

"You think you'll be gone all night?"

He pulls me into his arms and kisses my forehead. "Yes, it's...not good. I'll probably be late. If you need something and can't reach me, call Keegan. His number's on the fridge."

"Okay."

"I hate leaving you right now, so damn much."

I run my hand over his cheek. "I understand."

"Thank you."

He gives me one last lingering kiss before getting dressed and hauling ass.

CHAPTER TWENTY-ONE
LIAM

RIANA CONSUMES MY thoughts on the way to Urgent Care. Her scent saturates my skin. Her laughter rings in my ears. I hated leaving her.

Unfortunately, under the circumstances I need to focus on work.

Today, the Urgent Care center is crowded and chaotic, doing nothing to ease my mind about the possible child abuse case I was called down here for.

I meet up with Brady in the parking lot. Together we push through the front doors and past a few people waiting to see a doctor.

Of course, the first person to help us is Linda. Why not?

"We received a call for a possible ten twenty-five," Brady states without acknowledging that he knows her. Brady's a hurt-my-friend-and-you're-dead-to-me kind of guy. Not that Linda had *hurt* me, but he's still curt toward her.

I couldn't care less at the moment.

The second she looks up from her clipboard, she groans. "Figures you two caught this one," she says, sounding just as excited to see us. "Follow me." She leads us into a private consultation room, flipping on the overhead lights and closing the door behind her. "Four-year-old female. Orbital fracture."

I wince and dread settles in the pit of my stomach.

Focus.

Detach.

Facts.

"Dad says she hit her face on a dresser last night when she was jumping on the bed. Didn't bring her in until this afternoon. Claims his mom is a nurse and he took her there instead."

Jesus. I need a second to process the information. Who the fuck smashes a four-year-old in the face? Why?

Stupid question.

I've been doing this long enough to know I'll never receive an answer that makes sense.

Brady speaks up first. "You suspect the dad?"

Linda hesitates. "Well, when he left the room, I asked her if anyone hurt her and she said 'Daddy did it.'"

Not all that compelling. Children that age are notoriously unreliable witnesses.

Brady opens the door and steps into the hallway, but Linda blocks my exit. "So are you and the little princess together now?" she asks.

"Seriously? We have an injured child and you're playing jealous ex?" I growl out each word and brush past her.

"Does Vince know?" she persists, following me into the hallway.

Is she really doing this now? "Mind your own business."

"That's a *no*. Well, call me when he kicks your ass. I'll patch you up."

Brady hides his smirk behind his hand.

Their cavalier behavior is the result of too much detachment. You see enough of this shit and after a while you're not trying to help people anymore, you're just trying to make it through your shift.

Linda leads us down the long hallway. At the end, a large, angry, tired-looking young woman sits on a chair outside the last room on the left. The little boy in her lap keeps struggling and squirming to break loose.

"Dad's live-in girlfriend," Linda mutters. "And the patient's half-brother."

"Bio-mom?" Brady asks.

Linda shakes her head.

I stop and jot down a few notes and when I'm finished, Linda pushes the door open and holds it for Brady and me. A dark-haired little girl shrinks back against the white hospital bed. The young man standing next to her jerks his head in our direction, his mouth opening but no words coming out. He barely looks old enough to drive but has a four-year-old daughter.

A clear picture of what happened forms in my head.

"You called the cops?" he asks Linda, who snuck into the room behind me.

"It's standard procedure," she replies, completely unruffled. "Deputy Hollister and Deputy O'Connor, this is Allison's father."

We're running out of room in here, so Linda ducks outside. I approach the bed slowly and use a lowered voice. "Hey, little miss, you must be Allison?"

The girl slowly lifts her head, and I swallow hard. Struggle to keep my face an expressionless mask while I mentally catalog her injuries. Bruising around her swollen-shut left eye. A cut directly below that was bad enough to require stitches. My jaw clenches and I exhale slowly through my nose to calm myself and not scare her.

No child should suffer an injury at the hands of a person whose duty was to protect them.

Dad stands there, gaze skipping from Brady to me.

Outside the room, a shriek echoes down the hallway. "That your little brother out there, Allison?" I ask.

She shakes her head in response and her dad sighs. "He's her half-brother. Mine and Nancy's son."

"That's Nancy out there?"

"Yeah."

"Where's Allison's mother?"

"Your guess is as good as mine. Probably some crack house."

Wonderful. Perfect thing to say in front of your daughter, asshole.

Brady and I exchange a silent look. He doesn't have to say a word. We're both thinking the same thing. A side effect of working many long hours together over the last few years.

"Allison has a speech delay, so I don't know what you think she can tell you," Dad says.

"Do you go to school, Allison?" I ask.

She shakes her head and glances up at her father, but doesn't seem to be afraid of him.

"Excuse us for a second, Mr. Davis." Brady and I step outside the room, leaving the door open.

Nancy marches over as soon as she spots us, attitude and defiance written all over her face.

"I need to get my son home," she snaps.

I point her in the direction of a quieter location that's still in plain sight. "I understand. Can you tell me what happened?" I ask in my calmest, most reasonable tone.

"Well, Allie's real rambunctious," she hedges, eyes darting around, never actually looking at me. "She was jumping on the bed. I heard a thump and then she started crying."

"Where were you when this happened?"

"She ain't my kid. I have enough to do watching my own son." She jerks her head toward the little boy who's now showing Brady his stuffed dinosaur.

I pause to calm myself before asking the same question in a different way.

"Were you in the bedroom with her when it happened?"

"No. I was in the living room."

"Where was Mr. Davis?"

"The bathroom. The door was closed. But that's where he was," she insists. Obviously someone already questioned her version of the story.

"Why didn't you take Allison to the doctor last night?"

"His mother used to be an ER nurse. We thought she could treat Allison and not have to drag her down to the hospital. Then this morning, it looked so much worse that she forced us to at least take Allison here."

My radar's pinging like crazy. Sure, these are two stupid kids playing house. Unfortunately, they have children themselves. The way Nancy went out of her way to distance herself from both the girl and the incident bugs the hell out of me.

Overtaxed young mother.

Caring for someone else's daughter.

It doesn't take a rocket scientist to piece together what *could* have happened. I'm trying to keep an open mind. Not jump to the most cynical, jaded conclusion here.

Brady and I offer Nancy a ride home. In a hurry to leave, she accepts. The entire way home, she coos and fawns over her son. To someone else it might seem sweet, but it gives me the creeps.

Or maybe I'm just pissed that she didn't bother to say goodbye to Allison.

Stay objective.

My memory flashes back to Bree when she was little. No more than eight or nine. Red tear-stained cheeks and bruises circling her upper arms when one of her mom's boyfriends got carried away with the discipline aspect of parenting.

Shit. How did I forget that?

My father drove right over to the Avery house and had a not-so-friendly chat with the boyfriend.

Bree's mom didn't appreciate the interference. Vince and Bree stayed over at our house a lot until that boyfriend finally left for good.

Brady elbows me and points out the turn up ahead. Shoving those memories back to the past isn't as easy as I'd like.

The house is so far out by the county line, jurisdiction may end up being a question.

"Do you mind if we come in and take a look at the dresser she hit her head on?" Brady asks.

I quirk an eyebrow at the request but don't say anything.

"Uh, well the house is kind of a mess. But sure."

"We can do it later," Brady says, even though he's already halfway out of the car. As if he isn't as eager as I am to look at the scene before Nancy has a chance to clean it up.

"No. No. It's fine," she says, waving us inside.

Messy turns out to be an understatement. The house reeks of hell only knows what. Dirty dishes, laundry, diapers. Take your pick. The filth invades every inch of the house.

Nancy kicks toys, garbage, and assorted junk out of the way to lead us into the bedroom where Allison supposedly hit her head.

Only a grungy, faded pink comforter carelessly tossed over the bed indicates the room belongs to a little girl. White particleboard makes up the cheap dresser on the opposite side of the room from the bed. How the hell did the little girl go from jumping on the bed to hitting her head on the dresser?

I glance around the filthy, cluttered room. Plenty of things for a little girl to hurt herself on. A metal chair with rusted edges, wire hangers strewn all over the floor, a pair of scissors. She would have encountered any one of those items before the dresser.

"What made you so sure she hit her head on the dresser?" I ask.

Nancy shrugs. "She said so."

I lead her back into the living room, while Brady whips out his phone to grab a few pictures of the room. No doubt CPS will be called in here next, but just in case things are disturbed before then we'll have a record.

I almost step on something hard and plastic in the hallway. Bending down, I see it's an old, cordless handheld phone. The perfect circle of the earpiece looks awfully similar to the perfectly circular bruising around Allison's eye.

Slapping my hand against my chest, I let out a few phony-as-fuck coughs. "Nancy, would you mind getting me a glass of water?"

"Uh, sure."

The minute she turns her back, I take out my phone and snap a few pictures of my own.

CHAPTER TWENTY-TWO
Brianna

HOURS HAVE GONE by since Liam left the house.

After we made love for the first time.

He didn't ditch me. It was work. I understand that.

I do.

My stomach rumbles, leading me into the kitchen, humming a mindless tune. Kimber follows behind me, silently begging for treats with the power of her soulful eyes. The *limited diet* instruction is so not her jam.

Liam didn't give me any details about why he got called in. His pinched expression spoke volumes, though. His job has to drain him at times.

Can I be the girlfriend of a sheriff?

The wife?

Whoa. Slow your roll, girl.

One romp does not equal wedding bells.

Besides, aren't I always saying I don't believe in marriage? Isn't that what I told my friends at school when they asked when Chad and I were getting married?

It was a lie.

I want all those things. I convinced myself I didn't because I think, deep down, I knew Chad was wrong for me.

Why didn't I leave sooner?

I stop and think of something positive. Count the good things in my life. Something I learned in my group counseling sessions.

I end up eating alone and putting the rest of dinner away for Liam, even though the expression on Kimber's face clearly says she'd be happy to finish it.

Except for taking Kimber outside a couple times, I stay indoors.

I peek out the front door and notice a Sheriff's car cruising by the house. My heart speeds up, thinking it might be Liam stopping in for a quick hello.

But it's not.

When the same sheriff drives by an hour later, I know Liam's thinking of me. Must have asked one of the guys he works with to check on me.

A little while later I send him a text to say thank you.

But he doesn't respond.

We were on the same page about our relationship, right?

Stop. I am not some needy, clingy woman who falls to pieces if her boyfriend doesn't check in every fifteen minutes. Liam has an important, demanding job.

Unease settles over me.

What if something happened to him?

Who would think to let me know?

I could call his parents, but it seems shitty to worry them for no reason.

Except, now I can't stop thinking about all the awful possibilities.

CHAPTER TWENTY-THREE
LIAM

BEING SEPARATED FROM Bree for so long annoys me no end. But my job doesn't always have regular hours, something I know she understands and I hope she'll forgive.

Endless reports, interviews, more reports, reviewing medical records, accompanying a social worker to the hospital and then the residence.

Yeah, it was a long night.

Bone-weary, I finally clomp up the front steps only to find a solitary lamp lighting up the entryway.

My stomach tightens in disappointment, but I'm not surprised. It has to be close to five in the morning. I wouldn't want Bree to wait up for me.

The door to the bedroom is wide open, inviting me in. Bree's sprawled out on her stomach, her face half under her pillow. My lips twitch into a smile. She'd slept that exact same way as a kid. Drove my mom nuts because she worried Bree would smother herself.

I don't want to disturb her, and I figure she should be up in a few hours. I need to decompress anyway, so I strip down to a T-shirt and shorts, flick on the television, and stretch out on the couch.

Even though my plan was to wait for Bree to wake up, sleep comes swift and solid.

The same house surrounds me. The way it looked ten years ago. Faded, peeling wallpaper, rotted carpet, smoke-stench clinging to everything.

More garbage litters the floor than I remember. Walking through the rooms, they distort and morph into the house I investigated earlier.

Somewhere in the back of the house Brianna's crying.

No matter how many times I push garbage and debris out of my way, I can't reach her. I call out for Brady, but my voice won't carry over the mountains of stuff piled throughout the house.

Sounds of flesh on flesh reach my ears. Someone being hurt. Smacked. Punched. Hard.

Dread curls in my gut.

Did Chad find Brianna?

"Liam," she calls softly, sounding so far away.

"I'm here, baby girl." I can't make my mouth work, and the words just stick in my throat.

"Liam." This time her voice is sharper and cuts through the fog. Soft hands press into my shoulder. "Wake up."

"Huh?" I turn and almost fall off the edge of the couch. The filth is gone. I'm staring at gleaming hardwood floors and Brianna's feet.

"Why are you out here?" she demands.

"What?" I scrub my hands over my face, sit up, and try to make sense of my world.

"You were having a bad dream." The couch dips as she sits next to me, running her hand over my back.

I blink a few times and glance around the living room, then over at Bree. "Are you okay?"

She huffs out a laugh. The sweetest fucking sound in the world after the night I just had. "I'm fine. Worried as hell about you. Bad night?"

Intense relief pulses through me. I pull her into my arms, crushing her against my chest. She wraps her arms around me, hugging just as fiercely.

"I was worried about you," she mumbles into my shirt.

"Yes, it was a bad night," I finally answer her question.

"Do you want to talk about it?"

"No. I don't want that ugliness touching you."

Her hand stops moving over my back.

"I can't talk about an ongoing-investigation with you anyway, sweetheart."

"Oh."

"What time is it?"

"A little after eight."

I turn my gaze on her, taking in the tight workout pants that end right below her knees and the baggy shirt—one of my sheriff department T-shirts.

"Damn, you look good in that."

One corner of her mouth quirks up. "You don't mind?"

"Hell no."

"I was going to go to one of Sully's morning classes," she explains, gesturing to the outfit.

A prick of jealousy pokes at me, but I push it back.

"That's good."

She turns her head away but not before I notice the way her bottom lip trembles. "I can stay…if you want me to?"

The shy way she asks says she's afraid I'll tell her no. "Is there another class today? I really do want you to go. But I also want to be selfish."

"You do?"

I brush her hair out of her face so I can see her better. "Look at me."

When she finally meets my eyes, I lean in. "I missed you so much last night."

She runs her fingers over my cheek. "I missed you too. I tried waiting up for you, but…"

"I'm sorry. I should've called. I got your text so late, I didn't want to write back and wake you up."

"You had one of the guys check on me, didn't you?" she asks.

"Sure did. He didn't bother you did he?"

"No. Not at all. I just noticed the same patrol car go by more than once." She stands and holds her hands out to me. "Come on. You should lie down in the bedroom and get some more sleep. What time did you get home?"

The way she's standing there beckoning me to the bedroom is way too sexy to resist. I take her hands and yank her into my lap. I fall back against the couch and guide her until she's straddling me. "Five."

She opens her mouth, but I place my hand at the back of her head and pull her in for a kiss. My other hand slides up under the back of her shirt.

"You look hot in this, but I need it off," I say, tugging the shirt up. She lifts her arms and I slip it off and send it sailing across the room.

"Christ, you're perfect." My hands go to her breasts, encased in a neon-green sports bra that somehow pushes her tits up and keeps them in place. "This is sexy." My hands fumble at the back, seeking a clasp. "How the fuck do I get it off?"

She chuckles and points to the front where there's a small black zipper. "Oh," I say, working it down. "I was too busy admiring these." The bra comes off, and I fill my hands with her bare breasts.

"I did *not* spend enough time here," I warn her right before sucking one hard nipple into my mouth.

"Oh, fuck." She gasps and squirms against me.

"In a minute." I grab her other nipple, drawing it into my mouth and lashing it with my tongue. Turns out, I can't wait another minute. "Hold on to me."

She mumbles out a questioning sound, but I'm too busy throwing the blankets down, then wrapping my arms around her and taking us both to the floor. We're both franticly ripping at each other's clothes. Her sneakers get in the way of me stripping her pants off, and I don't have the patience to fuck around. Urging her to turn over, I squeeze her hip. "Stick your ass up in the air for me."

Dropping down to her elbows, she does exactly as I ask. Even gives me an extra wiggle. "Show off."

After whipping off my T-shirt, I shove my shorts down enough to free my cock.

"Ready for me."

It's more of a statement than a question. She answers by pushing back, silently begging me to fill her.

I don't take it slow this time. I thrust into her fast and hard. She lets out a sharp scream that turns into a moan as I draw back. "Too much?"

"No. Keep going. Just like that."

Like I'm going to say no.

Brianna

LIAM DIGS HIS fingers into my hips, pounding into me at a hard, steady pace.

Underneath us, the blanket slips on the floor, pushing me away.

He pulls me right back.

"Liam." I gasp and dig my fingers into the blanket.

"Fuck." He pulls out, leaving me empty and irritated.

"What are you doing?"

His hand squeezes my ass cheek in a quick, affectionate way. "Give me a second. Stay like that, though. I like the view."

"Deviant."

He huffs out a laugh while tugging off my shoes and pulling my pants all the way off. His body heat disappears from behind me, and I turn my head.

"Come here," he beckons, sitting on the couch and patting his leg.

Slowly, I kneel up to face him. I must seem unsure or hesitant, because he reaches out and takes my hands.

Confronted by all his male beauty in the middle of the living room, I stop and stare.

And stare.

"You're magnificent."

"So are you. Now come here. I've been thinking about this nonstop since the other night."

Heat burns my skin and I drop my gaze.

"Hey, I meant it in a good way. In an I-wish-I-never-opened-my-mouth-and-fucked-it-up way."

I take his hand and he pulls me closer. "Climb on up."

"What are you, a carnival ride?" I tease to wash away any unpleasantness from the other night.

"Yeah. Best one you're ever going to have."

Last one too.

But I keep that thought to myself.

"Arrogant much?" I joke instead.

He grins and rubs one hand up and down his cock, while gripping my hip with the other.

"That's it," he whispers as I lower myself.

Both of us gasp when I ease down. All the way down. My nails dig into his shoulders and I squeeze my eyes shut.

"Okay?" he asks.

"Good."

He moves his hips from side to side, helping me adjust. "Bree, look at me."

His hand cups my cheek, and for the longest time, he stares into my eyes. He slides his hand into my hair and pulls me to him for a kiss. I move up and down and he groans into my mouth. "That's good," he mumbles against my lips.

"You like that?" I ask, doing it again.

"Fuck, yes. Keep going."

We find a rhythm and keep moving together. His eyes never leave mine until he places one hand between my breasts. "Lean back. Hands on my knees. Want to see all of you." The clipped directions turn me on even more, and I immediately do as he asks.

"Beautiful." His hands are everywhere, cupping my breasts, thumbs brushing over my nipples, running up my legs and up over my back.

My orgasm builds with breathtaking intensity and I can't keep my eyes open any longer.

"That's right," he whispers. "Come for me."

I do. Hard. It's intense. Pleasure and relief mix together. My fingers dig into his arms, holding on for dear life. It lasts for so long, I lose track of everything else except how good we feel together.

"Beautiful, beautiful," he murmurs over and over. I fall forward, burying my face against his neck and his arms wrap around me, holding me tight while he pounds up into me.

"Hang in there, Bree."

My teeth sink into his shoulder and he groans, holding me even tighter. I shudder from another wave of pleasure washing over me.

He lets out a number of breathless curses, and I pick my head up. His fingers twist in my hair, pulling me closer, swallowing down my cries with a kiss. He moans into my mouth and stills. His hands clamp down on my hips, holding me tight to him while the warm rush fills me.

"Come here," he mumbles. "Kiss me."

We trade a few soft kisses before he lifts me off him. "I can't straighten my legs." A wobbly giggle bursts out of me as he massages my thighs. "Oh my God. This is what it means to be fucked so hard you can't walk straight." More giggles spill out of me.

Loud rumbling laughter comes from behind me, right before he stands and carries me off into the bathroom, setting me on the counter.

"I wish we could stay at my place," he says while adjusting the shower. "You're brother's going to kill me."

"Sorry."

"Hey. I didn't say that to make you feel bad."

"I know."

He brushes my sweaty hair back from my face.

"Do you?"

"Can we not talk about my brother right now?"

Instead of answering, he sets two towels on the closed toilet seat. "It's hard when I'm in his house and he doesn't know about us."

"You've never told him how you felt?"

Presumptuous much?

"I mean, back then. That you might have been interested in me...in us...dating or whatever?"

The serious expression on his face stops my babbling.

"I was way more than *interested* in you." He takes my hand and leads us into the shower stall. "But, no we never talked about it. He seemed to have such a bad reaction, and you left soon after, that I didn't see the point. I just tried to forget. Convince myself it was nothing."

As the warm water rains down over both of us, I wrap my arms around him and lay my cheek against his chest. After a second, his arms band around me, pulling me tighter. "I really screwed up," I mumble.

"No, you didn't. You were young—"

I pull back and the regret in his eyes weighs me down. The last thing I want to do is keep hurting each other with the past. "We were *both* young. Boys mature slower than girls, you know."

He huffs out a laugh. "Yeah, I've heard that."

"Trust me. I'm a professional. I know what I'm talking about."

His strong hands on my shoulders turn me to face the water and he pours shower gel into his hands, working it into a lather before carefully soaping every inch of me.

"Liam?"

"Yes?"

"Can we forget about that night? I forgive you and I hope you can forgive me."

"God, Bree," he breaths against my ear. "There's nothing to forgive you for."

"Well, pretend there is. Can we let go of that night?"

"Yes." He presses a kiss to my shoulder, trailing his lips to my neck where he leaves one more kiss before speaking. "I'll let go of the bad stuff that happened after. But that was the sweetest kiss I'd ever had until about twenty-four hours ago."

"Me too."

"I'll never let go of that kiss."

CHAPTER TWENTY-FOUR

Brianna

I DON'T MAKE it to Sully's class until the next day. In the driveway, Liam kissed me hard and told me to have fun at class before he left for work.

No jealousy. No warning me not to flirt with his friend. He encouraged me to go by myself. It's clear Liam trusts me. Trusts that he's the only man I want.

This is how love *should* be.

A serious vibe infiltrates the gym when I arrive. You have to be a determined person to get up this early on the weekend to punch, jab, and kick stuff, I guess.

It's intimidating and I squirm with unease.

Sully joins us and greets me warmly in front of everyone, which helps me relax.

"I'm glad you came back, Bree. I never know if I helped someone out or scared them off," Sully says.

His easy demeanor makes me laugh. "You definitely helped."

I straighten up and look more people in the eye after he moves away. Not that I'm here to win approval from strangers. No, I'm here to learn how to defend myself from them.

Liam says his dad was so excited that I'm finally willing to learn how to shoot. He can't wait for me to come back for more target practice. I have a feeling I'll be testing every gun in the Hollister arsenal at some point.

By the time I start graduate school, I won't even recognize myself.

Sully claps his hands at the front of the room, startling me out of my

Zena-the-warrior-princess daydreams.

"Partner up."

I'm momentarily lost while people who've already been coming here for a while gravitate toward their friends.

"Need a partner?" a deep voice behind me asks.

"Keegan? What are you doing here?" I ask, smiling at the friendly face.

His mouth quirks. "Liam didn't want you working with Jake," he explains in a conspiratorial way that makes me laugh.

"And you just happened to be here?" I ask. I can't believe Liam went out of his way to make sure someone he trusted would look out for me today. This is what it's like to be genuinely cared about. Chad only pretended to care about my safety when it was convenient for him or as an excuse to control me.

Keegan jerks his head in Sully's direction. "This dope makes me come help him out at least twice a month."

"In return for free gym time," Sully mutters.

"How's Kimber doing?" Keegan asks.

"She's awesome. You're not getting her back." Even though I say it with a smile, I think Keegan senses how serious I am.

"I'm glad you're getting along."

"Time to work, people," Sully says, clapping his hands again.

"Wait, Sully, we're not evenly matched." I take in Keegan's towering form. "Like, at all."

Keegan turns his head to the side and laughs.

Sully takes a few steps closer, his face slipping into teacher-mode. "An attacker isn't going to be a woman your size, Bree. More likely it will be a guy. I want you to learn how to take someone of his size down."

"So start with the biggest guy in the room?"

"Think how empowering it will be," Keegan says with a straight face.

"Okay." Doubt creeps into my voice. "I don't want to hurt myself."

"You'll be fine," Sully assures me before walking off.

"Sorry," I mutter to Keegan.

"Nothin' to be sorry about, darlin'. Just watch the important bits."

I snicker as I promise not to strike him anywhere too hard.

I'm not laughing for long.

Once Sully has our attention, we start with how to get out of a wrist hold. "Now, this can be as simple as someone grabs you in a night club and tries to pull you onto the dance floor. Your instinct is to pull back, pull away, right? But his grip will only tighten if you do that." With a warm smile, and crooked finger, Sully lures a short, wide-eyed girl to the front of the room to demonstrate. She looks mortified.

I shift back and forth on my feet. Sully better not even think about calling me up there to show off any moves.

"Here's what I want you to do," he instructs. "Yank toward his thumb, where his hold is the weakest. You can also bend your elbow toward his forearm. Hit him hard."

Sully repeats the directions a few more times before turning us loose.

"No fair," I say to Keegan when his hand encircles my wrist. "Your whole hand fits around my wrist."

"You'll just have to work harder."

Keegan plays the bad guy part well, dragging me away like a proper barbarian. I plant my feet into the mat and try to twist the way Sully showed us, but it's no use, I can't break free.

"Don't give up," Sully encourages. "Here." He comes closer. "Use your other hand to assist you in getting free."

He demonstrates and, when I'm ready, Keegan grabs me again.

This time, after a genuine struggle, I manage to get free.

"Good job," Keegan congratulates.

Pride wells up inside. *I did it.*

"Thank you for not going easy on me."

He cocks his head as if the thought never occurred to him. "It's meaningless otherwise."

Sully goes over all the soft spots where we should poke, jab, and kick an attacker next.

"Let's take a break and then we'll try the chokehold."

The young woman Sully called to the front earlier makes her way over to us. "Hi, I'm Aubrey. Is this your first time here?"

"It's my first official class. Sully gave me a private lesson the other day."

Her cheek twitches—as if that bothers her. "My boyfriend is friends with Sully. He brought me in for the lesson," I explain.

"Oh," she says, smiling brightly.

Wait, did I just describe Liam as my boyfriend? Out loud? In front of other people?

Keegan, who overheard everything, winks at me. "Finally work that out?"

My cheeks heat up and I just nod my head.

"About time," he mutters.

Sully doesn't provide us with too much downtime.

"All right, class." He claps his hands together to grab our attention. "Chokehold time."

I guess I wasn't paying attention or thinking about what chokehold time meant.

The second Keegan's hands settle on either side of my neck, cold tingles race down my spine. "Bree, you okay?" he asks, immediately removing his hands.

"I'm fine," I whisper.

"Too much?"

"No." In a stronger voice I add, "Let's do it."

He returns to the position, and I thrust my hands up, exploding outward, breaking his hold.

"Good," Keegan praises, even though I'm pretty sure he went easy on me.

"Let's do it again."

He narrows his eyes. "Are you sure?"

"Yes, and don't puss out on me this time," I challenge.

Keegan's not the kind of guy to fall for a challenge like that. He still takes it easy on me, but some of my fear ebbs and I'm really able to concentrate on the movements.

"All right. Good work, class," Sully calls out. He checks in with most of his students before working his way over to us.

"How'd you do? Too much?" he asks.

"No. It was good. I feel like I learned a lot."

Sully crosses his arms over his chest. "I don't want to give you a false sense of security, Bree. I want you to learn to react quickly. So it's instinctual. In an attack situation, you don't have time to process what's happening, it's all reaction."

"That makes sense."

"Think you'll be back?"

"Absolutely."

His lips curve up and he unfolds his arms. "Good."

I glance at the front desk. "Do you need me to…"

"Nope. All taken care of."

He glances up at Keegan, then back to me. "Liam working today?"

"Yes. Must be something big going on, he was gone all night."

Sully raises an eyebrow, and it occurs to me how domestic I just made our relationship sound.

Aubrey approaches the three of us slowly. "A bunch of us go to Friendly's after class. Do you want to come, Bree?"

I hadn't exactly been looking forward to going home to an empty house.

"Sure!" I answer a little too enthusiastically.

Aubrey shyly glances over at Sully. "Will you join us?"

"Yeah. I'll meet up with you later. I need to finish up here." He pats her shoulder as he walks by.

"Bree, I need to head out," Keegan says, drawing my attention away from Aubrey. "It was fun working with you."

"Thanks, Keegan."

Aubrey loosens up once we're in my car. "So, you know Sully outside of the gym?" she asks in a casual way that's obvious as hell.

"Not really. I've met him one or two times."

"Oh."

I glance over. "You have it bad for him, huh?"

"Am I that obvious?"

"Uh, yeah."

"Shit." She turns and grins at me, not offended by my honesty. "If I'd known he had a 'no dating clients' policy, I would have tried a different gym."

"He seems like a good guy. Give it time."

"Do you mind stopping at a salon after lunch?" she asks, flicking the ends of her hair with her fingers. "I need a trim and it's in the mall right next to Friendly's."

I glance at myself in the mirror. "Sure. I might even join you."

"Good." She flips down the visor on her side and makes pouty faces in the mirror. "I need something that doesn't make me look like I'm still in high school."

"How old *are* you?"

"Twenty-two."

Even though she's tiny, she doesn't look or act like a high school girl. "Well, you're twenty-two and you have a crush on your gym teacher," I tease. "Maybe the high school look works for you."

She bursts out laughing.

LUNCH IS FUN. Aubrey introduces me to her friends. Overwhelmed, I forget most of their names and can't keep up with their conversation. It's still a relief to be out and around other people without fear. Chad wasn't above having his brother or one of his friends sneakily follow me whenever I told him I was going out with friends. I never knew what completely innocent thing they'd report back that he'd twist to use against me as soon as I returned to our apartment.

It's over.

After an hour, Sully still hasn't arrived. Disappointed, Aubrey tilts her head toward the mall. "Want to go?"

"Sure."

It turns out Aubrey's older sister, Celia, works at the salon. It's a slow afternoon, so Aubrey asks to have her golden-brown hair dyed a deep chocolate-cherry brown and trimmed into long, swingy lawyers. I tuck myself into a chair with a few magazines and watch the process.

Maybe two hours in, I run down to Starbucks and grab iced coffees for the three of us. I'm waiting for my order when I swear I see a set of broad shoulders I recognize hustling through the mall. A brief glimpse and then he's gone.

A chill tingles down my spine.

"Miss?"

"Huh?" I turn and find the barista holding out a fistful of change.

"Thanks," I mumble, tossing it in the tip jar. "I'll be right back."

Darting into the mall, my gaze scans everything. I've only made it a few stores away from Starbucks when I spot my prey. Chad's brother, Chris, cowering behind a rack of clearance sneakers.

I'm so done with this shit.

I march right into the store. "Are you following me, Chris?"

His face turns red as soon as he makes eye contact. "No. I'm following the order. I didn't know you'd be here."

"What order?"

"Oh." He flashes a smug smile way too similar to his brother's for my comfort and I back up a few steps. "Your boyfriend didn't tell you? Yeah, he had me served at my parents'. So, thanks for that."

I'm beyond tired of people blaming me when their shitty actions get them into trouble. "Maybe you should have thought of that before sending me all those emails and leaving me nasty voicemails."

His gaze darts away. "I'm sorry, okay? He's my brother. I was upset. He's never been in trouble before."

"That's because your parents always cleaned up his messes."

He grinds his teeth and doesn't respond.

"Just leave me alone, Chris," I snap. Courage gone, I turn and run back to Starbucks. Grabbing the coffees, I hurry back to the salon.

"Were they packed?" Aubrey asks, accepting the plastic cup dripping with cold sweat.

I nod and hand a coffee to Celia and sit so I can sip my own.

When it's my turn, I tell Celia to go nuts. "Okay, not too nuts, I may be going on some job interviews soon."

She sifts through my long, thick hair. "A lot of my clients would kill for this."

"It grows back, right?" I ask with a raised eyebrow.

"I like your spunk, Bree. So, if you're feeling brave, I think you could totally pull off a long, inverted bob that's shorter in the back with longer layers in front."

"How short?"

A quick grin says she'd expected that question.

"Skimming your shoulders. A little higher in the back." She touches a spot below my neck.

"Do it."

With every snip, chunks of my hair tumble to the floor like all the bad years of my life falling away.

When it's finished and styled, Celia hands me a mirror and I admire her work. "I love it." Totally worth it. I admire the long, sleek layers that seem to make my round face look thinner and more mature.

"That came out beautiful, Bree," Aubrey says.

Feeling a little silly, I hold out my phone and take a quick selfie, then send it to Liam.

While we're ringing out, he replies:

Wow.

My girlfriend is hot.

Can't wait to see you later.

I guess Liam likes it.

"Is that the boyfriend?" Aubrey asks. "The one who's friends with Sully?"

"Yes." I suppress my laughter.

"Does he have any hot cop friends?"

I'm laughing so hard as we step outside, I almost stumble, catching myself on Aubrey's shoulder. She laughs with me for a second or two. "I'm serious. Don't hold out on me."

"Probably. I've met Sully's brother."

"Ooo, is he as hot as Sully?"

My shoulders lift. "I guess. In a smooth-guy, player sort of way."

"No thanks. Had enough of those."

"His friend Keegan is a fire fighter, but he's too old for you."

"I like older men. At least they know what they're doing and have their shit together. Usually," she adds. She glances over, big brown eyes, full of mischief. "You only have eyes for your man, huh? I can tell."

"Pretty much," I confirm.

I almost don't want to drop her off at her house.

"Thank you so much, Bree. This was fun." She hesitates before sliding out of my car. "If you want to hang out, call me."

"I will."

THERE'S NO SIGN of Liam when I return home. It makes me dread going back to school. We'll probably never see each other.

Kimber does her subdued version of a happy-doggy-dance at the door, her nub wagging so hard her whole rear end sways. After loving on her for a few minutes, I take her outside for a short walk around the back yard, then feed her a light dinner.

Still no sign of Liam.

Why am I obsessing over this? I think Liam made it clear this is more than a few rounds of hot sex. If it's meant to be, distance won't come between us.

Still full from lunch, I end up in front of the bathroom mirror playing with my new haircut. Staring at my reflection isn't as horrifying as it was when I first came home.

My phone buzzes, and I pull it out of my pocket.

LIAM: I miss you like crazy.

Wow. Five simple words do a number on me.

A few minutes later, I receive a follow-up from him.

Send me another pic.

I step out onto the porch for the natural lighting and snap a picture, sending it off to Liam.

He writes back. *Just made my night 1000x better.*

As I turn to go inside, something on the hood of my car catches my attention. Heart hammering, I push inside the house, locking the door. Kimber senses my anxiety and tries to nudge me over to the couch.

"No, girl."

I clip on her leash for the second time and take her out the back door. We circle around the house, and in the driveway she puts her nose to the ground like she's caught a scent. Once or twice she lifts her head to growl.

When we reach my car, a line of fur on her back stands straight up. She lets out a few deep barks, scaring the shit out of me. "Easy, girl."

The command dies in my throat as my gaze lands on my car.

Someone left four pink carnations on the windshield.

I hate carnations.

Especially pink ones.

Just like the ones Chad gave me for our anniversary every year.

CHAPTER TWENTY-FIVE
LIAM

ALL AFTERNOON, I wait for Keegan's call to see how Brianna did in the self-defense class. My phone finally rings as Brady and I are headed to interview Mr. Davis's mother.

"How'd she do?" I say into the phone.

"Whatever happened to hello?"

"Don't be a dick."

I should know better. Telling Keegan not to be a dick means he'll jerk me around for a few minutes before telling me what I want to know.

"I'm working," I prod, hoping he'll hurry up.

"Well, first, you're welcome."

"For what?"

"Sounds like you took my advice and finally pulled your head out of your ass since she's calling you her boyfriend."

"I…" I stop and roll the title around. Realize I like it a hell of a lot. Love that Bree's already comfortable describing our relationship to people.

"That's good."

"Second, Kimber's surgery has been pushed back."

"Fuck. How come?"

"The surgeon wants to take another look at her records and maybe do an MRI."

"All right. Just let me know when."

"I'll take her. You two are already doing enough to help me out."

"It's really fine. Bree loves her and I feel better knowing she's there when I'm working late." Like tonight. I have the feeling there's a long night ahead of me.

We talk for a few more minutes about the dog before Keegan finally shares the information I'm waiting for.

"Bree did well today. I didn't take it easy on her. She was nervous at first, but when she finally worked herself free of one of the holds on her own, she was pretty happy."

"Good." That's why I wanted Keegan to work with her. I trust him not to do anything inappropriate and I'm way too soft when it comes to her. One blink of her big blue eyes and I'd let her win every damn time. Besides, I sure as fuck didn't want to play the role of attacker with her. Keegan's detached enough to work with her and friendly enough not to freak her the fuck out.

A deep sigh comes over the line and I realize he's not done with his assessment. "One of the holds seemed to bother her—"

"Which one?"

Another sigh. "The chokehold. I tried not to make a big deal out of it, but you might want to talk to her."

Christ, I don't even know how to start that conversation. "Thanks, I will."

"I got a call in downtown Empire," Keegan informs me. "So that's where I'm headed for fuck knows how long."

"I hear you. I'm out in East Bumfuck all day."

After I hang up, Brady glances over. "Did I understand that correctly? You adopted a *dog* with this chick?"

"She's not a chick."

"So, is this the girl Linda was all bent out of shape about?" he asks, unable to let anything go.

"Yes. You want to maybe put on your cop hat so we can do our jobs?"

He lets it go for now, but I'm sure he'll needle me again at some point.

In our large, sprawling, but sparsely populated part of the county, the weekends can either be crazy or so boring writing tickets seems like grade-A entertainment.

After reviewing more medical records and trying to track her down for a couple days, Brady and I finally located Allen Davis's mother and are on our way to question her.

The supposed former ER nurse greets us in a gruff, no-nonsense manner.

We go through a carefully crafted list of questions, circling back a few times when her answers are evasive.

"Why didn't you insist they go to the emergency room right away?" Brady asks for the second time.

"They're in debt up to their ears. He didn't need another medical bill hanging around his neck," she explains.

"Mrs. Davis, your granddaughter's injuries were pretty severe," I say gently.

Her shoulders drop and her mouth twists as if she doesn't want to say the words forming in her head. "I warned them if they didn't take her in, I was going to call child services on them," she finally admits.

This is new information.

"I didn't want my son railroaded by the system."

Something about her answer seems off, but I let the comment go for now.

"Listen, I know he didn't hurt his baby girl. It was either an accident or *she* did it." Mrs. Davis hasn't once used the girlfriend's name and that deepens my suspicions of what actually happened. "I didn't raise my son that way."

Although she suffers from an inflated opinion of her son, she seems to care a lot about her granddaughter.

"Has Allison ever had any similar injuries?" Brady asks.

She clamps her lips shut. My fists clench at my sides and I fight to relax my posture. The kid's record was clean, but maybe we missed something.

"No. Nothing this bad," she answers after staring Brady down for a few seconds. She cocks her head. "Now, unless you two want to help me muck some stalls, I have horses to take care of." Mrs. Davis doesn't wait for us to leave. She simply walks past us and out to the barn without a backwards glance.

"We need to dig some more," I mutter.

"Still like the girlfriend for it?" Brady asks once we're back in the car.

"Something isn't right."

On the way back to the station we run over a few different scenarios.

"He had to be, what? Sixteen when the daughter was born? Maybe there's a neglect or endangering charge that was sealed. That might explain why he didn't seek medical help right away."

He nods, drumming his fingers over the notebook in his lap. "Why cover for Nancy if she hurt his little girl?"

"I've seen parents choose lovers over their children too many times to count." Starting with Bree's mother.

"I'll never fucking understand that," Brady huffs.

"Me either. Unless he really thinks it was an accident. He didn't strike me as particularly smart."

"No way. Medical report was clear. She didn't do that on the dresser."

"He's not the sharpest crayon in the box. You really think he read a medical report? Maybe he took whatever Nancy told him at face value."

He shrugs. "Still nail him on endangering. That house was fucking disgusting. No way to raise a kid."

"Can't argue with you there."

He scribbles down a few notes, then closes his notepad and sits back. "So, you're still babysitting?"

"I'm not babysitting. I'm helping out a friend."

"The friend you now have a dog with?"

"We're helping Keegan out by watching the dog. Not sure we're keeping her yet."

"Do you realize how many times you just said we?"

"No, please enlighten me."

He shakes his head, not offended by my sarcasm or deterred by it unfortunately. "You're in deep. This girl's why you haven't been to your apartment in days?"

"Stalker."

Brady snickers. "Ya live right next door. How am I not supposed to notice?"

"I don't know. Pay attention to your own shit?"

"You should've tried fucking her out of your system instead of getting a dog."

My fingers clench around the steering wheel. "You're lucky I'm driving or I'd punch you right now."

"Ohh, so you did fuck her."

"Is fucking your answer to all of life's problems?"

"Pretty much." A little quieter he adds, "Next thing you know, you'll be marrying this chick. Then who's going to be my wingman?"

"You'll figure something out," I answer, not bothering to deny his assumption.

I'M RELIEVED AND disappointed to find Bree asleep when I return to Vince's. I almost trip over Kimber, who's stationed outside the bedroom door.

"What's wrong girl?" I asking, crouching down to scratch her ears. She pushes her wet nose into my other hand and lets me love her up for a few minutes. "Were you a good girl? Did you watch out for Bree?" Her short nub of a tail wags harder with every word I say to her.

"All right, I guess you deserve a cookie." I pad into the kitchen and grab the box of dog treats, pulling one out.

Stems from a bunch of carnations stick out of the trash, catching my attention. I tug them out, wondering where they came from, then shove them back.

I'll solve that mystery in the morning.

I toss Kimber her treat and close the bedroom door behind me. Exhausted, I slide into bed, pull her into my arms, and immediately fall asleep.

Bree should never doubt how I feel about her because I wake up a few hours later with one of my hands under her tank top cupping her breast. Definitely the first time I've molested a woman in my sleep. Her nipple's hard against the palm of my hand and she moans, turning toward me. My hand skims down her belly, dipping into her underwear. "Bree, are you awake?"

She sleepily mumbles a few noises as my lips find their way to her neck, kissing and licking. Her legs spread and her back arches, inviting me to slip a finger inside. Christ, she's so hot and wet it fully wakes me up.

I drag her underwear down her legs, tossing them to the floor. We need to start spending nights at my apartment where she can sleep naked.

My mouth finds her nipple, sucking hard until she gasps, coming fully awake. "Liam?"

"Need you," I mumble.

She wriggles her tank top off, tossing it on the floor with her underwear. Next, her hands are at the drawstring of my shorts, yanking it loose and shoving them down my hips. We're warm and hot, skin on skin. Tangled up in the sheets.

"Bree." Her name comes out raspy and desperate which is exactly how I feel. It's so dark I can barely make out her features. My hands do the work, tracing every soft, heated curve, helping me position myself between her thighs. I press my cock against her entrance, the tight, wet heat beckoning me to take her hard and fast.

She wiggles under me and I drive inside her. "Fuck," I breathe out, stopping to enjoy the feel of her around me. I gather her in my arms, holding her tight.

My hips flex slow and steady, savoring this time with her.

"Liam. Wait. Stop, stop, stop."

Her words come out in a scared rush and I immediately pull out and draw back. "What's wrong?"

"Nothing. I can't." She's breathing hard and sits up, scooting back until her body hits the headboard.

I reach out and cup her cheek, trace my fingers down to her neck. It's so damn dark, I can't make out her expression, but her pulse beats wildly under my fingers. "Did I hurt you?"

"No. It's not that."

I reach over to flick on the lamp, but she stops me. "Don't. Please. Not yet."

The problem hits me like a freight train and all my rage roars to the surface. I've always suspected Chad didn't stop at hitting Bree.

I'm a fucking moron for not figuring this out sooner and being more careful with her.

I *knew* it. Knew this was too soon. Too quick. She can pretend she's okay until I do something to trigger her. I don't want to be the one to ever hurt her.

I knew damn well she wasn't ready for this, yet I went ahead and did it anyway.

"I need to see you, Bree." This time she doesn't protest when I lean over and turn on the small lamp on the nightstand. It throws off a bare circle of pale light, but it's enough to observe her panicked expression.

"Tell me," I say gently.

Her eyes squeeze shut and she ducks her head. "I can't, Liam. Please. Not right now. Not here with you."

"Sweetheart." I turn so I'm sitting next to her and throw the sheet over my legs, then pull her into my lap. She loops her arms around my neck and rests her head on my shoulder.

"You don't have to give me details." Because fuck, if I hear them right now, in this moment when I'm drowning in my love for her, in my guilt, in my need to do anything I can to make things right, I might lose my mind. "But I need to know what upset you so I don't do it again."

She clings to me even tighter, shaking her head.

I stroke my hand over her hair, now noticing how short she cut it. "I love the hair."

"Thanks," she whispers.

My hand continues rubbing her back, waiting for her to continue.

Finally, she takes a deep breath. "When you were…on top of me, holding me so tight. For a second I couldn't breathe and I panicked. That's all. I'm so sorry."

"Stop saying you're sorry."

"It's not you, Liam. It's me."

I don't know the right thing to say. It's not her. It's not me. It's neither of us, but it's both of us. If she's mine for real, then we need to work through this together.

"I'm sorry I ruined everything."

"Hey." My hand brushes over her cheek. "You didn't ruin anything."

"But I did. Please don't..."

"Don't what?" I ask when she doesn't finish her sentence.

"I don't want you to see me...think of me any different." Her mouth quirks. "Not when you're finally falling in love with me."

"Bree." I slip my fingers under her chin, tipping her head back so she meets my eyes. "I'm not *falling* in love with you. I'm already there. Been there a long time."

"Liam," she breathes out.

"And I still think you're the same sweet girl I've always known. Only difference is now you're mine."

"And you're mine." Her words come out somewhere between a question and a statement.

"Yes. I'm very much yours." I wait a few seconds for her to absorb that. "Tell me, was that the only time we've...been together that you had those feelings?"

"Yes." She shifts. "Only tonight. I think because I couldn't see you and I was sleepy." She hesitates and glances at the closed bedroom door "You stopped when I asked. That's all I need." She brushes her lips over my cheek. "Everything was so, so good before that," she whispers against my ear, scraping her teeth over my earlobe. "I loved waking up with your hand in my panties."

"Bree," I warn.

"Liam," she mimics. Another twist of her body and she's straddling my lap. She reaches down and lifts her hips so she can fling the sheet away.

"Bree—"

She places her finger over my lips, asking for my silence. "This was particularly good the other day. Let's try this."

Her fear and anxiety seem to have lessened. Even though she's playing naughty sex kitten, I'm having trouble catching up. "You need to give me a minute, sweetness. You scared me."

"*Hmm…*" She trails kisses down my neck and over my shoulder. "How's that?" she murmurs against my skin.

"Good." My dick stirs back to life. "Tell me what you like. Be specific."

Her eyes close as if she wants to call up the image in her head before sharing. "You. Behind me. Gripping my hips and pounding into me so hard."

Ding!

I fit my hands over her hips, holding her tight. "Like this?"

She answers by slipping her hand between us and stroking my cock. "Almost, except I want to see your face when you make me come."

My brain's too foggy, my throat too tight. I reach down and circle her clit with my fingers, loving the jolt and jerk of her hips. "Come on, baby girl." My ragged voice practically begs her to climb back on my cock.

She's done teasing me. With another soft press of her lips to mine, she braces her hands on my shoulders and lifts herself. I guide her way, and groan as she takes me inside her. "Fuck, that's good. Keep going."

The way she takes me is all consuming. Not the fast, desperate fucking of before. This time I hold her tight and let her take what she needs. Keep her grounded with my voice and hands.

"So good, Bree." I squeeze my eyes shut, trying not to succumb to the orgasm threatening to throw me over the edge. She gasps and grinds down harder.

"Liam."

"Right here, sweetness." I've never experienced this level of *wanting*. The intensity of needing to feel her come apart. Somehow I hold out until she's spent and then I blow like a volcano. My teeth scrape her shoulder. "You're mine, Bree. Mine."

CHAPTER TWENTY-SIX

Brianna

FINALLY, LIAM AND I have a morning together. All week he's been distracted with some case. I don't ask a lot of questions, but I can see the toll it's taking on him. That's why I don't want to dwell on last night.

I'm also embarrassed as hell.

"Are you okay?" he asks me first thing.

"I'm fine. Really happy you're still here this morning."

He presses a soft, slow kiss against my lips. "Me too."

Kimber's waiting by the back door with an eager expression.

"I think she's happy to see you too," I say as I clip on Kimber's leash.

Liam takes my hand and leads us outside. "She was glued to the bedroom door last night when I came home."

The backyard is small, but rests against a strip of woods that belong to the town, giving it a larger feeling. Knowing Kimber can't walk far but still needs to stretch her legs, we take it easy. "Do you...can you tell me about the case you've been working on?"

"I have a few at the moment."

"The one that's keeping you up at night."

His expression turns distant. "It's a child abuse case."

My hand flies to my mouth. "Oh."

"It's bad. We arrested the parents yesterday, but the whole thing's a mess."

"Boy or girl?"

"A little girl."

"Where'd she go? I mean, if the parents were arrested."

"Her grandmother's."

"That's so sad. But at least she's with someone she knows."

He nods once. "True. The woman boards horses at her farm and I guess the little girl is pretty horse-crazy."

"I think most little girls are. But that sounds promising."

He lifts his shoulders and I figure there's more to the story he can't share with me.

"Chad's brother hasn't bothered you anymore, has he?"

"Well, uh." I hesitate because I know Liam will be upset that I didn't tell him this sooner.

"Bree?" He stops and faces me.

"I ran into him at the mall yesterday."

"You what?" To Liam's credit, he doesn't yell, but he's clearly frustrated. "Why didn't you tell me right away?"

"He said it was an accident and I believed him. He was trying to hide from me when I caught up to him." Who am I trying to convince? Liam or myself?

"Yeah, right," he mutters, running his hands through his hair.

"He told me about the restraining order."

He stops and stares me in the eye. "I told you I was going to do it."

"I know. I'm not mad. He apologized, but it was pretty insincere."

Liam snorts. "What else?"

"Nothing." My lips curve as I remember how empowered I felt facing Chris head-on. "I think it shocked the hell out of him that I confronted him instead of cowering or running away. Heck, I surprised myself. Must have been left over adrenaline from Sully's class."

One corner of his mouth lifts, but I don't think he's ready to let me off the hook yet.

"Okay." He hesitates. "I don't want to encourage you to handle things alone, but I'm proud of you."

"I was in a public place."

His lips settle into a grim line. "That doesn't always matter. If you run into him again you have to tell me. Even if you think it's a coincidence."

"I will. Honestly, I had fun with Aubrey and her sister afterwards, so I ended up forgetting about it."

The tension in his face eases and his shoulders drop. "I'm glad you had a good time." He tucks my hair behind my ear. "I like this a lot."

"Thank you."

As we're walking back inside, he casually asks about the carnations in the trash. "They were on my windshield last night when I went outside to take the selfie."

"What?!" *This* time he raises his voice.

"Kimber pulled her Cujo thing. If it were Chris, he would've been crazy to stick around. I'm sure he didn't expect me to have a dog, so I doubt he'll be back."

He stares at me for a long time, studying my face. "What aren't you telling me?"

"Nothing."

"I'll decide if it's nothing. Spill."

I let out a sigh and fiddle with Kimber's leash that's still in my hands. "Chad used to give me pink carnations on our anniversary."

He grits his teeth. "When was your anniversary?" His jaw's so tight he can barely spit out the question.

"September."

That seems to relieve him. "That fucker's still in jail. I called down there yesterday to be sure. Obviously he needs his visits and phone calls monitored better," he mutters as he grabs stuff out of the refrigerator to start breakfast.

"Wait? You called the jail?"

"God damn right I did. They're supposed to give me the heads up if he makes bail."

I blink a few times, not sure how to process that. "Thank you."

Some of his irritation seems to drain out of him. "Can you think of anyone else who would've left the flowers?"

I consider his question, but come up blank. "No."

He crosses his arms over his chest and leans against the counter. "I'll look into it. If anything else shows up, you have to tell me immediately."

"After our four-pawed menace made her presence known, he'd be stupid to come back." I scratch behind Kimber's ears and she lifts he head as if she agrees.

Uncertainty and exasperation still surround Liam. Maybe it's better if I offer up the full truth. "Liam, I didn't say anything, because we…you and I just…I don't want to keep bringing up my ex all the time."

"Hey," he says, pushing off the counter and joining me at the table. "This isn't a matter of not talking about our exes so we don't hurt each other's feelings. I'm secure enough to know how you feel about me." He takes my hand, forcing me to look in his eyes. "This is about keeping you safe." One corner of his mouth lifts. "If it makes it easier, why don't you inform *Deputy Hollister* about anything pertaining to your case. That way you only talk about the fun stuff with your *boyfriend*."

The distinction pulls a chuckle out of me, but in a way it also makes it easier for me to separate the multiple aspects of our relationship.

"Well, in that case, Deputy, I took some pictures." I pull up the pictures on my cell phone to show him.

"Good job. Send those to me."

At least I finally did something right.

"Are we good?" he asks, leaning over to place a kiss on my forehead.

"Yes."

While we're finishing breakfast, my phone buzzes, and I pull it out of my pocket.

I glance down at the text. "It's Emily. She wants me to go out with her tonight."

He focuses his penetrating gaze on me. "No."

"Excuse me?"

He sighs and runs his hands through his hair. "I have to work to-night. I can't go with you."

"Who said you were invited, Officer Buzzkill?" I tease.

He huffs out a laugh. "This the one who wanted to go to the Lan-tern?"

"Yes."

"Christ, that place is a shithole. We get complaints from there every weekend."

"Liam," I say softly. "I'm not asking your permission to go out with my friends. I'm sorry. But I'm done doing that."

He reels back, staring at me for a few seconds before speaking. "Bree, it's not because I'm trying to control you. I want you to go out and have fun with your friends. I don't want you to get hurt. There's a difference."

I turn his words over in my head. He's sincere. His concern comes from a good place. "I didn't mean...I lived that way once. I won't do it again. That's all."

"I understand that," he says, using obvious restraint in his choice of words. "I don't like that you ran into Chris, and this shit with the flowers. It's creepy. I want you to be careful."

"Right. You're right." I peek up at him. "So, maybe it's better that I'm out with a group of friends instead of here like a sitting duck?"

Boy, I'm really pushing Liam's buttons this morning.

"Okay," he says slowly in a way that means it's not okay at all. "Can I say something without you getting mad?"

"Maybe." I cross my arms over my chest and nod at him to continue.

He sighs. "Remember what Sully said about not putting yourself in danger? I don't want you taking unnecessary risks because you want to prove how independent you are."

"It's just a nightclub."

"In a rough area of town."

"I'll be with a group of girls."

His stares at the ceiling, probably asking the universe to send him extra patience. "Promise you'll stick together?"

He really is only worried about my safety and I regret acting so prickly. I need to work on recognizing the difference between unhealthy control and acceptable concern. "Maybe you can meet us there when you're done tonight?" I try to hide the pitiful hopefulness in my voice, but it creeps in anyway.

His hard cop face relaxes into a semi-smile. "Yeah, baby girl. I can do that."

BY MID-AFTERNOON, I'VE persuaded Aubrey into joining us too. Liam chuckles when I call to tell him I'll have one more girl with me who knows how to kick ass.

Emily arrives in my driveway before sunset and I hurry out to meet her, careful not to trip in my high-heeled sandals. She climbs out of the car to hug me and wolf-whistles when she steps back. "It's unfair that you have such killer legs," she says, eying my gold short-shorts with envy.

"I'm not sure I should show them off when I'm this pale, though." I fiddle with the white, sparkly tank top. "Do you think this is too much?"

She runs her hands over her own short, red dress. "Nope."

"Damn, I thought this place was casual?" I nod at the dress. "You look hot."

Her lips curl into a satisfied smile and she gestures for me to climb into the car. A few of her friends are with her and she introduces us as I cram myself into the back seat and try not to flash my butt to the entire neighborhood.

"I need to look for my friend, Aubrey, when we get there," I remind Emily.

"No problem."

Liam wasn't kidding about the neighborhood. It's outside the town limits, so I probably haven't been here since high school and even back then it wasn't the safest area. The club itself isn't much better and I cast a suspicious look at Emily as the doorman waves us inside.

Even though she's a tiny, doll-eyed pixie, I manage to spot Aubrey right away. She runs over and hugs me like we haven't seen each other in months instead of days. "Holy hell, I'm glad I have pepper spray in my purse," she shouts into my ear.

I introduce her to Emily and even though they're exact opposites, they seem to hit it off. While the location is questionable, it's nice to be out, socializing with other women my age like a normal human being for a change.

"So, tall, dark, and deadly let you out of the house?" Emily asks after the other girls head off to the dance floor. "Do you have a curfew?"

"No, smartass, he's meeting me later."

Her eyes widen. "I was joking. Wow, you seem to be moving fast with him."

Emily had heard plenty of details about my relationship with Chad during our group therapy sessions. She'd also heard the counselors caution us about getting into another relationship right away. Part of me wonders if I can trust her not to rat me out at our next session.

"We've known each other since we were kids," I explain, wanting her to understand what Liam and I have isn't a rebound or a mistake.

"Oh, this is the one who was running hot and cold." She nods knowingly. "If that was still going on, I was going to suggest you bring a guy home tonight to make him jealous."

I blink and stare at her. Even if Liam and I hadn't…gotten together, that'd be a level of childishness I'd never stoop to.

"Well, I'm going to sample the goods."

I raise an eyebrow. She'd heard the same advice I had during group. "Not all of us have a knight in shining armor waiting for us at home," she explains.

"Be careful."

Emily assures me she'll be fine and pushes her way into the crowd.

I scan the room, seeking a familiar face. Aubrey's in the corner involved in what appears to be an intense discussion with an older guy whose features I can't quite make out in the low lighting. A steady stream of people comes in through the front door, filling the place to capacity.

Emily's in the center of the room now. I nudge and squeeze my way through a sea of grinding couples to reach her and her friends.

It's fun to let loose, even if I can't get quite as loose as Emily. Her enthusiasm for everything makes me happy we met, even if it was under crappy circumstances.

After a few songs, she drags a tall, lanky blond guy over to me. "This is my friend, Shane," she shouts over the music.

We end up dancing in a large group, but eventually the others leave to grab drinks. Shane and I keep dancing. The guy has panty-melter written all over his face, but he keeps a respectful distance.

"Do you have a boyfriend?" he shouts over the music.

"I do."

He nods even though I'm not sure he heard me. I'm wracking my brain trying to think of something else to say to keep the conversation moving, but his gaze is fixed on something over my shoulder.

Leaning down, he shouts, "There's a guy watching us who looks like he wants to rip my arms off."

Terror that Chad somehow wormed his way out of jail, grips me. Whipping my head around, my frantic gaze searches the bar. Through the throng of writhing bodies, no one stands out.

Cold ice knots in my stomach, even if I can't see Chad. I don't want to put Emily's friend in danger. Chad always swore he'd kill any man who touched me.

It was one of his favorite threats.

A familiar scent envelopes me right before a rough voice intrudes. "Excuse us."

My heart jumps and a relieved breath bursts out of me as I turn around. "Liam."

Shane taps my shoulder. "You all right with this guy?"

The corners of my mouth twitch. Liam's busy glowering at Shane. "Yes. Liam, this is Emily's friend, Shane. Shane this is my boyfriend, Liam."

They go through the firm-grip, male handshake process and Liam acts civil enough, but as soon as Shane leaves, Liam's intense gaze shifts my way. There's no anger though. Only heat and a glimmering possessiveness.

"You're here." My breathy voice barely carries above the music.

He clamps his hands over my hips and pulls me against him. "I'm here."

In the heels, it's easier to loop my arms around his neck and give him a quick kiss. "I've been thinking about you all night."

He responds by holding me even tighter.

There's no denying that the way he places his hands on me is his way of informing everyone I'm taken.

LIAM

AFTER A LONG day, I stopped by my apartment for something dressier than what I had stashed at Vince's house.

I enjoy dancing about as much as a good, swift punch to the balls, but I find for Brianna, I'll do just about anything.

Instant, primitive possessiveness flowed through me the second I spotted my girl on the dance floor.

With another guy.

And more guys checking her out that she seems oblivious to. Of course she attracts a lot of attention, she's the most beautiful girl in the room.

The way Shane stared at Bree made me want to punch the smug smile right off his face. Somehow, I hung on to the urge by sheer will.

No matter how much I don't enjoy random guys panting after her, I'm not about to act like a jealous dick after the stuff Bree confided in me about her ex. I trust her and that's all that matters.

"I've been thinking about you too," I admit. Wrapping my arms around her, I pull her close and we start moving to the music together. "Missed you."

"Missed you too."

"So, Emily's friend?" I work hard to keep my tone neutral.

A slight smirk turns the corners of her mouth up and she arches a brow. "Yes?"

"So much for girls' night out."

She rolls her eyes and pokes me in the chest. "For a guy who hates to dance, you're awfully good at it," she teases, ignoring my comment.

"Anything to keep that smile on your face."

She responds by pulling me closer and kissing me softly. "Will you take me home, Liam?" she asks against my lips.

Fuck, yes. I'm ready to toss her over my shoulder and storm out of the bar with her. "I'll take you anywhere you want."

She ducks her head and peeks at me through her lashes. "I want to be alone with you." The husky tone of her voice is a jolt of arousal straight to my groin.

My brain-to-mouth function has trouble forming an intelligent response. "Sounds good."

She gives me another sweet smile and a kiss on my cheek. "Let me say goodbye to Emily and Aubrey."

I examine the crowd again. People haven't stopped coming in the front door since I arrived. I'm off the clock, but can't help noticing the place is probably over capacity. I doubt the fire marshal's going to bother coming down here, though. "Do either of them need a ride?" I ask.

"Yes, but not the kind you're offering."

"What?"

"Nothing," she shouts, snaking through the crowd to the bar.

I don't want to lose sight of her. Her sparkling white tank top and gold shorts stand out, but I still follow.

When she realizes I'm behind her, she slips her hand into mine. The way she smiles up at me ties me up in knots. Why did I ever try to deny my feelings for this woman?

Vince. *Fuck.* I really need to call him.

Bree's elbow pokes me in the side and I realize she's trying to introduce me to Emily. "Do you need a ride home?" I ask the energetic redhead.

"Nope. My posse's here with me. Figured this one would ditch out as soon as you showed up," she laments, nodding at Bree.

So, Bree's telling her friends about us too? I like that. A lot.

Restless and eager to have Bree all to myself, I grip her hand and lead her to the door. She stays tucked behind me while I push our way through the crowd.

"Did you have a good time?" I ask when we step out of the stifling club.

"I did." She pulls her hair into a pile on top of her head and fans herself with her hand. The movement arches her back, pressing her breasts against her flimsy, sparkling top. The erection I was sporting in the club comes back with a vengeance.

Her head tilts. "What's wrong?"

"You're hot."

"I know. It was gross in there. I have sweat running down places I don't want to think about."

I groan at the visual that gives me, and her eyes widen. "Sorry, too much?"

She doesn't get it.

I take her hand and hustle her into the shadows by my truck. Using my body, I press her against the side. "All I can think about is getting sweaty with you now." Her hand's still in mine, and I guide it to the bulge in my pants.

Her mouth falls open, but before she says anything, I take a long, possessive kiss. My hands sweep her hair off her shoulders and I bend down to kiss her neck.

Under my passionate attack, she melts into me. Low, husky moans fall from her lips.

My hands drop to her legs, tracing my fingers against her smooth skin, to the edge of her shorts. I grip her ass and deepen our kiss. Her hold shifts from my shoulders to my belt and, fuck, do I want to strip her down and bury my cock in her right this second.

I've never wanted anyone so much I was willing to risk a public lewdness charge before.

She draws back and our eyes lock. "Let's go home before we get arrested, Deputy Hollister. I don't want you getting in trouble." She gives me a flirty wink.

"It'd be worth it."

ONCE WE'RE IN the truck—with the air conditioning on full-blast—I ask Bree about her night.

"It was fun. But you're right about that place. Can't say I want to go back any time soon. I like Emily a lot. Aubrey too. She's the one I met in Sully's class. I think she has a crush on him. Although, I saw her talking to some older guy tonight and it looked intense."

Warm contentment fills my chest as I listen to her describe her evening. What the hell am I going to do without her when she goes back to school at the end of the summer?

"Should I let Sully know he has an admirer?" I ask.

"Don't you dare."

She's quiet for a minute. "Were you mad at me?"

"Bree, I came damn close to fucking you in the parking lot. How can you ask that?"

A soft huff of laughter eases out of her. "You looked angry when I was dancing with Shane."

My hands tighten on the steering wheel, and I sigh.

"I didn't like it. But no, I wasn't mad at you," I answer after slipping the truck into park and shutting the engine off. The headlights stay on so I can search the front yard for any movement. After a few seconds, I shut the lights off and turn to face her.

She leans across the seat and feathers a kiss over my cheek. "Thank you."

"Stay there." I round the truck, open her door and lift her up.

"You can't carry me all the way into the house."

"Don't be ridiculous." I squeeze her ass. She hitches her legs around my waist and her arms around my neck. "I don't want your heels sinking into the grass and getting dirty," I explain.

"You're so sweet."

"Not really. I want you to leave them on when I fuck you," I murmur against her ear.

221

She gasps and throws her head back. Her laughter echoes through the still night. At the bottom of the front porch steps, I set her down and she hurries up the steps.

"Why're you running, baby girl?" I growl, grabbing her around the waist and bear-hugging her.

"You know why," she rasps, leaning her head back so I can kiss her again.

I take the key out of her hand and stare at her for a minute. A slight summer breeze picks up strands of her hair, moving them around her shoulders and across her face. I reach out and tuck a few loose pieces behind her ear. "You're beautiful."

"You don't think it's too short?" She shakes her head back and forth, letting the ends brush over her bare shoulders.

"Not at all." I lean in closer. "It's sexy as hell."

"*Mmm*, let's go inside," she says, taking my hand. "I have plans for you."

Brianna

INSIDE THE HOUSE, Liam turns and places his hands on my cheeks, tilting my head back so he can kiss me. I fall back against the door and he follows.

My fingers tug and pull at his crisp white shirt, revealing his tight, flat stomach with the trail of dark hair disappearing into the waistband of his gray dress pants.

"How is it that you're sexier every time I look at you?"

He presses more kisses to my cheek and down to my neck. "Thank you."

"Did you dress up for me?" I ask as I undo the buttons of his shirt.

"Yes." His answer ends in a groan as I lean in and place a kiss on his chest. The frantic beating of his heart beneath my lips says he wants me too.

Being so close, absorbing his woodsy, spicy scent, stirs my hormones.

Tipping my head back, I meet his dark gaze.

"Brianna." The aching whisper speaks volumes.

Kimber nudges us with her cold, wet nose, reminding us of her presence. "Sorry, girl. You need go out?" Liam asks.

Something about my big, hard sheriff speaking so gently to a dog is so sweet, I press my hand to my chest.

A loud thump against the front door startles me into Liam's arms. "What the hell was that?"

His face turns to stone and he pulls a small pistol from his waistband.

"You were carrying that all night?" I ask.

"Yes." His voice comes out clipped and harsh. "Stay here."

I step to the side, ready to hide in the closet. My legs shake as I hold the door open for Liam.

"What the hell?" he mutters, stepping onto the porch.

Kimber snarls and lets out a thunderous bark. "Holy shit. Calm down, girl."

Ignoring me, she squeezes out the front door. "Kimber, no!" I call, running after her.

"Kimber, come!" Liam shouts, but she keeps moving, leaping off the porch and landing in the front yard.

"Fuck!" Liam runs down the front steps.

Even though she's limping, Kimber rounds the house, running into the dark, pursuing hell only knows what.

I take a step forward and my shoe lands on something squishy. I glance down. "Eww." My stomach lurches when I realize what the thump against the front door must have been.

A dead bird.

CHAPTER TWENTY-SEVEN
LIAM

BETWEEN THE BIRD and Kimber reinjuring herself, Bree hasn't stopped shaking.

"I'm so sorry, Keegan," she says for the third time.

"It's not your fault, Bree. She was doing her job. Protecting you."

Kimber's at his feet, panting hard. I had to carry her back from the woods with no idea what she'd been chasing. We're waiting for a call back from the emergency vet.

"Who would do that?" Bree asks, gesturing toward the front porch.

Keegan catches my eye. "Probably just a sick bird that got confused and flew into the door," he says.

Bree's eyes widen. "Oh." She lets out a nervous laugh. "I didn't think of that." Her gaze swings to me. "You think that's what it was?"

No, I think Chad's in some way responsible, but no way am I saying that to her. "Could be."

Keegan's phone rings and he steps away to take the call. "Hey, Dr. Fischer, thanks for calling me back."

"Are you all right?" I ask Bree.

"No. I'm upset about Kimber." She lifts her foot and wiggles it. "And that I have bird goo on my going-out shoes."

Deep, rumbling laughter rolls out of me. I love her resilience. Only Bree could make a joke about bird guts on her shoes with a smile after such a weird night. Hooking an arm around her waist, I pull her toward me and press a kiss to her lips. "I love you," I whisper against her mouth.

Her eyes widen and her body melts against mine. "Love you too. You scared me when you took off."

"Nothing's gonna happen to me."

"Hey," Keegan calls out. "I'm going to run her into the emergency clinic. The doc who's doing her surgery is on call there and she's coming in."

"Do you want us to go with you?" Bree asks.

"Nah. It's going to be a lot of waiting around."

Releasing Bree, I help Keegan lift Kimber into the back seat of his truck. "You going to be able to get her out on your own?" I ask.

"Yeah, someone there will help." He lifts his chin at me. "I'll text you."

Taking Bree's hand, I lead her into the house. She follows me around as I turn on the lamps and check every window and door lock.

Uneasy, I'd rather take her to my apartment, but I don't want to scare her. She seems exhausted anyway. Tomorrow we're headed to my place.

After she goes to sleep, I call Brady to come over and help me search around the house.

CHAPTER TWENTY-EIGHT
LIAM

B RADY AND SULLY show up to help me search the woods behind Vince's place. Sully stays close to the house while Brady and I check out the woods. On the other side, there's a parking lot for people to stop and explore the nature trails. We find fresh tire tracks. Judging by the size and tread, they belong to a truck.

I researched everything I could on the Joseph family. No one owns a truck.

Not that it means much.

Frustrated and annoyed, I finally fall asleep as the sun's coming up, glad I have today off.

Bree's watching me when I wake a few hours later. Wearing an anxious expression, she questions me almost immediately. "Where were you last night?"

Shit. I thought for sure, she'd been asleep.

"A few buddies came over and helped me search the yard."

"Did you find anything?"

"Nothing useful."

She tucks her bottom lip under her teeth. I'll do anything to ease her anxiety today and make her forget the way last night ended. "Come on, I have the day off and want to spend it with you."

"Have you heard from Keegan?"

"He texted me last night. Kimber's okay. They numbed her up and they're transferring her to the regular vet today."

"I feel so bad."

"I do too. She has to stay there for a couple days, but he said we can go visit her in a day or two."

I have to drag her out of bed—who thought that would ever happen? We make a quick stop at the grocery store, where Bree raises an eyebrow at my purchases.

"So, are you planning to explain all the watermelons?" Bree asks as we leave the store.

"You'll see."

The humidity's already thick in the air this morning. Instead of the air conditioner, she chooses to roll the window down, pointing her face toward the breeze. Her hair swirls around her for a few seconds before she pulls it into a ponytail. Already, she seems more relaxed.

The temperature cools a couple degrees the higher up the mountain we go.

"You're sure your parents don't mind us up there when they're not home?" she asks as we approach their driveway.

"I promised them I'd check on the house while they were away this weekend."

"Oh. Okay."

Today I plan to familiarize Bree with handling a few more guns. Mostly long arms. I even tucked her brother's old shotgun behind my seat so she can learn to use it.

After a quick look around the house, Bree follows me to the shed where my dad keeps targets and other supplies. Together, we set up a series of spinning targets. They're all orange and shaped like various woodland creatures.

"This woodchuck looks rabid," Bree says, flicking her hand against it and watching it spin. "Is that so I won't feel bad about shooting it?"

I chuckle and kiss her cheek. "Probably."

"Can you staple the paper targets to the plywood there?" I ask, pointing to the spot.

While she wields the staple gun, I run inside. It feels weird invading my father's gun safe when he's not home, but I told him I planned to do this today and he encouraged it.

I return with a Ruger 10/22 rifle and my mother's .243 deer rifle, so

Bree can get comfortable shooting something with a little more recoil.

"You know," she says as I line the weapons up on the bench. A glint of mischief makes her eyes sparkle and she leans in close, lowering her voice to a hypnotic purr. "Freud said men with a compulsion to own firearms were compensating for small penises."

Fuck, do I love her. I do my best to hold in my laughter, leaning down to touch my forehead to hers. "Well, it's a good thing you know that theory is false."

Pink spreads over her cheeks.

"Besides, aren't his theories considered archaic and obsolete now?"

She raises an eyebrow. Guess she thought I wasn't listening when she was telling me about some of her classes. "That's true, although even I admit his take on memories and defense mechanisms still have some relevance."

"I'll let you measure me later. Now, we shoot."

Jerking her chin at the long arms I have laid out on the table, she comments, "Those guns are much bigger than last time." She throws her hand up. "Just an observation. Not a penis joke. I swear."

I roll my eyes even as I laugh. It's so good to see her smiling and teasing. Happy. This is what I want for her every day. "I'd like you to be familiar with multiple weapons and you don't have a pistol permit." What I *don't* say is that I feel today's lesson is a priority in case Chad's released from jail before her pistol permit gets processed.

Setting aside the threat of her ex, learning to shoot takes some skill and could be a good confidence booster for her. She's been attending group therapy and now I want to show her *my* version of group therapy—a target with a grouping of bullet holes dead center.

We start with the spinners. They'll give her the instant gratification of whirling around when she hits them, rather than having to jog out to check the paper after each round.

I pick up the gun closest to me. "This is a .22. Perfect for plinking, but it will also stop someone in their tracks. Might not kill them unless you get the right shot, but it'll hurt," I explain.

She takes it, weighing the weapon in her hands, studying each feature I point out.

"Ready?" I ask.

"Yes."

She blows through a lot of ammo in a short amount of time. She's laughing and having fun. Especially when she gets the little orange forest creatures to spin like crazy.

After she's used every bullet, she sets the rifle down on the bench. "I like this one better because it has the scope. It's so much easier." She glances at the empty boxes of ammo. "I can't believe we kicked two boxes."

"You were having fun. Ready to try Vince's shotgun?"

She pushes her bottom lip out. "There's no scope on that."

"I know. But I think you should learn how to use it. Plus, with bird-shot, there's less collateral damage because the pellets won't penetrate through walls. And in a home defense situation, you can do a lot of damage with a shotgun in a short amount of time."

She seems uncertain for a moment, as if she realizes we're not just out here for fun.

"Think of how surprised Vince will be when he comes home and you can outshoot him," I encourage.

Her eyes light up. "Ooo, yes. Let's do it. Show me."

I pick up the Remington 870. "This is a pump action shotgun. All the same safety rules apply. Always assume it's loaded. Never point it at anything you don't intend to kill."

"Got it."

While we're out here for fun and because I want to boost her self-confidence, I'm glad she also takes this seriously.

"Safety is here." I hit the release and pull the pump back to show her how to load it. "Keep the safety on to load the shells into the tube. Once it's full, you're going to rack a shell." I take a second to show her each of the steps. "Push it forward with authority. Don't short stroke it."

She wiggles her eyebrows. "That sounds dirty."

"Trust me, I don't short stroke anything, sweetheart." My voice comes out low and rough.

"Oh," she purrs. "I'm well aware you're all about the long and deep strokes."

I close my eyes and groan. "You're killing me."

"Come on, continue," she urges, all serious again.

"Pull the trigger, eject the shell, keep going until you're out of shells. It's that simple."

"Got it."

She takes a few shots at the metal gong my dad has set up about fifty yards out. It's fun, but after a few minutes I notice her losing interest.

When she runs through the shells already loaded, I hold up my hand for her to stop. "Leave it open so you know it's empty. I'm going to go grab something. Stay here."

I return with the watermelons and line them up on a board about fifteen yards out.

"Wait, are we shooting them?"

"Yup."

"Waste of good watermelon," she mutters.

"I left one in the house for later."

I stand back and watch silently as she picks up the shotgun and carefully loads each of the shells on her own, pleased she's already comfortable with the process.

After taking her time, she aim and fires. The first watermelon explodes. Bits of green and pink flying everywhere.

"Holy shit!" She pumps her fist in the air and then blows the next three melons off the board.

"Good job."

"Oh, sorry." Her gaze drops to the ground. "I didn't save any for you."

Brianna

THE INTENSE WAY Liam watches me sends a quiver of excitement up my spine.

"You're sexy as fuck when you're concentrating on hitting the target."

"Oh, yeah?"

"Yes." He hooks a hand behind my neck and draws me closer, giving me a deep kiss. After a few seconds he releases me and I sway on my feet.

"Help me clean up?"

We pick up the brass shell casings scattered around the area, take down the paper targets, and place the moveable targets into the shed. When we're finished, I run into the house to use the bathroom, then meet Liam in the kitchen.

"Mom said she left steaks in the fridge if we wanted to grill outside."

"Sounds good." I rub my hand over my stomach. "I worked up an appetite."

He flashes another simmering look my way. "So did I."

I don't think he means for dinner.

Together, we prepare the steaks and a salad, taking everything outside to eat at the table on the patio.

"Want to start a fire?" he asks after dinner.

Yes. Yes, I do.

While he lights the fire, I slice up the remaining watermelon and find a blanket. I carry both back outside with me.

"The lone melon that survived that massacre," I announce, holding the bowl up. Liam chuckles and takes the blanket from my arms, spreading it a safe distance from the fire.

I kneel down next to him and feed him a chunk of watermelon. The cool juice runs down my hand, over my wrist and Liam chases the trail with his tongue.

"You're getting me all wet." The protest is weak.

He raises an eyebrow and draws a piece of watermelon from the bowl, holding it to my lips. "Open."

I take it in one bite and he snaps, leaning in closer and gently brushing his tongue over the corner of my mouth. "Bree, Bree, Bree," he murmurs, moving to my mouth. Kissing me over and over. He slides his hands under my T-shirt and strips it off, tossing it in the wet grass.

There's a tug at my waist as he fiddles with the buttons on my shorts. "Bree." His voice drops into the deep, commanding tone that quickens my pulse. "Get these off."

I undo the button and he works my shorts down my legs and throws them on top of my shirt.

Nervous about being almost naked in his parents' backyard, I cross my arms over my chest. He yanks me closer and slides his hands under my ass, lifting me into his lap. His fingers dig into my flesh urging me to wrap my legs around his waist, and bury my face against his shoulder.

Ohmygod his scent. Bullets and grass and burnt summer air. He smells like my Liam.

He falls back against the blanket, leaving me straddling him. His hands cup my breasts, thumbs brushing over my nipples, straining against the lace of my bra. "I like this," he whispers. "I can see how hard your nipples are for me."

Reaching back, I unhook my bra and drop it on the ground.

"Even better," he groans.

Underneath me he tilts his hips, tipping me forward. His arms wrap around me and he rolls us until I'm completely covered by him. "Take your shirt off," I demand. "I want to feel you against me." My hands slide under his T-shirt, fingers trailing over hard muscle and hot skin. I help him drag it up and over his head.

"I need you, Bree."

"You have me." Does he ever. Wound tight and desperate to come.

The rough fabric of his shorts brushes against my bare legs as he undoes his fly, freeing himself.

I gasp as he slides my underwear out of his way and slowly pushes his thick shaft inside me. My hips rock, angling for more. He presses in deeper, filling me. His hands slide underneath my shoulders and lower back, protecting me from the hard ground underneath us.

"So good." He pulls back and slowly pumps in and out. Hip lips brush my jaw, stopping at the side of my throat where he places an openmouthed kiss, then gently sucks.

Under the weight of him, I thrash, working my hips against him. He lifts his mouth from my skin to stare into my eyes. "Need to come?"

"Fuck, yes. I'm so close."

All afternoon, he's had me dancing on the edge of orgasm. The intense way he watched me. Standing behind me to give instructions, so close I could feel his heat. Who knew target practice could be so exciting? A few minutes of his hips pistoning back and forth might be all I need.

Oh, the sweet, sweet friction. My muscles tense and a scream tears from my throat.

He moves faster in response, giving me the right rhythm to draw out my orgasm.

Our skin is slick with sweat but he holds onto me as he groans and comes in long, hard jerks.

When he's finished, he drops his sweaty forehead to mine for a second. We stay that way, holding onto each other until our breaths slow and our hearts stop racing. He releases me and rolls to his back and we both stare up at the sky. "You all right?"

"Mmmhmm."

He comes into focus, gazing down at me. I reach up and run my fingers through his hair. "You know, I used to fantasize about doing something like that with you all the time when we had these bonfires."

He raises an eyebrow. "Did I live up to your fantasy?"

I nod vigorously. "Oh yes."

"You're gorgeous all naked in front of the fire." His fingers trace the lines of my shoulders, down my arms, over my chest and down to my belly. "You're so soft."

"Weird, since I like it when you give it to me hard."

He bursts into laughter. "Careful, sweetness or you're going to get it hard again."

We trade silly jokes laced with sexual innuendo until I'm laughing so hard I can't breathe.

"Let's go inside before you get eaten up by mosquitos." He reaches over and plucks his shirt off the ground, slipping it over my head. "We can sleep in my old room," he says, picking himself up and pulling on his shorts. He leaves them unbuttoned and it's such an unconsciously sexy thing to do, I can't help running my fingers around the edge of his waistband. "That's a good look for you, Hollister."

He nods at the T-shirt I'm wearing that hits me at mid-thigh level. "You look damn fine in my shirt, Avery." He holds out a hand and I take it.

I follow him around the house while he sprinkles flakes of food in his mother's small fish tank and does a few other tasks.

"You're such a good son," I blurt out. Liam glances at me as if he thinks I'm making fun of him, but I'm not. "I mean it."

He gives a quick shrug. "They're good parents."

Is it possible to be any more in love with this man?

With Liam, I can vividly picture having a family. He'll be a wonderful father and protector.

"Hey." His hand taps my shoulder. "What's going on in your head?" He opens the door to his bedroom and leads me inside.

I doubt he wants to hear about my primal you're-a-good-baby-making-candidate instincts, so I go with something more lighthearted.

"Wow, I finally made it into Liam Hollister's bedroom. The best wide receiver Johnsonville High has ever had," I tease, glancing around the room that hasn't changed all that much from when he was a teenager.

"It's weird when you say my full name like that."

"I doubt I'm the first girl to say it."

"You're the first one to say it in here."

I decide not to pull at that thread. Nothing before us matters. Only our future.

He drops down on the bed and pulls me to stand between his knees. "I spent a lot of time in this bed thinking about you."

"Really? I thought I was like a sister to you?"

"No. Not at all." He cocks his head. "I told you I had a crush on you the first day we met."

I try to recall the conversation he's referring to. "You rescuing me from the playground bully?"

"Yes."

"I figured you were just trying to make me feel better."

He sighs and shakes his head. "What am I going to do with you?" His hands skim up the back of my legs, up under my shirt, and he slowly lifts it over my head. "You won't be needing this tonight."

THE NEXT MORNING, sunlight stabs me in the eyes much earlier than I usually prefer. I grumble and roll back over, shoving my head under the pillows.

Cold air rushes over my skin as Liam rips away the covers. "Noooo. It's too early," I whine.

Liam's warm body replaces the blankets. His hands roaming everywhere. Over my hip, my belly, up to cup my breast and nuzzle my neck. "Time to wake up."

I open one eye and peer up at him. "You kept me up half the night. I'm still sleepy."

"Come on. I want to take you to my apartment. We can stay there until Kimber's back from the vet. You can take a nap after I leave for work."

My lips push into an unhappy pout. "Do you have to go to work?"

"Yes, baby girl." He gives my butt a few affectionate pats before rolling away from me.

"I would like to finally see your apartment."

"Good. I'll go make breakfast while you get ready."

After breakfast, we tidy up the house and grab the mail, leaving it in a neat stack on the counter.

"First, let's stop at your brother's so we can get your things," he suggests.

"I do need some clothes," I grumble, staring at my grass-stained shorts and the shirt I borrowed from Liam since mine was damp with morning dew from sitting outside all night.

He settles his hand on my leg. "Bring anything and everything you want with you."

"Careful, or I'll move in with you."

He glances over. "Fine by me."

My stomach flutters and I rest my hand against his.

Everything seems exactly the way we left it at Vince's. Liam still stalks around the perimeter of the house to check.

Excited because I'm *finally* visiting Liam's apartment, I blow through the house like a tornado tossing stuff in my backpack and duffle bag.

Liam's footsteps thud over the hardwood floor and I glance up to find him standing in the bedroom doorway.

"Got everything?" he asks.

I pat the bag I have crushed to my chest and motion to the other bag strapped to my back. "Ready."

His mouth quirks. I probably look as eager as a kid headed to summer camp. Heck, I almost feel like one.

"Follow me over in your car. I don't want you to feel stranded."

"Works for me."

It's a short drive to the complex Liam calls home. His apartment is on the second floor. He gives me a quick tour. One bedroom. Nothing fancy.

"It's so neat and tidy."

My observation makes him laugh and he places his hands on his hips. "It sounds like you expected my place to be a pig sty."

"No, but you *are* a single guy."

He drops the teasing smile. "Not anymore. Never again."

Wow. I don't have time to fully absorb and appreciate his words before he pulls me against his body. "I can't believe I finally have you at my place and I have to go to work."

"I'll be here when you come home."

"I like that," he whispers, pressing a soft kiss against my lips.

After Liam leaves, I unpack a few of my things. I brought tea and decide to make that before flicking on the television.

At least I feel safe here. I didn't want to admit to Liam that after the last freaky occurrence, I was scared to be alone at Vince's house. Here, I'm safe. No one should be able to find me.

My phone beeps and flashes red, telling me it's almost out of juice.

Crap.

In my hurry to pack up my stuff, I forgot my cell phone charger. After rummaging through Liam's drawer of electronic odds and ends, I still can't find one to fit my phone.

"Shit." I need to charge it soon. My brother was supposed to call and let one of us know when he's finally coming home.

Will he flip out when he finds out Liam and I are together? Or will he act like an adult and be happy for us? I'm ashamed to say, I don't really know my brother that well anymore, so it could go either way, although I'm leaning toward *flip his shit.*

Never mind Vince. If Liam calls later and he's sent to voicemail, I don't want him to worry. I also don't want to miss any of the texts he might send me tonight.

I won't be the cause of any more stress in his life. His job is hard enough. So, I grab my keys, shove my almost-dead phone in my pocket, and trot downstairs to my car.

CHAPTER TWENTY-NINE
LIAM

"I NEED COFFEE. Stop at the Stewart's at the bottom of the hill," Brady directs, waving his hand at the windshield. As if I don't know which store he's talking about. Or why he really wants to stop there.

"Coffee my ass. You want to flirt with what's-her-face."

Brady chuckles, not offended because we both know it's the truth.

"I'll wait in the car. Don't want you to be embarrassed when you get shot down again." While he's busy getting the brush-off from the checkout girl, I plan to call *my* girl and make sure she's comfortable at my apartment.

She wants her independence, but the urge to protect her isn't ever going to go away. She might as well get used to it now.

Through the store window, I can see Brady chatting with the girl he's had his eye on for at least a month. With the way I've seen him go through women, watching him get shot down multiple times has been entertaining as hell. For me, anyway. Today, he's clearly working the Irish charm hard. If I had to guess, he's laying the accent on thick. Poor girl.

Chuckling, I pick up my phone and dial Bree's number, eager to hear her voice.

I'm greeted with her voicemail instead.

Dammit. I've asked her to keep her phone on in case of an emergency multiple times.

Immediately, I call back and still get her voicemail.

Frustrated, I set the phone down. How much shit will Brady give me if I say I want to swing by my apartment?

Do I really care what he thinks?

I ring Bree a few more times with the same result.

"Damn, I'm glad you stayed in the car," Brady says, flinging himself into the passenger seat. "She's a tough one."

Glancing down at his empty hands, I give him a light punch on the arm. "Where's my coffee, jerk? No wonder she keeps turning you down. You waste her time and don't buy anything."

Brady's eyes widen. "Fuck. Should I go back inside?"

"No," I answer, the smile fading from my lips. "I need to stop by my place real quick."

As he opens his mouth—to rib me, I assume—my phone rings. At first I'm relieved, figuring it's Bree. But I don't recognize the number.

"Hollister."

"Hey, Liam. It's Howard. The dude you wanted me to keep tabs on? He got sprung early this morning."

"What the fuck? How?"

"They got some sort of emergency bail hearing in front of another judge. Parents posted bail. He has to wear an ankle monitor and stay at their house, though."

Motherfucker.

"Why didn't anyone call us?" Bree certainly would've called me if she'd been told Chad was loose.

"Don't know. Sorry. I just got in. Called you as soon as I saw it."

"Thanks. Appreciate it."

"What's wrong?" Brady asks after I throw my phone on the dash.

I can't believe they let that asshole out of jail. Thank fuck I moved Bree into my apartment. To my knowledge Chad has no idea where I live. Probably the only time I'll ever be thankful Bree and I haven't had a lot of contact in the last few years.

"They let Bree's ex out of jail."

"Shit. He stupid enough to contact her?"

"He better not. She's at my apartment, though, so she should be fine. Supposedly they put an ankle monitor on him." Am I trying to convince Brady or myself everything's okay?

Brady snorts. "If he's crazy, ankle monitor won't mean shit until it's too late."

"Thanks a lot, asshole." I pick up my phone and my finger hovers over Bree's number. I hate to call and scare her with this news. Especially when she's alone.

On the other hand, there's a .38 and a box of bullets in my nightstand drawer and I want her to be prepared.

Just in case.

Brianna

THE HOUSE DOESN'T look any different than it did a few hours ago. For some reason, though, I'm uneasy being here by myself. There's no Kimber waiting inside to greet me at the front door. I can't believe how I attached I've gotten to her in such a short time.

For that reason, I pull my car right up over the lawn and park next to the front porch, crossing my fingers Vince is in a forgiving mood when he returns and won't mind the tire marks in his grass.

Rushing through the house, I finally locate my charger in the bedroom and stop to plug in my phone, which died completely on my way over. Since it'll take a while to give it enough juice to turn on, I stretch out on the bed and close my eyes for a few seconds.

A clink and rattle invade my mind sometime later. I blink and turn my head, searching for the clock.

"Shit!" I bolt upright, grab my phone, and yank the charger out of the wall socket. While my phone powers up, I slip my shoes on. I was out of it for less than thirty minutes, but I'm still eager to leave and return to Liam's apartment.

A squeak and clunk from the front of the house reminds me why I woke up in the first place. Vince has upgraded the place significantly, but it's still an old house. It sighs, creaks, and produces other random odd sounds all the time.

This particular creaking sounds too deliberate.

Stop it. You're being ridiculous.

Didn't Sully tell me to listen to my instincts? Hell, didn't I discuss it at length in group therapy?

Time to go.

The knock at the front door sends my heart racing. Did Liam drive by and see my car?

Liam wouldn't knock. No, he'd burst in and lecture me for not telling him I was coming over.

There's another knock at the same time my phone buzzes in my hand. Startled, I drop it.

Shit! I realize I'd been holding my breath, hoping whoever was out front would assume no one's home and go away. Hard to do when I'm making so much damn noise. And let's not forget my car parked haphazardly in the front yard.

Maybe it's a neighbor checking to make sure everything's okay?

This neighborhood's never been the kind to look out for each other—a painful lesson learned as a child—so that seems unlikely.

I snatch my cell phone off the floor and keep it in my hand as I creep toward the living room.

Another knock at the front door. No, not a knock. Three blunt pounds from the side of a fist against the hard wood. The small glass windows at the top of the door rattle.

The police?

No, they'd identify themselves.

A name forms in the back of my mind, but I refuse to allow the thought to fully form.

"Brianna," an agitated voice calls out.

No.

Chad.

I'd recognize that belligerent tone anywhere.

Heart slamming in my chest, hands shaking, I freeze. What the hell should I do?

Call 911?

"Bree, baby, I know you're in there." He chuckles softly. "Address was on the restraining order."

Liam had warned me about that. Another reason, I was happy to stay at his place.

Footsteps thud over the porch. Back and forth. Back and Forth. From experience, I know Chad's pacing. Something he does right before he loses his shit.

I'm too scared to make a sound.

Grab the shotgun?

911. Call Liam. Then shotgun.

Is that a good plan? Is calling 911 overreacting?

No, dumbass. There's a restraining order. He shouldn't be here.

This is what Sully meant about there being no time to process in an emergency. Mere minutes have passed since I woke up, but it feels like an eternity.

911 on the way to get the shotgun.

Yes!

As my thumb hits the last button, I realize the pacing's stopped. Not a single sound comes from the front porch.

Did he actually leave?

"911. What's your emergency?"

I peek out the window, but there's no one. Weird that I never heard a car leaving.

"Twenty-Nine Sand Lake Road," I rush to spit out the address. "My ex-boyfriend is—

Before I finish the sentence, there's a rattle, then a pounding at the back door. Seconds later a terrifying crashing and splintering of wood.

My back hits the wall and I slide along it until I'm tucked against the door of the entryway closet. Slowly, I peer around the corner as the back door bounces off the wall and Chad storms into the kitchen.

Shit. I pull back before he sees me and stand rock still.

My eyes focus on the door three feet in front of me.

Front door—outside?

My flight response is screaming *yes, run for safety!*

The part of me that's too terrified to move wants to duck into the closet door at my back and hide. My hand automatically reaches behind me, silently twisting the knob, opening the door a fraction of an inch.

Keeping my options open.

Ominous footsteps creep through the house. The place isn't that big. I'll be face-to-face with him any second now.

Move!

"Hello? Miss? Are you there?" the 911 operator's voice shouts from my phone.

Well, I guess hiding is no longer an option.

The footsteps rush closer. I sprint for the front door, snagging my keys off the entryway table as I go.

I wrench the knob and hurl myself through the open door, running onto the porch without looking back.

Behind me, Chad snarls.

Too close.

My feet pound down the first and second steps. Skipping over the rest of the steps, I land hard in the grass.

Don't look back. Keep moving.

I'll never make it.

"Help!" I scream, fumbling my keys in my hand.

"Shh, what are you shouting for?" Chad says behind me.

"How'd you get out of jail? There's a restraining order!" I shout, praying the 911 operator is still on the line and catches every word.

The alarm on my car chirps as I hit the key fob. I jam the phone in my pocket and yank the car door so hard I break my thumbnail. My body's between the car and the door when Chad grabs the top of the door, slamming it into me. My hip and thigh take the brunt of the impact. For once I'm glad I'm a little fleshy in those areas. It hurts, but I keep squirming into the car. My butt hits the seat and I kick my feet, pushing Chad back. "Get away from me!" I scream.

I try to jam my keys in the ignition, but my hands are shaking so bad, I don't make it on the first try.

And that's the only chance I have.

Chad wrenches the door open, reaches in, and grabs my hair, yanking me out of the car. I fall to my knees and as he reaches down to grab at me, I swing my keys at his face.

He recoils as the metal scrapes his cheek, but I don't carry many and they're not that heavy. The impact isn't enough to stop him. He slaps them out of my hand and they land in the grass with a muted jingle.

"I just wanted to talk to you. Why are you so hysterical?" he asks as if he didn't just slam a car door into my body and try to rip my hair out by the roots.

"You're not supposed to be here."

"I can't stay away from you. You know that." He crouches down in the grass next to me and lightly slaps my cheek.

Playfully, you know, the way a cat slaps a mouse around right before he eats it.

Playtime's over. He wraps his fist in my hair and his arm around my neck, pulling me off the ground with him.

Go limp.

I imagine my body boneless and try to get loose, but he tightens his hold.

I kick, sputter, and claw the whole time he drags me up the stairs. At the front door, I grab onto the doorframe and use what little strength I have to hang on.

He laughs and releases my hair, painfully prying my fingers loose.

Inside, he lets me go and slams the door shut. I back into the living room and he stalks toward me without saying a word.

Somehow that's more frightening. Chad's usually full of words. Especially when he's pissed.

"Why are you doing this?" A question I've asked so many times before.

"*What* am I doing, Bree? I just wanted to have a normal conversation with you. You're the one acting hysterical." That familiar manipulative tone fires me up again. How many damn times did he try to convince me I was the crazy one? That I somehow deserved being hit or punched. How many of our friends did he try to gain sympathy from by telling them he loved me so much, he put up with my over-emotional behavior?

Too many.

"There's nothing to talk about. We're done."

His expression darkens. "Don't say that."

He rushes forward and I dart to the right, heading for the kitchen, but he catches me easily, wrapping his hands around my upper arms and pushing me backwards until my back hits the wall.

"I'm sorry, okay? Is that what you want? Tell me you're not leaving."

"I'm already gone."

"It's your cop friend, right? The one who came to rough me up?"

My wide eyes meet his crazy ones. Liam did that?

It gives me the courage to push back, struggle harder. "No, Chad. *You* did it. *You* almost killed me! I'm done."

"You were planning to leave me!" he roars in my face.

I cringe and turn my head. "You hurt me. Over and over." There's no reasoning with him. I shouldn't even bother. But the alternative is worse.

"Bree," he murmurs, pressing his lips to my cheek. My shoulder draws up, squirming to get away from him.

"Not so fast, baby," he says against my ear, spinning me around.

My back hits his chest and an "uh" leaves my lips. He locks one arm over my chest and the other around my middle.

Oh God. I recognize the smell of him. The feel of his body. Hard. Terrifying. Breathing heavy.

"Let me go!" I scream.

"Feisty today. I like that, babe." His arms tighten around me like a damn python. "Feel that? I had lots of time to work out and think about you." He runs his nose along my neck, inhaling heavily. "You smell so good. I missed you."

His lips pull and suck at the skin below my ear and bile rises, burning the back of my throat.

"Let go." My nose twitches and my eyes water. I will *not* cry or beg.

Still bear-hugging me, he tries walking us to the couch. In a rush I remember a move from Sully's class. As Chad shuffles forward, I pick up my foot and slam it into his instep.

"Fuck!" he shouts.

Finally, his grip loosens. Frantic, I jab my elbow back into his chest. I turn and punch forward with the heel of my hand, catching him on the chin. I'd been aiming for his fucking nose, but I'll take it.

Chad's not used to me fighting back. He circles me. Eyeing me with caution now.

That's right, motherfucker.

Desperately, my eyes search the living room for anything I can use as a weapon.

"You're trying to hurt me today, baby." He lunges, grabbing my wrist and yanking me closer. I push forward instead of away and almost slip out of the hold, but he grabs my other arm right above the elbow, shaking me like a rag doll. "You want it rough? That what you want?"

He pushes me onto the couch and when I try to launch myself off, he uses his body to pin me to the cushion, straddling my lap.

I push and shove, wiggling and sliding my way out from underneath him, going limp and melting onto the floor.

Before I get my feet under me, he tackles me back down. Pain explodes through my skull as it thumps against the hardwood.

We grapple, me slapping at him and trying to get my feet up to kick him. Him trying to pin my arms down. He manages to trap my legs underneath him.

Soft spots.

As soon as I go for his eyes, he ducks and grabs my wrists.

"You think those cute little self-defense moves can stop me?"

With one hand, he pins my wrists above my head. His other palm comes flying at my cheek. This time it's not playful slaps he delivers.

One. Pain explodes over my cheek.

Two. Flashes of red burst behind my eyes.

It's jarring, but only a fraction of what he's capable of. My back arches and I wriggle my legs, my hips, my butt, anything to get out from underneath his heavy body. But his weight presses me into the floor and at a certain point all my squirming only seems to turn him on more.

His free hand wraps around my neck, holding me down.

"Look what you're making me do," he snarls.

"Don't." I choke out the word.

Can't breathe.

Desperate, hot, frustrated tears leak from the corners of my eyes, dripping into my hair.

Helpless and held down, my mind recalls other fights we've had.

Never like this.

This time, he's really going to kill me.

My terrified heartbeat pounds in my ear. *Help, help, help.*

He eases up the pressure around my neck and I suck and choke in enough air to clear my head.

"Keep fighting me, Bree." His voice grates over my nerves. "You know it only gets me harder."

Oh, how I knew.

I screw my eyes shut, unable to stand staring at him any longer. Once, I thought Chad was beautiful. Now, I know better. He's the fucking devil.

"Does lawman know what a dirty fucking whore you are?" He releases my hands and palms my breast, squeezing hard, pinching my nipple through my shirt. "Has he figured out all the dirty things that turn you on?"

He tightens the hand around my throat again.

I can't breathe.

The edges of my vision darken.

This is it.

Thank God. I don't want to be conscious when he rapes me this time.

"Please," I beg with the last bits of air I have before his fingers tighten around my windpipe and cut off my air for good.

"I love you so much, Bree." He whimpers the words and squeezes his eyes shut. "Why do you make me feel like this?"

This isn't love.

My hands tingle, but they're free.

Free.

My arms are lead weights as I raise them and slip them between Chad's arms, exploding outward like Sully showed me.

I don't have enough power or energy to knock him totally back, but he releases my throat. Coughing and gagging, I roll to the side and throw my elbow back, hoping to catch his face.

There's a satisfying crunch and I wriggle out from under him, kicking as I go. My foot hits something hard, his chin or his head, I don't know.

I kick again.

There's a thump.

Don't look back. Just move.

I'm still struggling to get air in my lungs, but I stagger to my feet.

The back door's straight ahead and wide open.

But so far away.

Run.

The closet where my brother keeps the shotgun is to my right.

Escape or shotgun?

CHAPTER THIRTY

LIAM

ON THE WAY to my apartment, the radio chirps and Brady turns the volume up. "911 Domestic Dispute. 29 Sand Lake Road. Female caller states..."

No.

Blood roars through my ears, drowning everything else out.

"That's Vince's house!" Brady shouts.

"Why is she there?" She should be safely tucked away in my apartment.

Brady picks up the call. "Car thirty-two, headed to the four-fifteen in progress." He pauses. "Send additional back-up."

"We're still at least ten minutes away."

"Liam. You need to chill. Don't do anything stupid. I'll handle it when we get there."

My entire body freezes. My vision's narrowed on the road in front of me, an object that stands in the way of getting to Brianna. "If he hurts her, he dies. Don't interfere."

Brady sighs but doesn't argue.

Not wanting to spook Chad, I flip the lights and sirens off as we approach the street.

I bring the car to a halt at the end of the driveway and throw open my door. The only other car is Bree's, parked right next to the porch. The driver's side door is wide open.

The front door to the house is closed.

"Easy," Brady mutters as we slowly approach.

From inside, there's a shotgun blast.

"Shit," he mutters. I take off, headed for the front door, Brady right behind me. At the door, I pause, listening for any sounds. I won't be any good to Bree if I get my head blown off.

Brady motions that he'll circle around to the back of the house and meet me inside.

I step over the threshold, checking carefully behind the door. The closet door's wide open and I check that too before closing it.

No one's in the living room, although it's clear there's been a struggle. Careful not to touch anything, I move farther into the house.

The back door is busted wide open, splinters of wood everywhere.

There's a shotgun blast in the wall next to the door.

"Bree!" I shout. "Where you at, baby?"

"I'm here." Her voice is so thin and strained, I don't realize it's her until she peeks out from behind the bathroom door. "Is he dead?" she asks as I approach, my gaze smoothly sliding over every nook and crevice of the house, freezing on the red droplets spattered across the white kitchen tile and out the back door. Dark spots mingle with a fine red mist on the wall.

Brady comes through the back door, shaking his head. "Where is she?

"I got her." I focus on her reddened face. "Bree, where are you hurt?"

"I'm alive," she answers, sounding as if she's going into shock.

"Liam!" Brady shouts from the back door.

I glance down at Bree. "Stay where you are."

Brady signals to me, and a second later I realize why. I jog over the wet grass to him. "This your guy?" he asks in a calm voice.

From the ground, Chad gasps for air.

"Jesus. He took it right in the gut," Brady mutters.

I stare down at Chad, not feeling a damn thing other than concern for Bree. "I told you to stay away from her."

Chad's eyes close.

"He ain't surviving that," Brady says. "I'll give it a few before calling the ambulance."

"Shit." I did not want Bree put through this. Being responsible for the death of someone—no matter how awful a human being—isn't something that ever leaves you. Someone she was in love with? I can't calculate the amount of emotional damage this might do to her. "Fuck!"

Brady watches my outburst with a passive expression. "Your girl did good."

I let out another string of curses.

"Go back and make sure she's all right," Brady insists, giving me a slight push away from the body. In a lower voice he adds, "You know there'll be a lot of questions thrown at her."

"Not tonight," I snap. "She needs to go to the hospital."

He shakes his head, knowing as well as I do that Bree will have to be questioned tonight. "I'll do what I can," he promises.

Sirens fill the air and the sounds of cars skidding to a stop on the street reach us.

"I'll take care of it. Go get her."

Bree's on the couch when I return to the house. Her cheeks are devoid of color and she looks so much like the frightened teenager she'd once been. I crouch down in front of her and place my hand on her leg. "Are you hurt anywhere?"

"Everywhere," she whispers through chattering teeth. "He hurt me. He kept coming at me," she says without meeting my eyes.

In a gentler tone, I say, "Bree, look at me." I give her leg a tender squeeze.

She blinks and stares right through me.

"I finally fought back."

CHAPTER THIRTY-ONE
Brianna

*P*AIN.

Crashing into me from every part of my body. Battering and dragging me into a dark undertow then spitting me back out onto a jagged shoreline.

I killed him.

A man I once thought I loved is dead because of me.

My hands ache and throb. They've fought hard and it shows. They've been tested for gunshot residue, even though I told everyone I did it. I shot him.

It was either him or me.

Those last few minutes are a whirl of pain and fear. So much fear that he'd reach me before I reached the shotgun. Fear that he'd pry the gun out of my hands and use it against me. So much terror racing through my body.

Then *his* fear as he realized, too late, that I wasn't fucking around. That I was done being battered by him.

Him or me.

More fear when I wasn't sure if I'd hit him or scared him off. If he'd been hurt or I'd just made him even angrier.

So much relief when I heard Liam's voice.

Then the horror of knowing I actually killed someone.

Liam stays by my side the whole way to the hospital. Refuses to leave while I'm questioned by the sheriff's office. They warn him the State Troopers will be called in because of our relationship.

He still doesn't leave my side.

My nails are ragged and torn. My cheek, throat, and jaw hurt. My knees, legs, hip all ache. Bruises are already showing, like a map of everything I endured tonight.

The painkiller they gave me barely took the edge off.

Nothing's broken. On the outside, anyway. Inside, I'm shattered and splintered.

I want to go home.

Wait. I don't have a home.

Liam brushes his hand against my arm. Afraid to touch me. Afraid he'll hurt me. "Let's get you home."

"I don't have a home," I utter the words out loud this time.

"Yes, you do. With me." He tucks some hair behind my ear and kisses my forehead. "Always."

"Liam," I croak. I want to tell him how much I love him and how sorry I am that it came to this. That if he needs to put some distance between us, it's okay. We both know that eventually my shitty life choices might end up costing him his job.

An imposing State Trooper steps into the small hospital room where I'm waiting to be discharged. I can't focus and my throat's so raw I'm barely able to answer his questions.

Liam fills in the blanks, which only seems to irritate our interrogator. I pick up on the subtle insinuations woven into his questions.

How did Deputy Hollister arrive first on the scene?

What's the nature of your relationship with Deputy Hollister?

How well did you know the victim, Deputy Hollister?

Victim my ass.

That last question, directed at Liam, pisses me off so much, it finally snaps me out of my fog. I throw the blanket off and point to my neck with one hand while holding out my other wrist. "Chad did this." I don't even recognize my voice, it's so scratchy and rough. "He was trying to kill me. It was him or me."

He finally seems satisfied. Or maybe it's the fact that the day Chad was released from jail for attacking me, he defied the restraining order and attacked me again. That can't look good for the judge who granted bail.

The hospital tried to call in a therapist, but I can't do any more tonight. Can't speak to another person.

Except for the bruising around my neck and every single part of my body hurting, I'm fine and the hospital finally releases me.

Liam drives us to his apartment while I doze on and off in the front seat.

"Did someone call my brother?" I ask when we step into Liam's apartment.

"I'll call him in the morning," he assures me and I'm too tired to argue otherwise.

"Can I...I need to take a shower."

"Okay." He leads me into the bathroom where we both undress and he flips the water on. I don't dare look in the mirror. I don't need another reminder of the damage Chad inflicted on me.

"He didn't... Did he hurt you? Anywhere else?" he asks, holding his hand out to help me into the shower.

"No." I flip both thumbs up. "I went for the soft tissue like Sully taught me." I try to force a smile, but it hurts too much.

He kisses me on the forehead. "Good girl."

This is no sexy-time shower. It's a please-wash-this-nightmare-off-me shower. When I'm clean from head to toe, I turn in Liam's arms and press my face against his chest. Under my cheek, his skin is slick and warm. His heart beats strong and steady.

A harsh sob breaks free from my throat, maybe from my very soul, it hurts so much.

The pain, anger, fear, uncertainty, all of it spills down my cheeks.

Liam holds me tighter.

"Shhh, everything's okay, Bree. You're safe. You did so good."

I know he's right, but I can't accept it right now. Instead, I hold on to him tighter, until the tears stop rolling down my cheeks.

When we're finished, Liam gently pats me dry and slips a T-shirt over my head. His jaw clenches with every new bruise or mark he encounters, but he doesn't say a word. He tucks me into bed and slides in next to me. Neither of us seem to be able to sleep though.

"I'm scared," I whisper.

"You're safe now," he assures me. I wrap my fingers around his. "I'm sorry I didn't make it there sooner. When I got the call that he'd been released, I hauled ass. That's when the 911 call came in." He pauses and faces me. "I thought I'd lose my mind if I didn't get to you. I'm so sorry I wasn't there."

"It's not your fault," I rasp.

"Why were you at Vince's?" he asks gently. "Were you uncomfortable here?"

"No. I forgot my phone charger and I didn't want you to try to call me and be worried if you couldn't reach me." Hot tears pour down my cheeks. I'm surprised I have any tears left.

He runs his hand over my hair gently soothing me. "Shhh, okay. It's okay."

"I'm scared—"

"You don't have to be scared anymore."

"Not for me." A little frustration enters my voice. He doesn't see the bigger picture. "I don't want this to ruin your career."

He reaches out and snaps on the light. The expression on his face is all intensity and passion. "Bree, please hear me when I tell you I don't give a fuck about my job or anything else. Your safety is the only thing I'm worried about."

"You might regret that one day."

"I'll never be sorry for loving you." He snaps the light off and pulls me into his arms. "You're worth any risk, and I'll protect you with my last breath."

CHAPTER THIRTY-TWO
LIAM

THE NEXT MORNING I call in to work and stay with Bree. She mostly sleeps and cries. I feed her soup, water, and pain meds.

On the second day, she seems better. I still call in to work.

On the third morning, someone's fist against my front door wakes me way earlier than I planned on rolling out of bed.

Brianna sits up and stares at the bedroom door with wide eyes and I decide I'm going to punch whoever's on the other side of the door.

I've been dreading this. So far, I've held off anyone coming to question her again. But that's only going to fly for so long.

"Bree," I say in my calmest voice. My gaze lands on the bruises around her neck and *fuck*, but I'm ready to explode. "It might be someone here to question you. I want you to stay here."

Her frightened eyes meet mine. "Why?"

I've thought about this a lot in the last few days, even paid a hefty retainer to the best criminal defense attorney in the area. Just in case. "I have an attorney I want you to speak with before you answer any more questions."

"Why? I didn't do anything wrong." Her lips settle into a grim line. At least her mood seems better today.

"Please. For me. Stay in here."

She runs into the bathroom and locks the door.

When I'm sure she's safe, I throw on a pair of sweats, pad out to the living room, and open the door.

Vince.

Fuck. He called yesterday. He'd gotten stranded at the airport in

Hong Kong.

Despite looking like someone who spent the last forty-eight hours sleeping in an airport and on a plane, he shouts as soon as he sees me.

"What the fuck!?" he explodes, shoving his way into my apartment. "You didn't say my house is a fucking crime scene. Where's Bree?" he asks, stomping from room to room. "Where the hell is she? Is she okay?"

"Calm down."

He rubs his hands over his face. "Don't fucking tell me to calm down. Where's my sister?"

"I'm fine, Vince," Bree answers from the doorway to my bedroom.

Match, meet powder keg.

My best friend's gaze goes from Bree—standing there in my shirt and nothing else—to me. "Are you fucking kidding me?" His voice drops to a deadly calm tone.

"Vince—"

His fists tighten at his sides. "Liam, so help me God if you offer up some lame excuse for fucking my sister, I'll punch you in the crotch." His angry glare swings back to Bree. "Get dressed and get in my car."

She takes a few steps closer until she's standing by my side. "No," she answers in the strongest voice I've heard her use in days.

"Vince," I snap, taking his attention off Bree. "She's staying with me. She's *with* me," I repeat. Fuck, it feels good to say that out loud. To finally say it to my best friend. Next to me, Bree bumps against my arm and wraps her fingers around mine. "We're together." I feel like shouting it a hundred more times.

"The fuck you are," Vince growls. "I asked you to look after her and instead you fuck her?"

"So help me, Vince, if you talk about us that way one more time, I'm tossing you out on your ass." Bree squeezes my hand. "Watch your mouth," I add.

"My love life is none of your business, Vince," Bree says.

Vince isn't used to backtalk from his baby sister. "The hell it's not. After Chad, you're out of your fucking mind if you think what you do isn't my business."

"Don't," I growl, stepping forward. "We're not just messing around. I *love* her and we're together. Deal with it."

His icy glare melts a little when he turns to Bree. "What the fuck!?" His eyes widen when he finally notices the bruises covering her legs, arms and neck.

"Chad attacked me. At the house," she answers softly.

He stomps over to us, and I push Bree behind me. "You were supposed to be looking out for her. You say you're with my sister and you let this happen? That's how you take care of her?" Venom drips from every word.

"Don't you dare blame him," Bree defends.

Vince doesn't need to blame me. Guilt's been wrapped around my neck since the moment I heard the 911 call. I did fuck-all to protect her and that stings more than any words or punches Vince might throw at me.

Brianna

IF VINCE HADN'T lashed out at Liam, I'd almost feel bad for him. Too stunned to say anything else, he drops down onto the sofa and shakes his head.

He throws another glare at Liam before settling his gaze on me. We stare at each other. Him taking in my injuries. Me taking in how much older and more tired he seems.

I swear my big, strong, scary brother seems ready to break when he says, "Come here. I'm sorry."

He stands and beckons me closer.

Still mad at him for blaming Liam, I approach slowly. Vince embraces me carefully and I let out a muffled sob. This is the brother I remember. I may have tried to convince myself otherwise, but I've missed him so much these last few years.

"Tell me what happened, Brianna. Please."

I sob harder and can't get the words out.

"That little shit got out on bail and attacked her," Liam explains for me.

"Where were you?" he asks, with less accusation than before, but I still don't care for his tone.

"It's not Liam's fault," I mumble against his shirt.

He makes a growly-grumbling sound that doesn't suggest he's convinced.

"Bree dealt with him," Liam says with a note of pride in his voice. I'm not quite there yet. I'm still too relieved that I'm alive. I don't think I'll ever be proud I killed someone. But I am proud that I survived.

Vince's hands lightly grip my shoulders and he pulls away. "Tell me everything."

I swallow hard. It still hurts to talk and it really hurts to go over the events again. "I stopped at the house to get something. He broke in. Tried to choke the shit out of me." I turn and take Liam's hand. "I broke free finally and went for the shotgun."

"Since when do you even know how to use a shotgun? I thought you were terrified of it."

"Liam taught me how."

His gaze darts to Liam. No wild interpretation skills are needed to recognize the accusation on his face.

"I'm fine," I say, pulling away. "Or I will be."

"Where's Chad now?" Vince asks.

"Dead," Liam answers.

A strangled cry rips out of my throat and Liam takes me in his arms.

"Jesus Christ," my brother breathes out. "What kind of bullshit is that, Liam? He was out on bail and attacked her. They better not even think of charging her with anything."

"They're investigating. The State Troopers were called in. But it's plain as day what went down."

"Will they question her again?"

"I have it covered."

"What the fuck does that mean?"

Liam grinds his teeth and steals a glance at me before answering. "I have Rob Glassman on retainer if she needs him."

"You do?" I ask.

My brother raises an eyebrow. Liam smooths his hand over my hair. "It's just in case."

Vince seems to have a little more respect and concern for his best friend now. "What's that mean for you?" he asks.

Liam hesitates to answer. "Nothing. I just can't be involved in the case."

"Bree, can you go get dressed?" Vince asks. "I'm still trying to deal with your...*relationship* and it'll be easier if you're wearing pants."

I cut a glare at him, and then to be a complete brat after that pants comment, lean up and kiss Liam.

LIAM

SINCE I'M PROBABLY receiving an ass-kicking either way, I take my time kissing Bree before she trots off to the bedroom.

"I think you owe me some coffee," Vince says.

We head into the kitchen. Once the coffeemaker's doing its thing, I turn and face him. The emotions flickering over his face stir up guilt in my chest. We've been friends a long time and I never wanted to betray him.

"Tell me," Vince says in a lowered voice that says this talk has nothing to do with Chad and everything to do with me and Bree as a couple.

"I meant to call you."

"Yeah, I guess you've been busy," he sneers. "You really couldn't keep it in your pants? She's not some badge bunny. You break her heart, I break your bones." This is Vince. Blunt. To the point.

Ignoring the badge bunny comment, I answer, "More likely, she breaks my heart."

He rolls his eyes. "I doubt that. I've never seen her so pissed at me."

"You *were* a bit of a dick."

"She's my little sister. The only family I've got left. What'd you expect me to do, congratulate you for nailing her?"

"Are you always this disgusting?" Bree says, sweeping into the kitchen and wrapping her arms around me. "No wonder you're still single."

I lean over and kiss the top of her head.

"Feel free to knock it off anytime," Vince grumbles.

"Can't help it. I've got it bad for her." It feels really good to admit that.

"The feeling's mutual," she murmurs.

Vince squirms in his chair. "Christ."

"Ooo, I'll be right back," Bree says, tapping my chest before she goes.

Vince watches her leave before asking his next question. "What are you going to do when she goes back to school?"

"I don't know. We'll work something out. Or I'll transfer to Empire PD." As soon as I say it, a weight lifts from my shoulders. It's the only logical solution. It's all so clear: I want to be with Bree. Bree needs to finish school. I find a job near her school. Easy as that.

"Shit." He sits back and stares at me. "You're serious. You'd leave our little Mayberry?"

"Yeah, Vince. For her, I'd do just about anything."

CHAPTER THIRTY-THREE
LIAM

I TAKE A few more days off and help Vince repair the damage at his house once we get the all-clear from the department. Sully and Jake also come over to help, so we accomplish the work in record time.

I leave Bree at my parents' house where she spends the days baking and talking with my mom.

When we're finished with the repairs, she asks to go to the house. She's surprisingly calm as she inspects everything.

"You guys did a good job," she mumbles, staring at the brand new back door and fresh, white wainscoting.

Vince gives me a look. Maybe it was too soon to bring her here. We move over to the kitchen table, which is now over by the window seat.

He reaches over and taps her shoulder. "By the way, you want to explain to me why I have a dog bed, dog dishes, dog treats, and toys in my house?" Vince asks.

The mention of Kimber seems to shake her out of her fog. Her mouth tips up in a sly grin. "We adopted a dog together," she explains. I'm pretty sure she said it that way to shock her brother, which I think it does because he reacts like she said "kid" instead of "dog." "A Rottweiler. We named her Kimber."

"Well, where is she?" he asks.

I explain the circumstances of Kimber's arrival leading up to the night she injured herself.

In the aftermath we found out it was Chris who flung the dead bird at the door, left the flowers, and followed her around the mall.

"Oh," I say to Bree. "Keegan said she should actually be ready to come home tomorrow."

"She can't stay at your place," Vince points out.

Bree turns her pleading eyes on her brother. "You want me to take her?" he asks. "I'm never here."

"I'll stay here with Kimber."

I raise an eyebrow at that.

"Oh, Christ, don't tell me. The two lovebirds can't be apart," Vince bitches.

Ignoring him, I reach out and take Bree's hand. "My parents said they'd watch her. I think my mom's pretty excited to have someone to dote on."

Bree's bottom lip juts out. "I guess that works."

"It's temporary until we get our own place," I assure her, which earns me another grumbly face from Vince.

"Go back to this dead bird thing," Vince says, waving his big, meaty fingers in my face to distract me from Bree.

Slapping his hand away, I explain in more detail how Chad's brother confessed to the bird and flowers. "And he *had* been following you that day, Bree," I say a pointed look.

"I should've known better."

"I think you confronting him the way you did scared the piss out of him. That's why he resorted to the sneaky-creepy shit."

Her mouth twists into a half-smile. "It felt good to stand up to him."

I place my hand over hers. "Chris didn't know about…what happened to…his brother at the time he confessed all this, so I doubt we'll be getting any more cooperation from him."

"We need to worry about him bothering Bree?" Vince asks.

I'm not sure how to answer that. Chris *should* be scared to come anywhere near Bree, but let's face it, the guy doesn't seem to be very smart. "I don't think so. They charged him with a few misdemeanors for the harassment and for violating the restraining order. Bail was low, he paid it and got out right away."

"You fuckin' kidding me?" Vince rages.

"He does it again, he's definitely going to jail."

"He does it again, he's fucking dead," Vince states. "Plain and fucking simple. Dead."

Bree stands and moves into the living room. Under the table, I kick Vince. "Ow, you fuck."

"Have some tact, asshole," I growl at him.

He seems to finally get it. "Come here, Bree." He wraps an arm around her when she reaches his side. "Are you okay? How you feelin' today?"

"Better."

My phone buzzes and I grab it out of my pocket. "Shit. I have to go in to work."

Vince's hold on his sister tightens. "She can stay here with me."

My gaze goes to Bree and she nods.

"Walk me out, V." I lean down and brush a kiss over Bree's cheek. "You sure you're all right?"

"I'm fine," she murmurs against my lips.

"For fuck's sake, he'll be back later. Jesus," Vince complains when we take too long saying goodbye.

Outside, I drop my best friend smile. "You two need to talk to each other. Heart to heart. Clear the air. Bond. Whatever. But I'm warning you, do *not* upset her or blame her or anything else. Watch your damn mouth."

His eyes widen and he takes a step back. "So this is how it's going to be? You're Bree's boyfriend now? Not my best friend?"

"Don't worry. Soon I'll be your brother-in-law." I enjoy a speechless Vince for a second or two before clapping him on the back and climbing into my truck.

As I back out of his driveway, I throw him a cocky wave and he gives me the finger.

Brianna

"WHERE ARE YOU?" Vince calls out when he comes back inside.

I'd been worried he and Liam were wrestling out in the front yard, so I'm pleased to see him come inside free of dirt and bits of grass when I emerge from the bathroom. "In here."

I stop and take in his perplexed expression. "I hope you two didn't argue outside."

Vince throws himself down on the couch, stretching his arms out over the back. "No. Your *boyfriend* just told me how it is."

"What does that mean?"

"That he'll be my brother-in-law soon." And no, he doesn't sound like someone who's thrilled with the idea.

Liam actually said that? I can't stop the smile from twitching at the corners of my mouth. "Did he now?"

"How long's this been going on, Bree?" he asks, wiping the smile right off my face. "Since high school?"

I move closer, sitting at one end of the couch and drawing my legs up, turning to face him. "No, you ruined that for us the night of my graduation."

He stares at me for a few minutes. "I thought he was taking advantage of you. I didn't know what was going on."

"You think that little of Liam?"

"No."

We're silent for a few minutes. Quietly watching each other. "I freaked out, Bree. You were so fragile. I knew how much you needed to get out of this house, out of this town. Away from mom. And Liam—fuck, I love the guy, but he's never had any ambitions beyond that badge."

"There's nothing wrong with that."

"No, there isn't. But I didn't want you getting trapped here because of him."

"I—" I can't think of a response. I kind of see where he's coming from, even if I'm mildly insulted.

"If I'd know you were going to hook up with that asshole and this was going to happen, I would've kept my damn mouth shut."

"Don't go there."

His hand edges closer to mine. "I've missed you, little sis."

I can't meet his eyes so I gesture to the rest of the house. "The house is amazing. Liam said you did the work yourself."

A hardened look crosses his face. "Had to."

"Why didn't you come home sooner?" I don't know why I bother asking.

"Figured Liam would take care of you." His mouth turns down. "Didn't know he'd seduce you too."

I snort with laughter. "Get over it."

My brother doesn't laugh with me. He's stiff, almost angry. He's always held in a lot of anger. Especially after our father died. But he was never that way with me. "What's wrong, Vinny? We used to be able to talk more than this."

"You've barely been home in four years, Bree."

"What do you care? You're always traveling, Mr. Big Construction Project Manager."

He huffs a laugh. "Yeah."

"I'm proud of you, Vince. I know how hard you work. How hard you've worked to get where you are."

"Thanks. Even if I'm not here, you can still come home, you know."

"This isn't my home anymore."

"No, I guess not." He tilts his head, whatever fondness we just shared disappearing. "How long was this going on?" he asks, pointing at my bruised neck.

I don't even pretend that I don't know what he's asking. "Too long."

"Why didn't you call me? Or if you didn't want to tell me, why not call Liam?"

"I was too embarrassed."

His fists ball up at his sides and he squeezes his eyes shut. "Fuck. I can't do this with you, Bree. Already been through it with mom."

Tears prick my eyes. "Maybe that's why I didn't tell you," I snap back. "I didn't want you to think I was like her."

"And yet—"

"Fuck you!" My fist slams into one of the couch cushions. "That's not fair."

"For fuck's sake, look at you!"

"He didn't drink." I think of how to explain why I didn't see the similarities between our parents' turbulent relationship and my relationship with Chad. "There were times when he was so sweet. Good to me. It wasn't like… It didn't feel the same. At first," I add.

"You should've left him sooner."

"Thanks, I hadn't thought of that."

We stare at each other for a few seconds.

"I'm sorry," he finally says.

"I didn't know what to do," I explain. "He always said it would never happen again." I shake my head and stare at our almost-touching hands. "I couldn't come back here."

He snorts. "Yeah. Got that loud and clear."

"You're mad at me?"

"No." He squeezes his eyes shut again. "Yes. I wanted you out of here as much as you needed to be out of here. But fuck, that first year after you left? Mom was a fucking nightmare to deal with. Then she got sick." He shakes his head. "I wanted you away at school. Was happy you were doing so good. But I was also pissed as hell I was the one who got stuck taking care of her. And I know that's unfair. It's not your fault."

"I'm sorry. I didn't know it was that bad."

"I didn't want you to know."

"Do you want to talk about it now?"

"Not really." He looks around the house. "I gutted this place. Erased it all."

"But it still haunts you."

"Don't fucking head-shrink me, smartass." The corner of his mouth pulls into a half-smile. "You been up to see Liam's parents yet?"

"Yes." My eyes water. "A couple times. I missed them a lot."

"Yeah." He smiles fondly. "Amanda was a big help toward the end. Helped me get mom into hospice care. Made sure I was eating." He huffs out a laugh. "Mom stuff."

"I always wished she was our mom."

"I know." After a second he adds, "So did I."

Speaking of things that haunt us, I have a question for my brother. "Did *she* ever ask for me?"

He rolls his lip and closes his eyes. "No."

"I figured."

He turns my way, dark-blue eyes snapping with fire. "She was a bitter, angry drunk, Bree. The woman drank herself to death and blamed everyone else around her for her bad decisions right until the very end."

It all clicks into place. Why Vince didn't call me to come home until my mother had slipped into a coma and was close to death. He knew there would be no loving, I'm-sorry-I-wasn't-a-better-mother-but-I-loved-you moment between us. He knew she'd only tear me down. My big brother wanted to protect me from the additional heartache seeing my mother would have caused, even though it meant he had to shoulder the entire burden on his own.

"I'm so sorry, Bree." His voice breaks and that's when I can't hold the pain in any longer.

He pulls me into his arms, rubbing my back, and lets me cry on his shoulder until I'm drained. "I'm sorry it all fell on you," I whisper.

His hand never stops moving over my back. "That's what big brothers are for."

CHAPTER THIRTY-FOUR
LIAM

W HAT I DIDN'T tell Bree and Vince was that I wasn't called in to my unit. No, I was summoned to headquarters to meet with the Chief Deputy.

I arrive at the station on time and am immediately directed into his office.

Chief Deputy Cain greets me with a grim smile and nods at the chair across from him. "Have a seat, Hollister."

I haven't been in here in a while, so obviously this has something to do with Bree.

"We got a problem," he starts.

I don't answer because I don't think he expects me to.

He taps the folder on his desk. "How well do you know this Avery girl?"

"Very well. We grew up together."

"Are you involved now?"

"Yes, sir." I'm not hiding our relationship from anyone.

"That why you went down to the jail and roughed up her ex?" He drops the question in a casual way, expecting me to be surprised he knows about my visit.

"I didn't rough him up," I explain. "I told him to stay away from Bree. That's it. I had to get a restraining order against his brother because he wouldn't leave her alone."

"I saw that. Entitled little prick that one."

Thank God this is finally going my way.

Or so I think.

"The victim—" he starts.

"He's not a victim. He's the attacker," I correct.

Cain raises an eyebrow. "The *deceased's* family," he continues. "have raised concerns."

"I'll bet they have," I grumble. "Maybe they should've been more concerned about raising their sons to respect women instead of turning out two psychos and unleashing them on society."

He ignores my outburst and continues. "They claim Bree lured Chad to the house. Then shot him in cold blood."

Fury shoots through my veins and I jump out of my chair, knocking it backwards. "That's fucking bullshit. You saw her. You saw what he did to her."

"Sit down."

I stare at him for a few seconds before taking my seat. "Where's the proof? A text? Phone call? How did she invite him over? Telepathy?"

Ignoring my sarcasm, he flips open the folder. "They haven't said yet."

"Right. They're not going to either, because it's a lie. A million pictures of her injuries were taken."

"They contend she got those injuries when he fought for his life."

"Oh, please. Nothing. *Not one thing* at the scene supports that."

He sighs and sits back. "I know. They won't get far, but until they accept reality I think you need to keep your distance from this girl."

"No."

"Excuse me?"

"No. I'm not abandoning her when she needs me the most. Absolutely not."

"Hollister—" he warns.

I unsnap my gun from its holster and set it on the desk. It's not meant to be some dramatic gesture. I'm dead fucking serious. I set my badge down next to the gun.

"You'd risk your job for this girl?"

"Absolutely."

He cocks his head and studies me through narrowed eyes. "You marrying this girl?"

"That's really none of your business."

"You're being a real insubordinate ass right now, Hollister."

"Yes. I'm marrying her."

He lets out a long, slow breath and flicks his gaze to the wall behind me. "Take a vacation."

"What? I didn't do—"

"It's not a punishment. You've racked up plenty of time. Use it."

"All right."

And I know exactly where my first stop will be.

THE JOSEPH FAMILY lives in an affluent suburb right outside Empire City. The homes here are not the run-of-the-mill McMansions you find in most suburbs. Most of them date back to the nineteenth-century. Federal judges, neuroscientists, and venture capitalists call this area home.

A lot of crooked-as-fuck politicians and their lackeys do too.

I park my truck in the circular driveway and stroll up the sidewalk. Officially on vacation, I'm wearing jeans and a simple, untucked, button-down shirt.

I ring the bell and a woman I don't recognize opens the door. "I need to speak with Mrs. Joseph about her son's case."

I hold the manila envelope to my chest and follow the woman further into the house. Mrs. Joseph is at the dining room table speaking on the phone in a low voice. She ends the call when I enter.

"I'm here to speak to you about your son's case."

No dummy, Mrs. Joseph looks me up and down. "Who are you?"

"Liam Hollister. A friend of Brianna's."

Her expression hardens and she stands. "Get out before I call the police."

"Ma'am, are you actually aware of what he did to her? Why he was in jail in the first place?" I ask as I approach the table.

"They got into a silly argument."

"He gave her a black eye."

"She probably provoked him," she argues.

That stops me cold. Is she that delusional about who her son really was? "Are you kidding, lady?"

I unclasp the manila envelope in my hand. "Sit down," I order in my hardest voice.

She sits and I lay out a row of photos in front of her. From the first beating. The one that landed Chad in jail.

They're harsh. Brutal.

"Please tell me what kind of provocation warrants this?"

She shoves the pictures away. "My son wouldn't do that. She must have done it to herself."

"That is a deep river of denial you're swimming in, lady."

I pull out more pictures. From the day her son was killed. The bruising around Bree's neck. "This is what he did not even two hours after you posted bail and he was told to stay away from her. You trying to tell me she deserved that too?"

"I…" Tears well up in her eyes, but I don't give a shit if I've upset her. Her son turned out to be a monster who tormented Bree and got what he deserved. I refuse to have Bree be bullied by this family ever again.

"You need to drop this she-lured-him-to-the-house bullshit and let them close this case. I'm sorry you lost your son, but he gave her no choice."

I place my hands on the table and lean forward. "Do you understand me?"

She glares right back.

I lower my voice because I want her to listen very carefully. "If you don't drop this nonsense, I will leak these pictures to the press and let everyone know what kind of son you raised. Not everyone's going to be as blind as you are."

She uses one finger to pull the first picture closer and studies it for a while. "I always thought she was so good for him. They seemed happy together," she says.

"Chad fooled a lot of people."

She winces. "I don't understand it. He wasn't abused. We raised him better than that, I swear we did."

I'm not here to dissect her parenting skills, but I can't imagine the pain she's going through right now. "Some people just aren't wired right, Mrs. Joseph. That's not your fault."

"We gave him everything."

Maybe that's the problem.

But I think I'm making progress with her so I don't voice that opinion.

"Will you do the right thing?" I ask.

Her jaw tightens and she meets my stare. "Yes."

"Thank you. Get Chris some help, Mrs. Joseph."

This woman's done taking orders from me. Her eyes narrow. "Get out," she spits at me.

I gather up all but one of the photos because she's still holding on to it. Maybe she needs the reminder, so I let her keep it.

CHAPTER THIRTY-FIVE

Brianna

AFTER A FEW weeks of moping around, I finally feel ready to do something besides hide out. Don't get me wrong, if a person needs to hide out there's no better place than the Hollister compound. But I'm also restless.

Liam and I are staying at his parents' to help Kimber with her recovery. I'm sure our friends think that's weird, but I'm happy and it feels like home. Always has.

It's also a way for us to save money since Liam hasn't gone back to work yet. Something that I know is my fault, but Liam assures me is fine.

It's a hot July afternoon, but up in the mountains there's actually a breeze, so Kimber and I are sitting in the backyard.

"Where are you, baby girl?" Liam calls out.

"Out back!"

Kimber picks up her head at the sound of Liam's voice and stares at the back door until he comes through it. I set my book down and turn around.

His lips curve into a smile the second he sees me, and he places a kiss on the top of my head. "Feel like going for a drive?"

"Sure."

Kimber and I follow him out to the truck. He hoists her into the back seat where she immediately sticks her head out the window and waits for the ride to begin.

"Where are we going?"

"You'll see."

When we're on the highway, I realize we're headed toward campus. "My Teaching Assistant job doesn't start for another six weeks," I remind him.

"I know."

Forty-five minutes later, he steers the truck onto a small tree-lined street near the university and pulls into the driveway of a modest brick bungalow.

"Where are we?"

"You'll see."

Kimber waits patiently for Liam to lift her out of the truck and set her on the ground. I take her leash.

"Who lives here?"

He answers my question by taking a set of keys out of his pocket. "We do."

"What?" I stare at the keys as he drops them in my palm.

His hand settles at the small of my back and guides me up the sidewalk. "Come on."

Inside, the place is empty. Light hardwood floors reflect the sunlight streaming in from the large bay windows in the front of the house.

Slowly, I walk through the kitchen, living room, and bathroom. "Liam, how?"

"I rented it. They allow dogs." He tilts his head toward the sliding glass door that leads to the fenced backyard. Kimber wags her nub as she stares through the glass at a couple of squirrels frolicking on the patio.

Liam chuckles and follows me to the bedroom at the end of the hallway. "This must be the master bedroom—" I let out a gasp when I see the built-in window seat on the left.

"As soon as I saw it, I knew this was our place." Liam's hands settle on my shoulders. "You like it?"

"I love it." I turn and stare up at him. "It's perfect."

"We can rent to own if you decide you really like it here."

A smile tugs at the corner of my mouth. "But I thought you hated the city, country boy?"

"Well, I better learn to love it, because I just got accepted into the

Empire Police Academy."

"Oh my God! You did?" I stop jumping around for a second. "But you loved your job. I don't want you to give that up because of me."

He pulls me into his arms. "I love you more."

"Liam—"

"Bree, this is a good change for me. It pays more. I have a better chance of being promoted. It's going to be good for us."

I raise an eyebrow and trail my fingers down his chest. "You won't be my sexy sheriff anymore."

His arms tighten around me. "I'll always be yours."

Hearing that never gets old.

"But wait, why do you have to go through the academy again?"

"It's not as intense, but some of the training differs. It's fine. I'm excited about it."

I start jumping around again. "Then I'm excited for you."

LIAM

Vince and I slap palms as I approach our favorite booth in our favorite bar later that night. "How'd it go?" he asks.

"Good. She loved the place." I slide into the booth across from him.

"Where is she?" he asks.

I point to the bar, where Bree stopped to talk to her friend. "I think she wants to play matchmaker tonight."

"I'm not interested." He glances at the girl and raises an eyebrow. "Maybe. She's tiny though. I'd break her in half."

"Jesus." I almost spit beer all over him. "Not you."

"Who?"

"Never mind. I want to ask you something before she comes over."

His blue eyes, so similar to Bree's, widen. "Oh, Christ, please don't tell me you're asking my permission to marry my sister."

I cock my head and stare at him.

And stare.

Because, yes, that's sort of what I'm doing. "I'm not asking your permission. I'm just giving you the heads up. If you have any objections, now's the time to spit 'em out."

It's probably the shitty lighting in here, but I swear Vince's eyes shine a little. "You've given her everything I always wanted her to have. How could I object?"

"Thank you."

Before we both start bawling and hugging each other, Keegan joins us. "Things look uncomfortable over here. I thought you were over it, Vince?"

"Shut up," Vince grumbles, shifting to the middle of the round booth to make room for Keegan. He lifts his gaze to me and I slightly shake my head. I don't want to tell anyone about my plan to propose to Bree in a couple days.

Sully approaches our table next and that's when Bree finally joins us, dragging her friend over. "Liam, you remember Aubrey? Aubrey, this is my cranky brother, Vince, our friend Keegan, and you know Sully of course." Then she not-so-subtly shoves Aubrey into the booth next to Sully.

I reach out and take her hand, pulling her down next to me. "Obvious much?" I whisper against her ear.

She shrugs and leans into me. "What were you and Vince talking about so seriously?" she asks.

"Nothing exciting."

CHAPTER THIRTY-SIX
LIAM

"BONFIRE AT MOM and dad's, we don't want to be late," I call out as I enter the house.

"I'm almost ready!" Bree shouts, hurrying into the living room to meet me. "Can you put this on for me?" she asks, thrusting a tiny silver necklace in my face.

She turns and sweeps her hair up, but instead of fastening her necklace, I kiss the back of her neck.

"Liam." Her voice quivers. I place another kiss on the side of her neck and she tilts her head to give me better access. I set the necklace on the table next to me and slide my hands up under her sundress.

Her breath hitches and she presses her butt against me. "What are you doing? You just said you didn't want to be late."

"I know, but I need to have you first."

A short moan slips from her throat as I dip my hand into her underwear. "Spread," I whisper against her ear and she inches her feet apart.

"You're all nice and wet for me."

"A common occurrence," she teases.

I form a V with my index and middle finger, slowly working them over her clit. She gasps and leans back against me, hooking one arm around my neck. "Like that?" I ask, kissing her forehead.

"Y—Yes. I…"

"Are you coming for me already?" I ask unable to keep the satisfaction out of my voice.

She rolls her hips, chasing my fingers and I press harder, rub faster until she explodes.

While she's still moaning, I tighten my hold around her waist and walk us to the couch, bending her over the back of it. Hooking my fingers in her underwear, I yank them to her knees.

"Ready for me?"

"God, yes," she gasps as I undo my belt, unzip and free myself.

My hands grip her hips, positioning her the way I need to, pushing myself inside her in one, long, slow thrust. "You have no idea. I've been thinking about having your sweet, wet pussy wrapped around my dick all day," I murmur into her hair.

Her fingers dig into my arm around her waist. "I love my dirty-talking Liam."

"I know you do, sweetness."

I stay at a slow and steady pace until she comes again, bucking against me. Triumph flows through my veins and I increase the power of my thrusts. I lean over and place my forehead between her shoulder blades. "You feel so good." My orgasm brews at the base of my spine, pleasure jolting through me while I lose track of everything except how good she feels. How good we feel together. I shudder and groan through my release, my breathing ragged.

It takes a few seconds to collect my thoughts and peel myself from Bree. "Are you all right?"

She pulls her dress up around her waist and bends to pull her underwear up, giving me one filthily-spectacular view. "I might need to go change," she says, tossing a teasing glare over her shoulder.

A short laugh bursts out of me and I reach out to squeeze her butt. "Come on, I want to take a quick shower before we leave anyway."

"Oh, no. I know what a 'quick shower' means in Liam-speak. It means 'quickie-in-the-shower.'"

I don't bother denying it.

Brianna

"WE'RE DEFINITELY GOING to be late," I say, glancing at the clock on Liam's dash once we're in his truck.

"I'll take the fall for it."

"You better."

A smile twitches at the corners of his mouth. He's up to something, I can feel it.

"What are you up to, Hollister?"

He glances over with a wide-eyed, *who me* expression. "When did you turn so suspicious, Avery?"

"Hmmm. We'll see."

His parents' driveway is blocked with cars and we end up parking on the grass. Liam helps me out of the truck and takes my hand. "What's going on?"

"You'll see."

Liam opens the front door and ushers me into the house.

My gaze lands on a big "Congratulations Graduate" banner hanging over the fireplace. There're wild claps and cheers from everyone in the room. Confused, I stare up at Liam.

"Mom wanted you to have a graduation party," he explains.

The room blurs from the tears gathering in my eyes, but I recognize Amanda's voice. "We're so proud of you, Bree," she says, giving me a tight embrace.

"Thank you." I tilt my head toward Liam. "What about him, he's graduating from the academy soon."

She reaches up and pats his cheek. "I know. I'm so proud of both of you." She gives me an extra squeeze and pulls me closer. "How are you really doing?"

"Good. Really good."

Liam leads me into the living room and I start to process who's here. My brother, Sully, Keegan, Aubrey, and Emily, along with a few people I don't recognize.

Vince sweeps me into a big hug. "How's the new place?" he asks, giving Liam only a slight glare this time. He's been swinging between happy for us and annoyed since we moved in together. I'm sure he'll get over it soon.

"I love it," I answer.

"Hey, Bree," a deeper voice behind me says.

"Marcel! You're here too?"

Amanda gives him an affectionate side-hug that totally surprises me. Liam raises an eyebrow.

"You were late," Amanda scolds her son. "Marcel was kind enough to help me carry in the bags of charcoal, since you were late," she adds again.

A bright smirk twists Marcel's mouth up as he meets Liam's stare. Amanda squeezes Marcel's hand and he gives her a genuine smile full of respect and affection. "Anytime, Mrs. H."

He silently laughs as Amanda heads into the kitchen.

Liam stands there working his jaw, while his mom heads into the kitchen and Marcel silently laughs.

"I didn't know you knew Liam's mom," I finally say to break the tension.

"Sure," Marcel answers easily. "She used to read to me at the library when I was a kid." He holds his hand down low to indicate how much smaller he was. He lifts his chin at Liam. "When he invited me, he said early afternoon, so that's when I showed up."

I turn to Liam. "You what?"

"Yes, I invited him," Liam admits grudgingly. "Although, now I can't remember why I thought it was a good idea."

Not offended in the least, Marcel chuckles and slaps Liam's shoulder. "Congratulations, Bree." He gives me a quick hug before moving across the room to talk to Sully and his brother.

Next, Liam takes me over to meet his former partner, Brady. "Lost my wingman and my partner, you know. But I can definitely see why," he says, letting his gaze roam over me.

"Are you flirting with his girlfriend right in front of him?" Sully asks, coming over to join us.

Liam laughs and gives Brady a friendly punch on the shoulder.

The rest of the night is celebrating with friends and family. Eating, drinking, dancing, and goofing around.

Much, much later, after Liam's parents have retired to their room, a few of us are still outside sitting around the fire. Liam and I are snuggled up in one of the larger Adirondack chairs.

Vince walks by and drapes a blanket over us.

"Keep your hands where I can see them, Hollister," he growls.

Liam obliges by flipping my brother off.

"Some things never change," I mutter.

Liam chuckles and reaches into his pocket. "I have something for you."

"Now?" I whisper. "With my brother like three feet away?"

He snorts and shakes his head. "No. Here." He presents me with a small, white velvet box. "I want to marry you and love you for the rest of my life, Bree."

I swipe a few tears off my cheeks and open the box. "Oh, wow. Oh my God. I can't believe you're springing this on me now. You've been holding on to this all day?"

"Was waiting for the right moment." He glances at the guys. "When *people* weren't up in our business."

I chuckle and continue staring at the ring. The fire's bright enough for me to make out the simple but elegant details. "It's beautiful."

"It's a fire opal surrounded by diamonds," he explains, plucking it out of the box and taking my hand. "My mom said you once told her opals were your favorite stone." He slides the ring on my finger.

I hold my hand out and wiggle it around, loving how the ring sparkles in the firelight.

"I did and I do. I love it so much."

"You didn't say yes yet."

I throw my arms around his neck and pepper his face with kisses. "Yes, yes, yes! Is that better?" I tease.

"It's perfect," he answers.

The End

RESOURCES

If you or someone you love needs help, please consider reaching out to one of the following organizations.

National Domestic Violence Hotline

1-800-799-7233 | 1-800-787-3224 (TTY)

http://www.thehotline.org

https://www.domesticshelters.org

A NOTE FROM AUTUMN

If you've read my work before, you know I'm very passionate about my series, the Lost Kings MC. What you might *not* know, is that at the time I started writing what became *Slow Burn (Lost Kings MC #1)*, I was also working on this book called *Alone Together*. I loved this idea of the older brother's best friend helping his friend's sister through a difficult time. The tension of being alone in the house together. The struggle between doing what Liam wanted to do and what he thought he *should* do. I worked on it for a long time, but could never figure out how it ended. I had editors who requested it and was determined to finish it and send it to them (sorry!) But then Rochlan "Rock" North and his MC brothers started speaking to me and they stole both my heart and my focus.

But I never forgot about Liam and Bree.

Alone Together was written in third person, as I used to write everything. After attending a workshop late last year, I went back to my hotel room and pulled up *Alone Together* and doodled around with re-writing it into first person.

I went home and played with it some more, liking it better and better. Then Teller showed up and *Alone Together* had my complete attention. This was a problem, because, I had just released *White Knuckles (Lost Kings MC #7)* and I was committed to getting Teller's book out next (I already had his cover photo and everything) but the little bastard wasn't speaking to me or maybe he was speaking to me too much. His book has a lot going on. But in *Alone Together*, he was the confident, cocky, lovable guy I knew well (for Lost Kings MC readers who are wondering, *Bullets & Bonfires* fits in somewhere between *White Heat* and *More Than Miles* time-wise.)

After that, I started working on Alone Together in earnest. Then I changed the title. That title still wasn't right. Once I heard Brantley

Gilbert's *Bullet in a Bonfire*, the book got another title change, and the rest of the story came pouring out.

I hope you love Liam and Bree's story as much as I do. I wanted a heroine who learned to stand up for herself but wasn't weak or bratty with Liam. I personally love over-the-top, loving alpha heroes (not the abusive assholes that people sometimes confuse alpha heroes with) but I worried about Liam being *too* overbearing, considering the relationship Bree just came out of. Bree is also smart and knows what she wants. Of course, everyone has their opinion on what the right amount of love or dominance is, but I always leave it up to the character. In particular, I worried readers might find the scene where Liam pushes her against the door troublesome considering what Chad had done when Bree tried to leave him. This is why it was important to me that the scene was in Bree's point-of-view. That way you knew she wasn't threatened. Nothing about his behavior frightened her. That's one of my favorite scenes in the book.

If you've read me before, you know I'm not big on what I call "manufactured conflict." I've taken a lot of workshops on "story beats" etc. Romance usually follows a certain, specific progression leading up to a "black moment." In my opinion, few writers actually do this well— although the ones who do, do it fabulously. I normally hate that progression and have always struggled to get those beats "right." I've found my best work comes out when I say "fuck the beats" and just write the story the way I want to write it. I could have easily added a "black moment" where Bree thinks Liam is going to choose his job over her. But when I read that sort of contrivance in other books, I always feel that it cheapens the whole love story. Instead, I liked a hero who fought for the woman he loved and gave up some*thing* he cared about for some*one* he cared about even more. That's true romance to me. Some people like my style. Some people find it lacking.

If you enjoy my style—thank you! I love writing. I've given up my legal career to write full-time, so I'm definitely invested in earning a living with my writing. But at the same time, I write to amuse myself first and foremost. One of my husband's favorite things is when I'm sitting next to him typing away and suddenly break out into giggles over something one of my characters says or does. I write the kind of stories I want to read, not what I think I *should* write to make more money. If the two things happen to coincide, then that is my perfect definition of success.

During the beta process I received a lot of questions about whose book was next. This is funny because, Keegan, is someone I had in mind for an entirely different series (my eagle-eye LOKI readers will recognize him from *White Knuckles*.) I always had plans for Sully to have a book, even back when this was *Alone Together*. Regular LOKI readers probably also recognize Jake from Wrath's gym. I think he might need a book soon too.

Then Vince. Oh, Vince. For someone who was away for 95% of the book, I had a lot of questions about when he'd get his own story. He's a good big brother. I think he deserves an HEA of his own.

Well, these notes ended up being longer than I planned. So, if you're still reading—thank you!

ALSO BY AUTUMN JONES LAKE

If you'd like to learn more about Teller and Murphy, they are prominent characters from my Lost Kings MC Series.

Murphy's book, More Than Miles, is already available.

Teller's book, Beyond Reckless, will be available September 18, 2017.

Find out more on my website. www.autumnjoneslake.com

Jake, Sully, and Keegan also appear throughout the Lost Kings MC series.

THE LOST KINGS MC SERIES

Slow Burn (Lost Kings MC #1)

Love Doesn't Obey the Law

Forced to represent an outlaw biker, a married attorney must come to terms with her feelings for her client while avoiding the danger he brings into her sedate life.

Corrupting Cinderella (Lost Kings MC #2)

Love is the ultimate outlaw.

Although widowed attorney Hope Kendall cares deeply for President of the Lost Kings MC, Rochlan "Rock" North, the truth is they come from completely different worlds. Add to that the fact that they are also both headstrong people, and they have a very rough road ahead of them.

Strength From Loyalty (Lost Kings MC #3)

As a dark cloud descends over Hope and Rock's already precarious future, will a long-hidden secret push them both past the point of no return?

Tattered on My Sleeve (Lost Kings MC #4)

Eight years ago, the Lost Kings, MC was recovering from turmoil within the club Wrath and Trinity met. Their connection was instant and explosive.

After three perfect nights, Wrath knew she was the one. But Trinity's dark past was about to catch up to her and the Lost Kings MC was her only hope for protection. One misunderstanding leads to a mistake that locks both of them into a war to see who can hurt who the most.

Can they move past their horrible pasts to become better people and ultimately forgive each other?

White Heat (Lost Kings MC #5)

THE QUEEN ALWAYS PROTECTS HER KING.
For straight-laced attorney, Hope Kendall, loving an outlaw has never been easy. New challenges test her loyalty as she discovers how far she's willing to go to protect her man.

IF YOU HAVE HOPE, YOU HAVE EVERYTHING.
MC President, Rochlan "Rock" North finally has everything he's ever wanted. Hope as his ol' lady and his MC earning money while staying out of trouble. The only thing left is to make Hope his wife. But as their wedding day nears, an old adversary threatens Rock's freedom, the wedding, and throws the Lost Kings MC into chaos.

LOVE MAKES THE RIDE WORTHWHILE.
While the club waits for Rock's fate to be decided, Wrath has to balance solidifying his new relationship with Trinity and fulfilling his president's orders.

LOYALTY GIVES AN OUTLAW STRENGTH.
Threats from unexpected places will challenge every member, but in the Lost Kings MC, brotherhood isn't about the blood you share. It's about those who are willing to bleed for you.

More Than Miles (Lost Kings MC #6)

Forbidden love is the hardest to forget...

Blake "Murphy" O'Callaghan, Road Captain of the Lost Kings MC, has the world by the balls. Money. Women. The wide-open road. It's all his, everything he wants...except the one girl he loves, the one girl who's off limits. His best friend's little sister, Heidi.

Abandoned by her mother when she was little, Heidi Whelan's familiar with heartbreak. Especially the heartbreak of falling in love with her big brother's best friend. When Murphy pushed her away, it broke her heart. Now, on her eighteenth birthday, he claims he loves her? Growing up around the Lost Kings MC, Heidi's witnessed his manwhoring ways. He'll never give that up for her. Besides, he's too late: Heidi's in love with her high-school boyfriend Axel.

White Knuckles (Lost Kings MC #7)

TWO TATTERED SOULS
After countless detours, Wrath and Trinity's wedding is only ten days away. Together they've battled their demons and are ready to declare their commitment to each other in front of their entire Lost Kings MC family.

ONE BITTER ENEMY
No one is prepared for the threat that crawls out of the shadows and issues an evil ultimatum. One that places Trinity's future in danger and jeopardizes the entire club. Trinity's more than ready to put her life on the line to save the club.

AN IMPOSSIBLE CHOICE
Wrath's role as protector of the club forces him to choose between the safety of his angel or the future of the Lost Kings MC and all they've built together. But Trinity won't relent. A queen always fights for her king.

FAITH IS STRONGER THAN FEAR

When evil takes her for a ride, will Trinity's faith in Wrath and her faith in the Lost Kings MC be stronger than her fear?

Beyond Reckless (Lost Kings MC #8)

Teller's Story, Coming September 18, 2017

ABOUT THE AUTHOR

Autumn believes true love stories never end. She's easily amused, a procrastinator, and adores romances with true alpha heroes who cherish the sassy women they fall in love with.

Her past lives include baking cookies, slinging shoes, and practicing law. Playing with her imaginary friends is her favorite job so far.

Autumn prefers to write her romances on the classier side of dirty, and she's a sucker for a filthy-talking, demanding alpha male hero. The bigger the better.

Autumn loves to hear from her readers:
autumnjlake@gmail.com

Visit Autumn:
Website: www.autumnjoneslake.com
Facebook: www.facebook.com/AutumnJonesLake
Twitter: @AutumnJLake
IG: @AutumnJLake
Facebook Group: facebook.com/groups/LostKingsMC

Follow Autumn:
Goodreads: www.goodreads.com/AutumnJonesLake
Amazon Author Page: http://bit.ly/AJLamazonauthorpage
Bookbub: bookbub.com/authors/autumn-jones-lake
Subscribe to Autumn's Newsletter:
http://eepurl.com/_4-T1

Made in the USA
Middletown, DE
29 July 2017